'You and I are going to dance a waltz together at the ball,' Brett said.

'A waltz?' Diana swallowed hard. 'I have no idea how to waltz.'

'I suspected that. It is why I am here.' He held out his arms. 'I plan to educate you on the finer points of the waltz.'

'You must be joking. It is a highly improper suggestion. I won't waltz.'

'But you agreed, Miss Diana. You agreed to dance with me at the ball.' His voice was smooth but there was a steely determination. 'Unless you want me to choose another forfeit? A forfeit more suited to a wager between a man and a woman? You were the one who lost the wager. It is up to me to name the terms.'

'You wouldn't dare.'

'Try me.'

Author Note

One of my favourite museums in the North East is the Beamish Open Air Museum, where they have several very early locomotives. It is possible to ride behind a replica of the Steam Elephant through a recreated Georgian landscape. As I did my research, I was surprised to discover how early the engines were developed, and that hundreds of miles of railway existed before George Stephenson developed the first public railway in 1823. As with many things, the Napoleonic War, with its restrictions on manpower and grain, provided the spur to develop the steam engine, and the first travelling steam engines date from around 1813.

Please be sure to look out for Simon Clare's story, coming soon, because the only way I could get him to be silent in his sister's tale was to promise him one of his own.

As ever, I love getting reader feedback— either via post to Mills & Boon, my website, www.michellestyles.co.uk, or my blog http://www.michellestyles.blogspot.com

A QUESTION OF IMPROPRIETY

Michelle Styles

MILLS & BOON®
Pure reading pleasure™

First published in Great Britain 2008
Large Print edition 2009
Harlequin Mills & Boon Limited,
Eton House, 18-24 Paradise Road, Richmond, Surrey TW9 1SR

© Michelle Styles 2008

ISBN: 978 0 263 20657 9

Set in Times Roman 16 on 17¾ pt.
42-0309-78480

Printed and bound in Great Britain
by CPI Antony Rowe, Chippenham, Wiltshire

Although born and raised near San Francisco, California, **Michelle Styles** currently lives a few miles south of Hadrian's Wall, with her husband, three children, two dogs, cats, assorted ducks, hens and beehives. An avid reader, she has always been interested in history, and a historical romance is her idea of the perfect way to relax. She is particularly interested in how ordinary people lived during ancient times, and in the course of her research she has learnt how to cook Roman food as well as how to use a drop spindle. When she is not writing, reading or doing research, Michelle tends her rather overgrown garden or does needlework, in particular counted cross-stitch.

Recent novels by the same author:

THE GLADIATOR'S HONOUR
A NOBLE CAPTIVE
SOLD AND SEDUCED
THE ROMAN'S VIRGIN MISTRESS
TAKEN BY THE VIKING
A CHRISTMAS WEDDING WAGER
    (part of *Christmas By Candlelight*)
VIKING WARRIOR, UNWILLING WIFE
AN IMPULSIVE DEBUTANTE

For Lydia Mason, whose unerring eye for plot problems, challenging questions and enthusiasm for my stories continually inspires.

Chapter One

*September 1813—the Tyne Valley,
Northumberland*

Diana Clare fought the overwhelming temptation
to swear violent, inappropriate oaths, oaths of the
type that no one would even consider a spinster
such as she would know.

One tiny scream of frustration and the merest
hint of a word passed her lips. Jester, the piebald
mare, turned its head and gave her a disgusted
look. Diana shifted uneasily in her seat on the gig.
Jester was correct. She had given in to her anger,
and had broken one of her cardinal rules—a lady
never allows passionate emotion to overcome her
sensibilities.

She drew a breath, counted to ten and concentrated hard on a serene outlook. But the gig

remained held fast in thick oozing mud and the tug of pain behind Diana's eyes threatened to explode into a full-blown headache. Adding insult to injury, Jester began to munch another clump of sweet meadow grass, daintily choosing the last few remaining daisies. Diana tucked a stray lock of midnight-black hair behind her ear and peered over the side of the gig. It was her fault that it had become stuck. No one else's. She accepted that, but accepting, and wishing to admit it to the general populace, were two entirely separate matters.

Diana knew she ought not to have been reading and driving at the same time, but she had needed something to erase the full horror of visiting Lady Bolt's At Home as the congregated gaggle of gossips had blithely torn another woman's reputation to shreds.

That the third and final volume of *Pride and Prejudice* had been waiting for her at the circulating library she took as providence, a way to restore her temper. Normally she scorned novels as frivolous and refused to open them, but Mrs Sarsfield had insisted she read the first page, and Diana had discovered that she'd had to read on and on. She had not bought the book, but done things the proper way—waiting her turn for each volume. And finally it was here, on the seat beside her in the gig. As she often joked to her brother Simon, Jester knew every step of the way home.

And what possible harm could come to her in the country?

Slack reins and the temptations of late-summer meadow grass had proved too great for the mare and Jester had pulled the gig into the mud pool just as Diana reached another scene between Miss Elizabeth Bennet and Mr Darcy.

Diana straightened her straw bonnet and measured the distance from the gig to solid ground.

She could do this—easily, with dignity and in a ladylike manner. One long leap. She pushed off from the gig and hoped.

Her half-kid boot caught in the oozing mud, several feet short of dry land. Diana gave a small cry as her bonnet tilted first one way and then the other before sliding off into the mud, taking her cap with it. Gingerly, Diana picked the bonnet up by one ribbon and stuffed the cap inside. Mud dripped from it, splattering her dress.

'Beauty in distress,' a low voice drawled behind her, cultivated, with more than a hint of arrogance. A masculine voice. A stranger's voice.

Her throat constricted and every particle of her froze. Her situation had suddenly become a thousand times worse.

'Distress fails to describe my predicament.' Diana refused to turn. Spoken to in the correct manner, the stranger would depart. Nothing untowards would happen to her as long as she behaved like a lady. She had to believe that, otherwise what had been the point of the last few years? 'My gig has become stuck, and I am solving a problem with calmness and fortitude. There is a difference.'

Diana concentrated on finding the next halfway decent place for her foot, rather than glancing over her shoulder at the owner of the voice. If she ignored him, there was a chance that he would depart and everything would be fine. Her ordeal would end. It was her actions that mattered. Her balance altered slightly and she was forced to make a windmill motion with her arms in order to stay upright.

'As I said—definite distress.'

'Nothing of the sort. I am finding my way out. It is simply proving trickier than I first imagined.' Diana put her foot down hard and heard a squelch as brown liquid spewed up. Her feet slipped. An involuntary shriek emerged from her throat. She flailed her arms about, trying desperately to regain her balance, before the mud sucked her down and destroyed all her dignity and decorum.

Her fingers encountered a solid object and she

grabbed on with all her might. She rebalanced and looked, hoping for a branch. But instead her hands clung to the sleeve of a white travelling cloak. It was a choice between two evils—the indignity of falling into the thick black mud and the impropriety of clinging to an unknown man's arm. Impropriety won.

'It would be a shame to stain your dress, I believe.'

Without waiting for a reply, the man's hands moved to her waist, and lifted her up. Her breast and thigh grazed his broad chest. Her senses reeled, then righted. She refused to give way to panic. She kept her body rigidly still and willed him to release her, but the arms stayed strong about her.

'You may let me go.' Her voice resounded, high and shrill, in her ears as she glanced up into deep grey eyes. A strange sensation stirred, deep within her, curling around her insides with insidious slowness. She swallowed hard and beat it back. 'Please.'

'After I have had my reward.'

'Reward?' Her tongue seemed to be three times thicker than normal. The day was rapidly becoming a nightmare. Surely this man, this gentleman, had to understand that she was a proper lady? She was not going to be punished. Again. 'Why do you insist upon a reward?'

'For rescuing you. Surely my gallant action warrants the merest trifle.'

He lowered his lips and his mouth skimmed hers—a brief touch, but one that sent a blaze of fire coursing throughout her body. Panic engulfed her. She turned her head and beat her fists against his chest.

'Put me down this instant!'

'If that is what you truly desire.'

Diana gulped and struggled to hang on to some sense of dignity. It was the only thing that could save her. A truly worthy and refined woman was never in danger. Ever. 'It is.'

'Never let it be said that I do not accommodate a pretty wench's wishes.'

Her rescuer withdrew his arms and she was unceremoniously deposited on a green knoll. Her skirt flew up and revealed her legs up to her calves. Diana hurriedly pushed it back down and hoped that the man had been gentlemanly enough not to look. Silently she promised never to read novels again, never to utter oaths, if only she would be delivered from this nightmare. It was all her fault. She had broken her rules of ladylike behaviour and this was what happened to women who behaved inappropriately.

Diana forced her breath in and out of her lungs and

regained some small measure of control. She could not show that she was discomforted. Exhibiting emotion only made situations like this one worse.

'I did not mean quite so quickly.'

'But I did as you requested. Beauty, thy name is perverse.'

'You have rescued me. Now you may depart.'

His black boots remained still. She glanced up at her rescuer, praying that he was a stranger, someone she might never encounter again. Broad shoulders filled out the finely cut white coat with fifteen capes and two rows of pockets. Tapered down to buckskins and the pair of black Hessian boots. He sported a white neckcloth with black spots, immaculately tied. Diana's gloom deepened. It was the sort only worn by a member of the Four Hand Club, the premiere carriage-driving club in the country.

She studied his dark features again and recognised the distinctive scar that ran from his forehead to his cheek.

Her insides twisted. That little place inside her that she normally kept locked and barred cracked opened. The man was Brett Farnham. Had to be. Diana pressed her hands into her eyes. She slammed the door of that place shut and willed the terror to go.

'Is something troubling you, Beauty?' The warmth in his voice lapped at her senses. 'Forgive me if I have offended, I merely sought to assist you.'

'Nothing, nothing at all.' Diana forced her face to relax and her lips to smile. Politeness must be her shield. A lady was always polite. 'Why should anything trouble me? Today has been without blemish or stain.'

'Aside from becoming stuck in a pool of mud.' A smile crossed his features.

'Aside from that.'

Diana resisted the temptation to bury her face in her hands. She had allowed herself to be carried and kissed by one of the most renowned rakes in the country, a man who had founded the notorious Jehu driving club at Cambridge University and who had set the fashion for speaking cant, tying neckcloths, a close confidant of both Brummell and Byron. Her late fiancé had revered him, and ultimately that reverence had been responsible for his destruction.

After all the years she had spent here, trying to forget that London had ever happened. Then Brett Farnham appeared and everything came crashing back as if it were yesterday. But whatever happened, she had to remember that it was *her* actions that decided her fate. If she held fast to her rules, she would be safe. If she had learnt one thing in London, it was that. 'Please, I beg you—go and forget about my predicament.'

He continued to stand there, looking down at her from a great height. 'I am no fool. You disliked being rescued.'

'Normally a gentleman waits to be asked.'

'A gentleman acts when he sees a lady in distress. He attempts to prevent greater harm.' His gaze roamed over her body. And Diana was fervently glad that she was wearing her dark brown gown with its high neck. 'It would have been a shame if your dress had become mud-splattered.'

Diana forced her eyes from his face. She struggled to breathe as her throat constricted again. It was nothing more than polite words, the sort that rolled off his tongue a dozen times a day. She was a fool to worry. This encounter would not happen again. London remained in her past. All was safe here. Her place in society was secure as long as she maintained her poise.

'Thank you,' she said quietly. Polite. Calm. She had to banish any hint of emotion and behave as if they had encountered each other at a tea party or some other social function. It was the only way.

'Remain here and I will free your gig.' A dimple

showed in his cheek. 'You may thank me properly…later.'

'You do not need to do that. I am perfectly capable of freeing my horse.' She struggled to stand and started forwards, but he blocked her way, preventing her from reaching the gig. She cleared her throat, and tried to ignore the sudden trembling in her stomach. 'If you would kindly move, I have no wish to be in your debt.'

He lifted one eyebrow. 'Ah, so you intend on ruining your boots after all the trouble I went to. And your…uh…pretty dress. I wouldn't let a Beauty do that.'

'I am quite capable of getting myself out of the difficulty.' Diana crossed her arms, ignoring his flirtatious tone. A Beauty, indeed. She was no pretty farmer's daughter or green girl ripe for the plucking. No doubt in another moment, he would give his dishonourable intention speech and steal another kiss. This time, longer, deeper. The thought of the consequences made her blood run cold, even as a tiny piece of warmth curled around her. She regarded her hands. This was all her fault. She should have been paying attention to the road. This is what happened when she forgot her rules of ladylike behaviour.

'It looked different to me. It appeared as if you

were heading for deep water and sinking fast.' He put his hand on his heart and made an exaggeratedly contrite face, no doubt expecting her to smile. 'Consider my reputation as a gentleman. How could I allow a Beauty such as yourself to meet with such a fate?'

'I am hardly a fainting violet who does not know how to handle the ribbons. I can free the gig…in time.'

He cleared his throat and looked pointedly at the vehicle with its wheels half-submerged in the mud. The position made it perfectly clear that she had driven straight at the puddle. She hated to think how long it would take to clear it. Or the difficulties she would have with Jester, who appeared intent on devouring every last speck of meadowsweet grass.

'I like to have my roads free from hazard. It could have been worse. I intend to rattle down this road today at high speed. If a carriage had encountered the unexpected obstacle, there would have been an accident. A bad accident.'

'It is a public road.' Diana lifted her chin a notch. His road indeed. Arrogant. Concerned with only his pleasure and comfort. Her heart rate slowed. She was back in control. Brett Farnham and all his kind were in her past. She was immune from such men now. She knew what danger they represented. But they also understood the code. Ladies were to be respected.

'I have never driven into a mud puddle, intentionally or unintentionally.'

'You think I intended on driving in?'

'As I am not privy to your thoughts, I remain unable to discern them. Mind-reading is, alas, not one of my talents. Dealing with horses is.' But within a moment, Brett Farnham had moved around the gig and with a few whispered words coaxed Jester back towards the road.

The pool gave up its hold on the gig with a great sucking sound. Diana reluctantly admitted that he had done it far more efficiently than she could have. And except for the splashes of mud on his gleaming black Hessian boots, Brett remained spotless.

'I must thank you for that. Very neatly done.'

'You climb back in and then we will depart.' He gestured towards the gig. 'I will drive.'

'Go? Where?' Her throat closed around the word and she was suddenly aware how deserted the road was, how far she was from any cottage. Alone with this man. Vulnerable. 'I refuse to go anywhere with you.'

'I am taking you home. You drove into a mud pool. Anything could happen.'

'My competence as a driver has never been questioned before.'

He pursed his lips and his face assumed a sceptical expression. 'We have a difference of opinion on competence, I fear. Your horse is a placid and serene animal. Easily managed.'

'It is not what you think. I can control Jester.'

'And now you know what I am thinking? Mindreading *is* a talent of yours. How marvellous.' His eyes pierced her. 'Do let me in on your secret some time. But for now, I will settle for your explanation.'

'I failed to pay attention.' Diana hung her head and her cheeks grew hot. 'I was reading a…a book.'

'Indeed. There is no book in the gig.'

'But it has to be there,' Diana said in dismay. 'The last volume of *Pride and Prejudice.* I left it on the seat when I jumped. I had to know the ending. The author writes so well. I shall have to search out more of his books.'

'I have it on good authority that the author is a woman.'

'The author's identity is a closely guarded secret, but I understand from Mrs Sarsfield that it is a man.'

'Shall we wager on that?' His grey eyes twinkled. 'A simple wager. With a suitable reward.'

He held out his hand. Diana kept her hand firmly at her side. No wagers. Ever. A simple enough rule to remember. She raised her chin and stared directly at him. 'I suspect you would not offer unless you knew the truth. I accept the author is a woman.'

'It does help to know the publisher and his habits.' He gave a small laugh. 'Never wager on facts you are uncertain of or have not independently checked. It helps keep people honest. But I shall agree with you—*Pride and Prejudice* is well written.'

'I had assumed that members of the Jehu club disdained reading and education, Mr Farnham.'

'How do you know I have anything to do with the Jehu club?' His eyes changed instantly and became cold slate.

'My fiancé was an admirer.' Diana spoke around the sudden tightness in her throat. 'Algernon Finch.'

He drew his eyebrows together before shaking his head. 'I have no recollection of the name.'

'He was younger than you at Cambridge, but he used to speak about the doings of the Jehu club.' Diana clenched her fist. The man who had done so much to encourage Algernon's folly and ultimately his death had forgotten his existence. 'He even introduced us five years ago.'

'Five years ago is a long time. I regret that I cannot remember the occasion.' Brett's voice held the faintest note of hesitation. A smug satisfaction swept through Diana. It was beneath her, but she did enjoy the feeling of wrong footing a rake. 'I look forward to renewing my acquaintance.'

'He died five years ago, Mr Farnham.'

'My condolences. But people will talk, and they do sometimes exaggerate the acquaintance.' He gave a slight shrug of his perfect shoulder, once again every inch the arrogant gentleman. 'You must not believe everything you hear. Remember that the next time. The Jehu club disbanded years ago. And it is no longer *Mr Farnham.* I am now the sixth Earl of Coltonby. Have been for the last six months.'

'My mistake. Lord Coltonby.' Diana inclined her head. 'I am sorry for your loss, but my answer remains the same. A title does not give one licence to seduce.'

'I can only apologise for the gross ineptitude of my sex.' A faint dimple showed in the corner of his mouth. 'It is lucky that I was not intending any such stratagem.'

'I am relieved to hear it.'

His eyes slowly travelled down her body, lingered on her curves. Diana reminded herself that this was a simple round gown, nothing too flattering. Suitable for visiting the Bolts and others in the neighbourhood, but it would appear dowdy and misshapen in Newcastle, let alone under the bright lights of London. Demure. Modest. Unassuming. His fingers trapped hers, curling around them and holding them fast. He brought them to his lips as his eyes watched her with a steady gaze. 'You will take driving lessons. I insist. Public safety demands it.'

'The public make no such demand.' Diana withdrew her hand and ignored the faint tremor that ran up it. 'I doubt our paths will cross again.'

Brett Farnham stared at the woman in front of him. This interview was not going the way he had planned when he'd glimpsed her ankle and the slight curve of her calf as she'd drawn her hideous dress up to avoid the mud. 'And if I say that the stories about me are exaggerated?'

'My answer would remain the same. In any case, London is your natural habitat. Your stay here will be a short one.' The Beauty's bee-stung lips were turned down. They were the most exquisite colour of rose pink and Brett wondered what it might be like to taste them again. But he decided against the notion. He would be a fool to try such a thing without knowing her antecedents. She claimed an acquaintance. Brett took pride in being discerning. He had never toyed with a woman whose thoughts might legitimately lean towards marriage; women who understood the nature of the game were infinitely preferable.

'It may be longer than you expect,' he said, keeping his eyes away from the swell of her bosom. Until he knew the exact nature of her status, he refused to risk any consequence. Silently, he prayed that she might be a legitimate pursuit, rather than one who was off limits. 'I recently won a highly desirable piece of Northumbrian property.'

'Did you, indeed?' Her blue-green eyes became cold. Her eyebrow arched. 'It appears to me that you play for very high stakes. Far too high.'

'Cuthbert Biddlestone had had rather too much port and challenged me to a race. I am hardly one to back down. I held his vowels, you see, and it was double or nothing. Now I hold the title to Ladywell Park.'

'You raced a noted drunkard? That must have been challenging.'

Brett brushed a speck of dust from his travelling coat. 'He was the one who insisted. He was the one who became a vice-admiral in a narrow ship. I did warn him what would happen. He chose not to believe me. I do warn people of the consequences.'

'And do you intend to keep this estate or will you wager it again on another race?'

'I never drink too much port. What I have, I hold…Miss…' Brett held out his hand and prepared to recapture her fingers.

She smiled and managed to sidestep him. 'You will not achieve my name by such stratagems.'

'You claimed acquaintance earlier.'

'You denied all knowledge.'

'Perhaps I spoke too hastily.' Brett dropped his voice to a husky rasp. 'Enlighten me, O Beauty of the wayside, so that I may worship you properly.'

'I shall wait until we are properly re-intro-duced—' she tilted her chin and her eyes became glacial '—when the proper order has been restored, if indeed you have won the Park.'

Brett smiled inwardly. One of the local gentry. Unmarried as she did not bother to correct him. He had anticipated, given the ugliness of the dress, that she was a farmer's daughter, rather than a social equal. But now that he listened to her tones, he conceded that it was a probability. Annoying, but true. There again, she had mentioned a former fiancé—perhaps there was a stout husband in the background? Or, better yet, she could be widowed. Brett smiled. Possibilities remained. He would play the odds. Five years was a long time. A woman who showed a zest for life like this one would not have remained unmarried.

'I believe your book has tumbled into the mud.' Brett reached down and picked the mud-splattered volume up.

The lady held out a hand. 'My book, if you please.'

'I would not want you to be distracted.' Brett pocketed the volume. 'I will arrange for it to be delivered if you will divulge your name.'

'For propriety's sake, stop this funning and give me my book back…' Her lips became a thin white line, but her cheeks coloured.

'I much prefer impropriety.' He gave a half-smile at her outraged expression.

'My book, Lord Coltonby, if you please. I have tarried here long enough.'

Brett ignored her outstretched palm, and placed the volume in his pocket. 'I have no intention of keeping it any longer than strictly necessary, but for now I feel it would be a distraction.' Brett made a bow as she opened and closed her mouth several times. 'Your servant, ma'am. I look forward with great anticipation to our next encounter.'

Her response was to twitch the carriage ribbons. Brett stood and watched it. She would find an excuse to come to him. It was only a matter of time.

Chapter Two

'Rude. Arrogant. Impossible.' Diana threw her gloves down on her dressing table and finally gave vent to her frustration. Passion and emotion were permissible in private.

Lord Coltonby actually thought that she would seek him out! And the worst thing was that he possessed the same sort of lethal charm that Algernon had oozed from his every pore. But she had learnt her lesson about how quickly such things vanished. Her rules had kept her safe since then. Diana concentrated on taking deep calming breaths.

'Who?' Rose, her maid asked, looking up from her pile of mending. Rose coming into her life was the only good thing that had happened in London. Sometimes, Diana felt that the world would have gone entirely black if not for Rose's practical approach to life and her sense of humour.

'What edict has the master issued now? You were displeased with him at breakfast. I could tell by the set of your mouth when he went on about you going to visit Lady Bolt. Why he should be interested in the Honourable Miranda, I have no idea. The woman is a menace. She is the sort who considers every cold a lung fever and faints at the merest hint of anything untoward.'

'It is not the Honourable Miranda's charms that interest my brother, but the possibilities of using Sir Norman's landing on the Tyne if he makes an offer. Business, always business with Simon.'

'Your brother should make other things his business. That son of his needs a mother. You do your best, Miss Diana, but you ought to have a life while you are young enough to enjoy it.'

Diana gave a short laugh as she gazed with fondness at her maid who sat sewing by the window. 'I have discovered someone worse than my brother—an unadulterated rake who goes by the name of Brett Farnham, the sixth earl of Coltonby. He thinks all he has to do is click his fingers and women will fall at his feet.'

'And do they?' Rose laid her mending on her lap. Her placid face crinkled up. 'I have often longed to meet one and to see if such a thing is really possible. What was he like, your mysterious rake?'

'He is no rake of mine. He will have forgotten my existence by the time my gig turned the corner, and certainly once he encounters the next skirt.'

'You judge yourself too harshly. You have done so ever since you returned from London.' Rose made an impatient motion with her hand. 'And what do you know of rakes and their doings? You resolutely refuse to read the Crim. Con. papers.'

Diana gave a small shrug as she stared into the large mirror that hung over the mantelpiece. Her features were ordinary: dark hair, reasonable eyes and an overgenerous mouth. They had not been what had caught the eye of Algernon Finch. He had been attracted to the size and newness of her fortune. And his determined seduction and easy manner had dazzled her. She had never thought to question his stories until it was too late, far too late. But she had learnt her lesson. 'Brett Farnham is a rake, Rose. His exploits with gaming, carriage driving and women were the talk of London five years ago. But simply because *other* women fall at his feet, there is no need to think that I should.'

Rose made a noise at the back of her throat. 'How has he behaved? Tried to flirt with you a bit? You never used to mind such things, Miss Diana…'

'That was a long time ago, Rose.' Diana tucked a tendril of hair behind her ear as she tried not to think about the girl she had once been. 'I am no longer a green girl, ready to believe the lies that drop from a man's lips, particularly not when he appears sophisticated and charming. And I have better uses for my fortune than buying a bankrupted title.'

'Is Lord Coltonby bankrupt?' Rose's eyes widened. 'You know a great deal about a man in whom you profess no interest, Miss Diana.'

'The state of Lord Coltonby's finances fails to intrigue me. I simply know what sort of man chased after me in London. Bankrupt. Let in the pockets. They saw only my fortune and not my face or personality.'

Rose shook her head so that her ribbons bobbed. 'You should judge each man on his own merit. And stop seeing yourself as a plain old maid, an ape-leader who is on the shelf. Abandon your caps and embrace life. There, I have said my piece, Miss Diana, and it has been a long time coming.'

'Please, Rose. You have it all wrong.' Diana briefly related what passed between her and Lord Coltonby. Her voice faltered briefly when she neared the kiss, but she pressed on, avoiding any mention of it. If she did not think about it, it would be as if it had never happened. 'I shall enjoy seeing his face when he realises who I am.'

'Why would you want to do that?' Rose finished darning a stocking. 'I thought you were not interested in the man's opinion—good or otherwise.'

'I can hardly allow Lord Coltonby's arrogance in the matter to continue.' Diana pressed her palms against her eyes, trying to think straight as Rose's lips turned up into a smug smile. 'I do have my pride, Rose. Simon is a man of consequence in this county.'

'It is a start.' Rose shifted the mending off her lap and smoothed out the wrinkles in her apron. 'You should borrow one of those lady magazines and see the latest fashions. One of Mrs Sarsfield's daughters-in-law is sure to be willing to lend her copy of this season's *La Belle Assemblée*. I could easily alter one of your London dresses.'

Diana shook her head. She had lost count of the number of rules she had broken today. Wearing clothes that made her fade into the background was vital, a constant reminder of what happened when one let one's guard down. 'My clothes suit the life I have chosen.'

'It is such a pity. All those lovely silks going to waste.'

'They stay where I put them—in the attic.'

'You have mourned your fiancé for too long,

Miss Diana. No one expects it. Not after the manner in which he died.'

Diana froze. How could she explain to anyone that she went down on her knees every night and thanked God for her lucky escape? That she had no intention of being caught out again. Ever. There were things about the past that even Rose did not know. Diana forced her fingers to pick up a pile of letters from the dressing room table. 'The post has arrived. You should have said.'

Rose tightened her lips and showed that she remained unmoved by Diana's sudden enthusiasm for her letters. 'Doctor Allen has written. Already.'

'What has Robert done now? It is barely a week into term.' Diana tore the seal on the schoolmaster's letter. 'He promised me when we said goodbye that there would be no repeat of last year. He would attend to his studies. Simon will be so cross.'

'It would be better if—'

Rose's words were drowned out by a door being flung open. The noise resounded throughout the substantive house. Diana gave Rose a startled look and hurried out of the room.

'He's gone and done it! Lost everything! On a horse race!'

'Who has gone and done what, Simon?' Diana regarded her brother's thunderous face as he strode about the entrance hall, his black coat flapping and his neckcloth wildly askew. 'You will make yourself ill, if you continue in this manner. Be calm and collected.'

Simon gave her a disgusted look.

'Cuthbert Biddlestone has wagered his fortune on a carriage race. And lost.' He handed the cane and top hat to Jenkins, the butler. 'He lost his entire Northumberland estate, everything that was not in the entail.' Simon Clare shook his head as his dark green eyes flashed emerald fire. 'He wagered the whole thing on his ability to handle the ribbons against one of the best horsemen in the country! His father would be turning in his grave if he knew.'

'I suspect he did know. It is why he put off Sir Cuthbert's majority until he was thirty.' Diana forced her lips to turn up, but saw no answering smile in her brother's face. If anything, his face became darker. 'You always predicted such a thing would happen. What was it that you called Sir Cuthbert—a witless fop?'

'He was a fool. He claimed in his letter that it was my fault as he wanted the money to invest in the travelling engine.'

'That is complete nonsense!'

'But it is exactly like Biddlestone. And he did

not listen to what I said. I only wanted a bit of his money…for my new engine. Then with the proceeds from the investment, he would have been able to build that new Italianate manor he was always on about. I was even prepared to sell him that parcel of land overlooking the Tyne—you know, the one where the old wooden wagon-way used to run—at a knockdown price.' Simon ran a finger about his collar.

'But what does this have to do with the new owner?'

'He wants to buy the land. Says Biddlestone and I had an agreement. Goodness knows what arrangement he will then strike with Sir Norman Bolt. Bolt's been after that land for years. About the only spark of intelligence Biddlestone showed was his loathing of Sir Norman.' Simon's lower lip stuck out. 'Is it any wonder that I am furious? Get me the latest copy of *Debrett's,* Jenkins, I want to know the measure of this Earl of Coltonby.'

Diana reached down and gave Titch a pat on the head. Lord Coltonby had told the truth—he was their nearest neighbour. The terrier looked up with big eyes. The simple act eased her nerves. She would be practical and she would not give in to her fears as Simon appeared to be overwrought enough for the both of them. Calmness and tranquillity were the keys to an orderly life. 'Why should it affect us? Why shouldn't we be able to go on as before? The colliery is profitable.'

'Everything has changed, Diana. Everything.' Simon's lip curled back slightly and his eyes became even greener. 'The bloody Earl of Coltonby now demands that I dance attendance on him and listen to his scheme for improving the area. I dare say that he will tap me for money. These aristocrats are all the same. Jenkins, I want my copy of *Debrett's* now, not in a month's time!'

'I am trying, Mister Clare.' The butler's voice echoed from the library. 'It does take time.'

'I know of Lord Coltonby,' Diana said quietly as Simon looked about to explode and the butler wore a hurt expression. The last thing she wanted was to have to find yet another butler. Jenkins was the third butler they had had in a year. 'He was there when Algernon died. One of the seconds… for the other man. It was all in Algernon's last letter. Then Brett Farnham…'

Diana hated the way her voice trembled. She swallowed hard and steeled herself to explain about today, but Simon held up his hand, preventing her from speaking further, from telling him about her earlier encounter with Lord Coltonby.

'By all that is holy! Brett Farnham…' He made

a disgusted noise in the back of his throat. 'I never realised your fiancé knew him. I would never have listened to Jayne and agreed to the match if I'd known that.'

'You never wished to know much about him,' Diana replied carefully. She refused to speak ill of the dead—neither Algernon nor Simon's late wife, Jayne. 'Perhaps it would have been better if you had. How do you know Brett Farnham?'

'Farnham and I were at Cambridge together. He with his drawling voice and oh-so-smooth manner as he threatened to dunk me in the Cam for wearing the wrong cut of coat.'

'It was mostly likely a joke, in poor taste, but an idle boast.'

'The water was ice cold, but I swam to the other side while he and the rest of his cohorts stood braying on the bank.' Simon's eyes flashed a brilliant green. 'The man is debauched, Diana. He bragged about his gambling prowess and how well he drove carriages. And the women. You should have seen the parade in and out of his rooms. He and his kind are one of the reasons I detested Cambridge.'

'It may not be as bad you fear. Rakes are ever in need of money.' Diana kept her head high and her voice expressionless. She wanted to shake

Simon. He should have questioned her chaperon in greater detail before entering into negotiations about her marriage.

'Why me? Why now when the engine design is beginning to show its true potential? Why am I being punished in this way?' Simon slammed his hand down on the mantelpiece, making the Dresden shepherdess jump. 'I should have insisted on the agreement being formal, but Sir Cuthbert hemmed and hawed about being honourable gentlemen. Honourable! Him! My great-aunt Fanny! He wagered his entire estate on a daft horse race. How can that be considered honourable?'

'He was not the man his father was.' Diana closed her eyes. 'The ways of the aristocracy are very different from ours. They always honour their debts to other gentlemen.'

'And never to their tailors. Papa finished being a tradesman before you were born and I am no tradesman's son.' Simon waved an impatient hand. 'I do not need the lecture, Diana. We both know what they are like, despite our dear papa's desire to become one. Coltonby is the worst of the lot. Mark my words. He will be up to some deviltry.'

'You don't know that.' Diana laid a hand on her brother's arm. She had to get Simon out of his black mood. A fit of the blue devils was not what anyone needed. The entire house's routine would be upset for days on end. 'Think logically, Simon.'

'You are against me as well! My own sister.' Simon slammed his fist against the table, narrowly missing the alabaster lamp.

'Simon Clare. Do not pick a fight with me, simply because you are cross with Lord Coltonby and his treatment of you years ago. You will find the finance for the engine. Perhaps Lord Coltonby is keen on all these new machines. Maybe he, too, sees the possibilities of steam and iron. Ask him. Maybe he will want to invest.'

'Ask? You never ask Farnham anything. He always declined politely to remove his boots from the stairwell, to not hold drunken parties, to stop fraternising with coachmen. He simply curls his lip and laughs at you.'

'You could try. People do change. You have.' Diana regarded her brother with his expensive frock coat and well-tied neckcloth, the very image of a prosperous landowner. 'You are no longer a student at Cambridge with little consequence. You do have a name and standing in Northumberland. You have a reputation for innovation and resourcefulness. The earl will listen to reason in time. You are under no obligation to sell that parcel of land.'

'I hope you are right, sister.' Simon's face closed down. 'Is there a method you would like to suggest?'

'Yes, wait and see.' Diana popped the final bit of toast into the terrier's mouth. 'Time has a way of solving problems.'

Brett paced the library of Ladywell Park, side-stepping the boxes of books that needed to be re-shelved and the portraits of Cuthbert Biddlestone's ancestors that needed to be sent on their way. The Beauty of the road invaded his thoughts, preventing him from learning more about the estate and how mismanaged it was, from planning his new house overlooking the Tyne, one which would be free of damp and mismatched rooms. He had had plans drawn for one years ago, something he had promised himself when he finally succeeded in restoring the family's fortune. And the outlook here was perfect. Biddlestone had been correct about that.

Who was she? Her eyes haunted him. Blue speckled with green, fringed with dark lashes. He had seen them before. He idly took down a book. 'Finch, Finch. Should I know the name?'

'You won't find songbirds there, begging your pardon, sir,' Hunt, the butler, put down the tray of port. 'Birds and natural history have always been kept at the other end of library. Shall I fetch you a book on the subject?'

'Songbirds?' Brett snapped the book and turned to face his new butler. 'Admirable insight, Hunt. You must tell me how you do it some time. Songbirds, indeed.'

'I do try, my lord.'

Brett waved a hand, dismissing the butler. Then in the stillness of the room, he poured a glass of port from the decanter and swirled the ruby-red liquid.

Songbird. Finch. Algernon Finch. Son of Hubert Finch, Viscount Whittonstall. He'd died in the duel. That dreadfully pointless duel over a disputed Cyprian. How could he have forgotten the name of Bagshott's opponent? The man who had unwittingly changed Brett's best friend's life and his own. A stupid boorish man who'd got everything he'd deserved.

It bothered Brett that the detail of Songbird's name had slipped away. He had been so sure that he would remember everything. The mud, the mist and the absolute horror of a life ended in such a way. Bagshott had already been up to his neck in debt, but it had not stopped him from quarrelling with Songbird. Standing on the dock after he'd bundled Bagshott into a ship, Brett had vowed that he would make a new start, that he would succeed and would restore his family's fortune. That he would not waste his talent, waste his life; but would use it wisely. But he had forgotten Finch's first name. And that of the man's fiancée.

How much else had he forgotten? Brett pressed his knuckles into his forehead.

Now all he had to do was remember her name, and why she was off limits to him.

'A man approaches,' Rose said the next morning as Diana sat re-trimming her straw bonnet in the dining room. 'He is driving one of the smartest carriages I have ever seen.'

'Since when were you interested in carriages, Rose?'

'I have an eye for a well-turned carriage, same as the next woman. My uncle used to work at Tattersalls. You should have seen them come in their carriages.' Diana's maid gave a loud sniff. 'Which admirer of yours drives such a thing?'

'I have no admirers, as you well know.' Diana bent her head and concentrated on the bonnet. A large silk rose now hid the mudstain and the ribbons were a deep chocolate brown instead of hunting green. More sombre. Less noticeable. By following her rules, her life was returning to its well-ordered pattern. 'It will be someone coming to see Simon.'

'The master is at the colliery. Where he always is these days. Why would a man not call there?'

Diana stood and went to stand by Rose. Her breath stopped. Lord Coltonby neatly jumped down from the high-perch phaeton and handed the ribbons to his servant. Diana drew back from the window as his intense gaze met hers. Her heart skipped a beat, but ruthlessly she suppressed it. She began to pace the drawing room. 'Lord Coltonby, Rose. He has come to call. What has Simon gone and done now? I told him to wait.'

'Shall I inform his lordship that both you and the master are not at home, Miss Diana?' Jenkins asked, coming into the dining room.

'No, no, Jenkins. I will see him. I want to know why he is here. I can only hope that Simon has not done anything rash.' Diana's hands smoothed her gown and adjusted her cap so it sat squarely on her head. Although some might have argued that at twenty-two she was far too young for a cap, Diana had worn it ever since that dreadful day in London when she had received news of Algernon's death. There was a safety of sorts in caps. 'You may show him into the drawing room if he asks to see either one of us. Else you can take his card if he asks to see Simon.'

'Should I stay with you, Miss Diana?'

'That won't be necessary, Rose. I believe I have the measure of the man,' Diana dismissed the maid. The last thing she wanted was some subtle interference from Rose.

Diana forced herself to wait calmly and to rearrange the various vases on the mantelpiece as she strained to hear the conversation between Jenkins and Lord Coltonby. Why had he appeared today and what would he say when he realised who she was? Diana gave a wry smile. She doubted that he would call her Beauty any more. She would be proper and hold her temper—the very picture of a spinster, an ape-leader.

Brett followed the butler into the Clares' drawing room. The house exuded new money, rather than old. The drawing room, with its multitude of alabaster lamps, Egyptian-style chairs and green-and-gold striped walls, was the height of fashionable elegance, even though the colours were enough to make a grown man wince in pain. He could well remember Clare revelling in his wealth at university, always going on about his latest acquisition or his father's newest business. A man who knew the price of everything and the value of nothing. A man without bottom. He had not changed.

'I wish to speak with…' Brett arched an eyebrow

as his gaze took in Diana Clare. Even her badly fitting dress in a green that rivalled the chocolate brown she had worn the other day for sheer horror and the oversized cap with ribbons did little to diminish her memorable eyes. Their almond shape and the curve of her mouth had plagued his dreams last night. Clare's sister. And a woman with a delectable bottom. 'How pleasant to renew your acquaintance, Miss Clare. I believe we once had correspondence on a less happy occasion.'

'I thought you had no recollection...' Miss Clare's pale cheeks flushed.

Brett inclined his head. 'I regret that it took me a while to connect you with Songbird's demise. I had quite forgotten that his fiancée was from Northumberland. Forgive me.'

He watched her intently. The aftermath of that day lived with him still. His determination to do more than simply chase skirts and play at gaming tables stemmed from the moment he'd seen Finch breathe his last. He had seen how quickly the dead and the departed were forgotten, not even a ripple on time.

'Songbird?' A puzzled frown appeared between her brows, marring her perfect skin. 'I am afraid that you are now the one who holds the advantage, Lord Coltonby.'

'Algernon Finch, as was. I only recalled him by

his nickname, more's the pity. I had thought every detail to be emblazoned on my mind and now find that certain details had slipped from my grasp. A thousand pardons.' Brett tightened his grip on his cane and prevented any words from slipping out. The irony of the situation did not escape him. The whore had taken a new man within hours of the duel, despite her protestations of undying devotion to Bagshott. And yet, Miss Clare, the innocent fiancée, who had had no party in the action was here, alone, apparently living a retired life. 'A sorry business that day. Totally unnecessary. Both men were insensible to reason. They paid a high price.'

'You do remember.' Her blue-green eyes widened slightly.

'It took me until the early hours of this morning to recall the precise identity of the fiancée,' Brett explained smoothly. 'It was a nag at the back of my mind that prevented me from sleeping. I then felt compelled to apologise for my behaviour. It was unforgivably rude of me to question your source of information. Although I would contend that Songbird was not the most reliable of men when alive. And people change over the years. You should not judge me on his tittle-tattle.'

'I am surprised that you troubled yourself with the recollection.' Miss Clare gave a bright smile, but her hand played with the ribbons of her hideous cap. 'It was most impertinent of me to bring the connection up. I was out of sorts from my difficulty with the gig. Please accept my apology for referring to the matter.'

Brett stared at her. Today all the life seemed to have gone out of her. The vibrant woman of yesterday had vanished and in her place was this shadow. How long had she been like that? And which was the true Miss Clare? He knew which one he preferred.

'It is I who must apologise,' he said at last. 'That particular duel has long played on my mind. It should never have happened and I most sincerely regret that it did. Hopefully, it does not impinge upon your present circumstances. And although I once presented them in a letter, again let me offer my sincere condolences on your most grievous loss.'

'Five years is a long time. I have quite recovered from the shock of it all, Lord Coltonby. You do not need to allude to the matter in oblique terms. I know my fiancé fought the duel over a courtesan. I had friends in London who took great pleasure in explaining it all. And I see no point in pretending that the duel did not take place.'

'I regret your choice of confidants, then. It was supposed to be a private matter.' Brett cleared his throat. It was all too easy to imagine. And even though this woman was innocent of any connection with the duel, people would have drawn their skirts back and whispered behind their hands. 'Those concerned with Songbird's death did everything in their power to keep the affair hushed. You must believe that. I know I never breathed a word.'

'A death such as Algernon's was never going to be private, Lord Coltonby.' Diana kept her head erect, but her insides trembled. She had never spoken of the hours that had preceded Algernon's death and she did not intend to start now, particularly not to a man such as Lord Coltonby. 'Whatever was said about me years ago is long forgotten. The wags and the wits found fresh victims to flay.'

'I can only recall pleasant things. You were quite right in thinking that we had been introduced before. I particularly remember Vauxhall Gardens. You commented on the brilliance of the fireworks.'

'I did?' Diana's feet felt rooted to the ground. Ice crept down her spine. Had he been there as well? That fateful night before the duel? How close had he been? Had he heard her cries and mistaken them for pleasure? And what would he say if he knew the full truth behind that night? She pressed her fingers to her temple. She would have to hope that he meant some other night. 'I have no recollection…'

Brett's eyes became a soft grey as he shook his head. 'Songbird was a scandal waiting to happen. He would never have done for a husband.'

'I didn't ask for anyone's pity.' Diana pressed her hands together. Privately she agreed with Lord Coltonby. But she could not make any excuses for Mrs Tanner, employed to keep fortune hunters away from her. The chaperon had failed miserably. 'My only excuse was that I was naïve and unused to the ways of the world. No doubt most young women saw him for what he was. I only regret that my chaperon did not.'

Lord Coltonby's mouth turned down at the corners. 'What a pity *your* friends did not speak up. His situation was no dark secret.'

'The *ton* is not so forgiving when one is only clinging to the edge.' She kept her head high and refused to allow the old feelings to swamp her. Calm. Tranquil. Her rules had protected her ever since that night at Vauxhall. She forced her mind to clear and then continued. 'I much prefer the peace of Northumberland. Society here may be an altogether duller affair, but the quality and quantity are at least known.'

'Why go to London in the first place?'

'My father had his heart set on brilliant matches for his children. My late sister-in-law's mother advised him to send me down there. I was to share the Season with her niece. Unfortunately the girl became ill and was forced to abandon the project. My father determinedly pressed ahead.'

'Did your father take the disgrace well?'

'My father died of lung fever, in the same epidemic that took Jayne. He never knew. When my brother's letter arrived, my duty to return to Northumberland was clear.' Even as she said the words, she knew they were a half-truth at best. Simon's letter demanding her return had been a godsend, a chance to lick her wounds and to dedicate her life to being sensible and calm. It was wrong of her to think that their deaths had been providence, however much it felt that way. 'I learnt my lesson the hard way, and have no regrets.'

'No regrets.' His eyes swept down her body, lingered on the neckline. 'That is good. I had worried. Songbird would not have wanted it.'

She paused and smoothed out the lines of her green round grown. 'Is there some other reason you called, Lord Coltonby? Surely it is not to reminisce over departed friends. I have turned my face towards the future. Life has been good to me.'

'Your book, Miss Clare, as you did not call for it. I felt certain you had need of it now that you were safely home.'

'My book.' Diana stared at the volume and then back Lord Coltonby. 'Of course, my book.'

She reached out to take it and their fingers touched. A small shock jolted her arm and she fumbled with the book, sending it tumbling towards the ground. Brett smoothly caught it and placed it gently on the small table.

'I had expected you to send a note, as you held the advantage,' he said into the silence.

'I had no wish to trouble you or your servants with such a trifling matter,' Diana breathed.

'And here I thought you would want to see me again.' His eyes became hooded. 'We have unfinished business, you and I.'

'We have no business.' Diana cleared her throat, ready to send him on his way, before she asked him to stay. With every breath she took, that little reckless piece of her seemed to once again grow stronger. She had to slay it before it led her back down the road to ruin and scandal, a road she had blithely trod before. Her heart pounded in her ears.

'I intend on teaching you to drive, Miss Clare. I have no wish to discover the roads cluttered with all manner of gigs and carriage simply because of your inattention.'

'It will not happen again, I can assure you. In any

case surely you will not remain in the neighbourhood for long. A few weeks at most.'

'You know my schedule? Intriguing. Is this
some party piece of yours? Or do you wish me ill?'

'Sir Cuthbert always complained of being buried
in the countryside,' she said quickly to cover her
faux pas. 'He only spent a little time here each year.'

'I am hardly Sir Cuthbert. His figure is far more
rotund than mine. I do not think there is any
danger of anyone mistaking us.' Lord Coltonby
smiled. Diana found it impossible not to answer
his smile with one of her own. 'I find the air very
agreeable here.'

'On that we hold the same opinion.'

'Shall we be friends as well as neighbours? Put
the past behind us?'

Diana drew in a breath. Friendship? Since when
did a man like that seek friendship from a woman?
'We are neighbours.'

'And how shall we celebrate this neighbourli-
ness? How shall we seal our friendship?'

Diana licked her suddenly parched lips. Sealed.
The back of her neck prickled as a distant memory
woke. Warned her. She held out her hand. 'As a
gentleman and a lady.'

He regarded her hand, and then his gaze lifted
to her mouth, made it tingle under his gaze. A

smile transformed his features. He reached out and touched her hand. Held it for a moment longer than strictly necessary. 'A pleasure as always, Miss Clare.'

'Welcome to Northumberland and the neighbourhood, Lord Coltonby,' she said gravely, trying to ignore the sudden pounding of her heart, and withdrew her fingers.

'I look forward to discovering everything Northumberland has to offer. To deepening our friendship.'

'There are neighbours, and then there are friends.'

'I trust we can be both.'

Diana adjusted the ribbons of her cap so it sat more squarely on her head. 'My brother will be sorry he missed your visit.'

'It gives me an excuse to come by another time.' Lord Coltonby's deep grey eyes met hers.

'If you wish,' Diana replied and made a mental note to add another rule—Lord Coltonby represented danger and was to be avoided. Her survival depended on it.

Chapter Three

'Have you heard about the exciting development, Miss Clare?' The tinkling tones of the Honourable Miss Miranda Bolt assaulted Diana's ears as she left the circulating library the next morning.

Pride and Prejudice had been safely returned to the library, and Diana had no reason to even think about her new neighbour. Her well-ordered life would go on as before. She would be able to concentrate on things like needlework and visiting the houses of the colliery's employees, tasks that today held about as much appeal as getting her teeth pulled. But good tasks, worthwhile ones.

'What news? What has happened?' Diana asked cautiously as she turned to greet the impeccably dressed Miranda Bolt. Already she could feel a distinct pain behind her eyes. 'Is it anything untoward, Miss Bolt?'

'Positively the most important thing that has happened in the district for the last century.' Miss Bolt gave a toss of pale yellow curls. Her tiny mouth quivered with excitement. 'My parents are to give a ball in honour of our new neighbour. I fainted when I heard the news. Mama had to call for the smelling salts. Papa has agreed to the ball.'

'You mean the most important thing to happen to the district since the Napoleonic War.'

'War is utter tedium and boredom.' Miss Bolt gave a tiny shrug of her shoulders. 'The only good part is the number of men in uniform. Both Carlisle and Newcastle are full to the brim with soldiers. Lovely, lovely red coats and gleaming buttons. They add such colour to a party.'

'We received our invitation yesterday.' Diana forced her face to stay bland. Penning her regrets was a task for this afternoon. Simon might go if he liked, but she would find a reason to avoid the ball. She always did.

'You and your darling brother must come. You missed the St Nicolas Day ball in Newcastle last Christmas and you must not miss this one.' Miss Bolt gave a clap of her hands. 'I knew if it was in the neighbourhood, all the eligible bachelors would come. I shall be quite in demand. I told Mama that. A woman who is in demand soon attracts the eye. It is only a matter of time before I make a brilliant match, one which is well suited to my station. Forgive me, Miss Clare, if you think me proud, but I only speak the truth.'

'Indeed.' Diana's jaw tightened and she forced her smile to remain in place.

'It would be so lovely if we had more entertainment in the district. Then, we should not have to venture quite so far afield in search of culture.' Miss Bolt stuck her chin in the air. 'Culture is very important to me. It is the foundation of society.'

'You are forgetting about the Grand Allies routs. And the Sarsfields' *musicales*.' The idea that the Bolts were the final arbiter of culture in the Tyne Valley grated on Diana's nerves. They had only arrived here when Sir Norman's great-aunt had died and he had finally come into his inheritance. 'The elder Miss Sarsfield plays the spinet beautifully.'

'True, true, but I thought her Chopin was a bit sharp last week. It laid waste to poor Mama's eardrums.' Miss Bolt tapped a finger against her mouth. 'There again, you were absent, weren't you?'

'Unavoidable. One of the servants had come down with a chill.' Diana forced her lungs to fill with air. The excuse was threadbare, but she had discovered it was far easier to keep to her rules if she avoided entertainment wherever possible. 'It sounded pleasant enough to me when I heard the dress rehearsal.'

'Dear Miss Clare, if you could but hear what passes for music in the great drawing rooms of London…'

'I have been to London, Miss Bolt.' Diana held back a stinging retort. A lady must be polite, but Miranda really was insupportable. 'I even managed to attend several *musicale* evenings there when I had my Season.'

'The London Season. I have tried and tried to convince Mama of the necessity of a London Season. A proper one, with vouchers to Almack's.' Miss Bolt put her hand to her mouth. 'My dear Miss Clare, I nearly forgot how trying the mention of London and the Season must be to you. Mama has warned me and warned me, but my tongue goes flippety-flop.'

'Why should the mention of London be trying?'

'You know *the disaster.*' Miss Bolt lowered her voice and her blue eyes shimmered as she put a hand briefly on Diana's elbow, a show of false concern. 'Every time I think about it I want to weep. Mama remarked on it the other day and how it should be a lesson for me, a lesson I intend to take to my heart. Dear, dear Miss Clare, when I go to London, I shall be a success. I will not be a wallflower.'

'I wish you every opportunity.'

'And I will take every single one, I can assure you of that. I am meant for a viscount or an earl at the very least. It is too bad that the royal dukes are so very old.' Miss Bolt gave her curls a little pat. 'With my looks, breeding and Papa's fortune, a title should be within my grasp.'

'One should always aim for the attainable.'

'How very witty of you. The attainable, not the unattainable. I will remember that. I collect witticisms so that I can repeat them to my friends.' Miranda Bolt gave another trill of laughter. 'There again, did you?'

'Did I what?' Diana stared at Miranda Bolt. Was Miss Bolt entirely without reason this morning? The young woman seemed intent on ignoring all of Diana's attempts to end the conversation.

'Aim for the attainable,' Miranda Bolt replied with maddening complacency. 'Is that why it was a disaster?'

'My situation hardly compares to yours.' Diana gritted her teeth. 'I returned to Northumberland for family reasons.'

'It must be so hard getting old.' Miss Bolt tilted her head to one side and gave her parasol a twirl. 'Every broken sleep shows. Mama told me. It is why I take such care with my complexion.'

Diana counted very slowly to ten. Passionate

emotion was the enemy of reason, but the thought of Lady Bolt and her odious daughter pitying her after all these years was insupportable. 'I believe your mother will be looking for you.'

'Mama is always searching for me. It is part of our little game.' Miss Bolt gave a gasp and a tremulous giggle as she lifted her reticule. 'Is that...? Can it be Lord Coltonby's carriage?'

Diana felt a prickling at the back of her neck and turned to see a smart yellow curricle. A tiger held the heads of two sleek bay horses. The lines of the horse proclaimed speed and the need for a firm hand on the ribbons. 'It may be.'

'He made his own fortune, you know,' Miranda Bolt continued on, her cheeks becoming infused with pink. 'Papa said that all he inherited when his brother died was a bankrupt title. Luckily Lord Coltonby had already won his fortune. He apparently has an eye for the horses. Papa is very much hoping to persuade him to support him in a business venture.'

'Lord Coltonby is a force to be reckoned with.'

'Have you met him? He is your nearest neighbour, after all.' Miranda Bolt clasped her hands together. 'I do think he is the most handsomest of men. He called on Papa the other day and we were introduced. Mama is most hopeful.'

'How pleasant for you.' Diana tapped her finger against her mouth, determined to make her voice sound casual, but to gently lead the subject away from Lord Coltonby. 'The horses have good lines as well.'

'How can you tell?'

'It is the way they hold their heads and shift their feet. They have a bit of spirit. In the right hands that curricle would fly over the ground.'

'I knew you would know about carriages and that sort of thing. I have heard Papa converse with you about them before.' Miss Bolt gave a little wave of her hand as if discussing the speed of carriage and horses were somehow slightly *outré*. 'I will confess that they bore me senseless. All a carriage does is get you from one place to another and wild horses scare me. But if they are Lord Coltonby's passion, I suppose I must assume an interest. It will be expected.'

'Horses are noble creatures. They deserve better than the conditions they are currently subjected to.' Diana tightened her grip on her reticule. Rules. An accepted mode of behaviour. She must not give way to her anger and keep within the bounds of society. It was the only thing that protected a lady. Why did she always come so close to forgetting the basic precepts of etiquette in Miss Bolt's presence? Diana strove to keep her voice light and bland. 'Do you know how many horses are lost because of the mail coaches each year?'

'Mail coaches, Miss Clare, are a necessity.' Miss Bolt looked down her nose. 'How else would I know which regiments were in Newcastle?'

'How, indeed?' Diana hid a smile and felt the tension ebbing from her shoulders. She would now bring the conversation to a close and everything would be well.

'I do believe he has glanced this way.' Miss Bolt rapidly smoothed her skirt and readjusted her bonnet. 'Mama says that his fortune exceeds that of Lord Allendale and Lord Carlisle combined. Mama is always right about such things. Marriage is not something that should be left to the young. She is singularly determined.' Miss Bolt gave another trilling laugh. 'But I forgot, dear Miss Clare, you are unlikely to marry. The ever-so-sensible Miss Clare. Does it pain you when other people speak of marriage?'

'It does not affect me in the slightest, Miss Bolt. I take little notice of such things. If you will forgive me, Robert requires a few sweetmeats from the grocer's. He particularly asked for candied peel in his last letter.' Diana started to move away from Miss Bolt, but the young woman clutched Diana's arm.

'Wait, please, Miss Clare. Your dear sweet nephew can have his things later. My need is at present the greater one.'

'Miranda Bolt, kindly contain your gesticulations.' Diana stared in astonishment at the young woman. And slowly Miss Bolt released her vice-like grasp. Diana rubbed her arm, trying to get the blood to flow again.

'If I have given offence, I most humbly beg your pardon, but please remain here with me.' A faint glimmering of tears shone in Miss Bolt's eyes. 'Do not desert me in my hour of need!'

'Why? What is so urgent? What disaster can possibly befall you on Ladywell's High Street?' Diana struggled to contain her temper. She started to fumble in her reticule. 'Are you feeling unwell? Do you need smelling salts?'

'Lord Coltonby is going to acknowledge me. I know he is. He is coming towards me. We met the other day when he called on Papa. It was a very brief meeting, but somehow I knew.' She gave a huge sigh. 'It is in the way he says hello. And he is attainable, I know he is.'

Diana's hand stopped halfway out of her reticule. Someone had to warn the girl before she did something foolish, before she made a life-altering mistake. Rakes only brought scandal.

'Miss Bolt, Lord Coltonby is definitely not one of the attainables. You will have to trust my judgement on this matter.'

'We shall see.' Miss Bolt nodded towards where Lord Coltonby had emerged from the livery stables. His black coat contrasted with the cream of his breeches. He appeared every inch the gentleman, but there was something more in the way he moved, something untamed, something that called to her. Diana forcibly wrenched her gaze away and filled her lungs with steadying breaths. She tried to remember all the reasons why Lord Coltonby was dangerous, and found she could only think of his smile.

'It does appear that he is coming towards us, but it could be that he wishes to visit the circulating library.' Diana prayed he would nod, acknowledge them both and move on. A civilised way out of her predicament.

'My knees grow weak. Mama will be ecstatic.' Miss Bolt hurriedly pinched her cheeks and straightened her gown. 'To be favoured in this way by Lord Coltonby. Do you know how far his lineage stretches back? Mama had me learning it the other night. Fortune favours the well prepared.'

'You hardly need me here.' Diana prised Miss Bolt's fingers from her sleeve. 'Your mama has brought you up properly. Eschew the vulgar and you will prosper.'

'I have heard of his reputation and do not wish him to say anything untoward,' Miss Bolt whispered. 'Mama insists that there always be a witness. A woman of quality cannot be too careful, particularly when she means to catch an earl.'

Diana pressed her lips together, holding back the words of warning. Poor foolish Miss Bolt. She had never expected to feel pity for the young woman. Someone needed to explain about the consequences of trying to capture a rake. Someone—but not her. Miss Bolt would dismiss her as a jealous spinster. And what could she say without betraying her own experience?

Diana wrinkled her nose and looked again at the figure striding towards them. His top hat shrouded his expression. The only thing she could do was to try to subtly protect Miss Bolt. It was her duty.

'You always have a choice, Miss Bolt. Your mother will not be the one married to him.'

'But will I make the right decision? My future husband needs to be someone special, someone who will put me on a pedestal.' She shook her head. 'It is a matter that vexes me nightly. I must marry well, Miss Clare. A title or a fortune, preferably both. It is expected. Mama will not have it any other way. And sometimes I dream of dashing redcoats and faraway places.'

'Sometimes, the unexpected happens.' Diana kept her voice carefully neutral, but felt her throat tighten around the last words. Suddenly she wanted Miss Bolt to experience happiness. 'Hold fast to your dreams, Miss Bolt. Never settle for second best.'

Miss Bolt gave a small squeak in response and grabbed Diana's arm again.

'Ah, Miss Clare, how delightful to see you again.' Lord Coltonby captured Diana's hand and brought it to his lips. He held it there for an instant longer than was proper. Diana gave a little tug. His thumb lightly caressed her palm as he released it. She was grateful that the shadow of her bonnet hid the sudden flame of her cheeks. She regarded his black boots, counted to ten and regained a measure of control.

'Lord Coltonby. I have returned the book to the library. It will trouble you no further.'

'I can only hope you enjoyed the ending as much as I did.' His rich voice rolled over her. 'I enjoy a happy ending.'

Miranda Bolt gave a soft cough and pointedly held out her hand. Her eyelashes fluttered and her soft blonde curls quivered. 'Lord Coltonby, it is marvellous to see you again. Such an unexpected pleasure.'

'Miss Bolt.' Lord Coltonby inclined his head, but made no move to take the outstretched fingertips. 'I trust your mother is well. The fruit basket she sent over was such a thoughtful, welcoming present.'

'Mama will be so pleased.' Miss Bolt swept into a deep curtsy. 'She told me to ask specifically after your health if we should meet. She has several tonics that you might wish to try if the Northumbrian air proves to be too chilly…'

'How kind of Lady Bolt. I have no need of attention at the moment.'

Diana breathed a sigh of relief. Perhaps Miss Bolt was not in his sights. She could safely take her leave, if Miss Bolt would let her have a word.

As Miranda twittered on about the weather, Lord Coltonby languidly reached into his pocket and withdrew his snuffbox. Diana's eyes narrowed and her body tensed as she remembered Algernon had once used that stratagem. Should she intervene? She could see Miss Bolt at war with herself over whether or not to take the proffered snuff. Diana gave a pointed cough and shook her head. Miss Bolt's face fell, but she made no further move towards the snuffbox.

'You do not approve, Miss Clare. I can tell from the set of your eyebrows,' Lord Coltonby said and a faint smile touched his lips. 'The ever-so-faintly censorious Miss Clare. Always so determined to do what is right and proper.'

'Whether I approve or not is immaterial as you appear intent on taking snuff.' Diana kept her chin up and made her gaze meet his, forced herself to ignore her natural inclination to walk away as quickly as dignity would allow. She would protect Miranda. She refused to allow an innocent to be drawn into his web. No true lady could ever do that.

'But I desire your good opinion. Your smile is so much prettier than your frown.' Lord Coltonby slid the snuffbox back into his pocket. 'I bow to your knowledge of the local situation as I do in all things. What is permissible in London… And it was a gift from Brummell.'

'The rules of society seldom change that much, Lord Coltonby.' Diana drew a deep breath and tightened her grip on her reticule. Protecting herself had to come second when she was faced with a situation like this. Miss Bolt stood poised on a precipice. She did not understand the danger. Surely a small sacrifice on Diana's part was worth preserving Miss Bolt's reputation. 'I find if one exercises common sense and courtesy, most situations resolve themselves.'

'What sound and estimable advice, Miss Clare.

Is it any wonder I hang on your every word?' A dimple flashed in his cheek.

'Insincere flattery does you no favours, Lord Coltonby.'

'How do you know it is insincere?'

'It was the upward twitch of your lips that gave me the final clue,' Diana said with crushing firmness. All she wanted was to end this exchange, to get back home where she was safe.

He gave a barely suppressed snort of laughter. His grey eyes shone like opals. 'As ever, Miss Clare, I find it difficult to disconcert you…but it is so much fun to try. I can't remember when I have been so amused.'

'My existence does not revolve around your amusement.'

'It could be arranged, if you desired it.' His voice lowered to a purr, one that played on her senses and made promises of sensual delights, if only she'd accept. As if she were some naïve débutante to be led astray during a visit to Vauxhall Gardens.

Diana shook her head. She'd never forget. She knew him for what he was—a leader of the Jehu club, the prince of rakes. Such men spelt trouble for the unwary woman. They were only interested in their own pleasure, and took rather than gave.

But a tiny piece of her wanted to believe that he was different.

'Ignorance is bliss, as some say.'

'But I thought you enjoyed being educated, Miss Clare. A denizen of the circulating library?'

Diana struggled to contain her temper. He delighted in provoking her.

'I was unaware that you were familiar with Lord Coltonby, Miss Clare. That you were *intimate* friends.' Miss Bolt's voice held an edge to it and her tiny mouth turned down, giving her the appearance of having swallowed a particularly sour plum.

She elbowed her way so she was standing between Diana and Lord Coltonby. The feathers on Miranda's bonnet tickled Diana's nose and she fought against the urge to sneeze. She stepped to one side.

'Intimate? Are we?' Lord Coltonby raised an eyebrow, regarded her with a faintly sardonic look. 'You must inform me of the Northumbrian definition of *intimate,* Miss Clare. I wish to see if it coincides with mine. As you know, I never like to disappoint a lady.'

'She hasn't said anything. She simply let me make a fool out of myself,' Miss Bolt cried. 'She has been keeping secrets!'

'Miss Bolt, Lord Coltonby and I were acquainted in London,' Diana replied, swallowing hard, scarcely able to believe it was her own voice. 'Lord Coltonby was good enough to call on me the other day as he happened to be in the neighbourhood and we renewed our acquaintance. He seeks to tease. It is his way. You must ignore him.'

'I always like to renew acquaintances where I can.' A bright light appeared in Lord Coltonby's eyes. 'Particularly when they are as charming as Miss Clare. It was one of the bonuses of coming to reside in this neighbourhood, to be able to renew an acquaintance that was cruelly cut short.'

Diana tilted her head and peered at him from under her lashes. This time his face, save his dancing eyes, was a mask of sincerity. No one would guess that it was an act. Her heart thudded in her ears. She played with the button of her glove, wishing she knew why he seemed determined to play this game.

'Lord Coltonby seeks to flatter, but one must never believe insincere flattery.'

'You sought Miss Diana Clare out? Deliberately?' Miss Bolt gave a little stamp of her foot. Diana noted her face did not appear nearly as angelic. 'You went to visit her? But I always understood her time in London to have been a complete and utter disaster.'

'You were misinformed, Miss Bolt.' Lord

Coltonby made a deep bow. 'She was one of the highlights of the Season that year. Unfortunately, duty called her home and the capital became a little greyer, a little less pleasant.'

'Duty…yes, I suppose.' Miss Bolt tapped a finger against her folded arms. 'Poor Mr Clare's wife died, leaving him that…that boy. I had never considered. It makes a great deal of sense now that I think of it. Dear Miss Clare was truly selfless.'

'Every time I have encountered Miss Clare, I have noted her quality. It is only increased if she also manages an impossible child.'

'Robert is far from being impossible,' Diana protested. 'He's lovely, if a little high spirited. I am very proud of my nephew.'

'High spirited? He put beetles in your sugar bowl and frightened poor Mama half out of her wits.'

'He had thought the bowl empty.' Diana stifled a smile as she remembered the incident from earlier that summer. Robert had sworn that it was a natural history experiment, but neither of the Bolts had been amused, particularly as one of the beetles had found its way on to Miss Bolt's new straw bonnet. Simon had claimed he'd been able to hear the shrieking all the way from the estate office. 'He did apologise.'

'Only because you demanded it.' Miss Bolt gave

a loud sniff. 'I can never look at that particular bonnet without a shiver going down my back. If you hadn't plucked the beetle out!'

'It is good to hear that Miss Clare had the situation well in hand. Quick thinking and a calm head are qualities to be admired.'

Diana lifted her gaze and met Lord Coltonby's steady one. She nodded her thanks. She bit her lip. She had been so quick to believe the worst of him. What if she had made a mistake? What if he truly sought only friendship?

'I must confess to having never given it much thought. A cool head in a moment of crisis. You could describe it that way.' Miss Bolt drew her top lip over her front teeth, giving her face the expression of a startled rabbit, and brought Diana back to reality. 'Mama can be wrong in her assessments of people sometimes.'

'I consider it best to judge people as individuals. To eschew cant and hypocrisy whenever possible.'

Miss Bolt's smile vanished as she looked quickly from one to the other. 'I don't listen to gossips.'

'You have a wise head on your young shoulders, then, Miss Bolt. Discover the true person. That is the key to success.'

Diana knew the words were for Miss Bolt's benefit, but to her surprise a tiny piece of her wanted them to be true. She wanted him to think well of her despite the long-ago gossip from London and Lady Bolt's pronouncements.

Diana put a hand to her face and mentally shook herself. Soon she would wish to believe in impossible dreams again. There was safety in the everyday world. Its strictures and structures prevented impulsive action. Impetuosity had led to her downfall before. It would never do so again. She had conquered it.

'It was lovely to meet you again after so long, Lord Coltonby,' she said, inclining her head. 'And to know that your feelings remain the same.'

'My feelings towards you have never changed since the day I first glimpsed you,' he murmured, capturing her hand again and bringing it to his lips.

Diana forced her body to stay still as his mouth touched the small gap left by her undone button. Heat washed through her. Rapidly she withdrew her hand and did the button up. When she glanced upwards, she discovered he was watching her with a sardonic twist to his lips.

'Oh, oh, I see Mama. She will need to know…to know…' Miss Bolt hurried away.

A smile tugged at the corner of Lord Coltonby's lips as they watched Miss Bolt run to her mother, obviously bursting to impart the bit of gossip she had learnt.

'That went delightfully well. Now I look forward to exploring your Northumbrian definition of intimate.'

'I have no idea what sort of game you are playing, but I don't like it.' Diana took a long steadying breath. 'We are not having and never will have a flirtation. How dare you imply otherwise?'

'Did I? You must be reading too much into my words. A very bad habit, Miss Clare. I always mean precisely what I say. I find it saves trouble.'

'I have shopping to do. I do not have time to discuss the precise meaning of words with acquaintances on the High Street.'

'And here I had anticipated that we might become friends.'

'I fear, Lord Coltonby, that we are destined for ever to remain acquaintances.'

Diana straightened her back and, with a sigh of what she convinced herself was relief, walked away from him. She refused to look behind her even when she thought she heard the word—coward.

Brett swirled the amber liquid in the crystal glass and gazed at the darkening landscape through the study's window. All the land the eye could see—

his, and unencumbered by a mortgage or debt. He had kept his promise, the one he had made on that windswept field and on the dock as he'd waved off Bagshott's ship. He had turned his fortune around. He had not sunk into the mire like his brother, and neither had he needed to run to the Continent. And he had achieved it in his own way. And yet, the victory seemed hollow in some fashion. He pushed the thought aside. It was a victory, and that was all that mattered.

All things considered, today had gone well. He had enjoyed crossing swords with Diana Clare, far more than he ought to have.

She might not have conventional beauty, but it was her prickly exterior that intrigued him. Why was she so set against him? What had he ever done to her?

'Simon Clare to see you.' The butler had barely uttered the words when the tall man brushed past him. The cut of the coat might be better and the boots shinier, but Brett felt he would recognise the intensity of Clare's eyes anywhere—and the feebleness of his manners.

Brett pursed his lips. The days when all he'd had was his name and a good eye for the horses were long gone. He refused to be intimidated by a man wearing the latest of everything and boasting about it. Clare always assumed that having money meant you could forgo the niceties of polite society.

'Ah, Clare,' he said, reaching for the decanter. 'It has been a long time.'

'I have come to discuss your latest demand.' Clare ignored the decanter and waved a piece of paper. 'I assume it is why you called at my house yesterday.'

'To see if things could be settled satisfactorily without calling in the lawyers.' Brett paused. How to say it? How not to antagonise Clare? 'Between landowners. Disputes have a terrible way of getting out of hand.'

'You mean amongst the aristocracy.' Clare snorted. 'Don't worry. I know where I fit in. And I can guess what flim-flam Biddlestone said, but I have no intention of selling that piece of land. I might have use for it sometime in the future.'

'Doubtful.' Brett swirled the brandy. Clare was the same jumped-up *arriviste* with his eye on the main chance that he'd been at Cambridge, lacking in bottom. Dog in the manger. The land was lying derelict. 'You have not used that wagon-way since you built the new staith. You have no use for it. I have offered a fair price in the circumstances.'

'You know all about coal mines as well as horses now, do you? Once I have a travelling engine up and running, that old wagon-way could be highly desirable.'

'I can tell when a man seeks to take advantage. Travelling engines are notoriously unreliable.' Brett regarded Clare. At university, Clare had gone on and on about this investment and that investment, always seeking to further his own ends. 'I want the land for the view over the Tyne. Not that you would understand that. The pursuit of pleasure is nothing compared to the pursuit of wealth. Wasn't that what you proclaimed on the staircase? That first day at Cambridge?'

Clare made a disgusted noise. 'You have a better memory than I. Is this derisory sum your final offer?'

'It is a fair sum. Consider it. That is all I ask.' Brett reached for the brandy again, preparing to pour Clare a glass. He and Clare were neighbours after all. They would have to put Cambridge behind them. 'I enjoyed speaking with your sister when we met at your house.'

'And spoke to her again on the High Street.' Clare crossed his arms and glowered. 'What sort of game are you playing at, Coltonby?'

'We were introduced in London. I had no idea at the time she was your sister. She is somehow much more...'

'Refined? Is that the word you were searching

for? My sister was educated at a ladies' academy. She is young enough not to remember how my father had to scrimp and save for every penny.'

'Convivial was the word I was looking for.' Brett permitted a smile to cross his face. 'It would have been vulgar of me to cut her. Don't you agree, Clare? I do despise vulgarity.'

A muscle in Clare's cheek twitched. 'I know what you and your kind are like. You are trying to use her.'

'Am I?' Brett managed to hang on to his temper. 'Pray tell me how.'

'My sister is a lady. Remember that.'

Brett stared at the man in astonishment. 'Tell me how I have behaved inappropriately.'

'I know what you're like. I remember you and your deeds from Cambridge.' Clare leant forward. 'Your business is with me. Keep away from my sister. You are not fit company for her.'

Clare stalked out. The door slammed behind him.

'And what will you do if I keep company with her? How will you stop me? What price will you be prepared to pay?' Brett asked quietly in the empty room. 'Will you sell me the land? No, you will give the land to me, Clare.'

If ever there was a woman who needed a bit of romance and flirtation in her life, it was Miss Clare. All Ladywell society would thank him if she abandoned her hideous caps. He would do it. It would prove a challenge. But in the end, Simon Clare would surrender.

Brett raised his glass. 'To this week's quarry—Miss Diana Clare.'

Chapter Four

Diana balanced the empty basket on her hip. When she had started out this morning, it had been full to the brim with gifts for the sick, and hard to carry, but after visiting the miners' cottages down by the wagon-way, it weighed hardly anything. It had been a productive morning concentrating on other people's problems and once again her mind was free from outlandish thoughts.

'Miss Clare, wait a moment and I will walk with you.' Lord Coltonby called from where he stood, chatting with one of the farm labourers. His hat was slightly pushed back and his cane dangled from his fingertips. The cream of his breeches outlined his legs perfectly. He seemed so entirely different from the men who surrounded him and yet he appeared perfectly at ease.

Diana shielded her eyes. She could hardly cut

him now that he had called out. She attempted to ignore the sudden thump of her heart. She had nothing to fear here, not with all the children running about the lane and playing in the dust. 'Lord Coltonby, what a surprise. I did not think to find you here. That is, Sir Cuthbert never came here if he could help it.'

Lord Coltonby covered the distance between them in a few strides of his long legs. 'I believe you and my tenants will discover that I am a very different sort of landlord. Crop rotation, corn yields and stock breeding excite my interest. I vowed a long time ago that I would not be an absentee landlord when I came into an estate, but instead would nurture it. The land responds to care and attention.'

'Then you plan on doing the repairs to the east cottages?' Diana asked, unable to disguise the scepticism in her voice. The answer was far too pat and too easy. Care and attention indeed. Sir Cuthbert had never given a jot about his tenants. 'A number of the miners and their families rent rooms there. I quizzed Sir Cuthbert about the repairs, but despite his assurances, nothing was done.'

'Repairs cost money.'

'Having unlivable hovels costs even more in the long run—the landowner has a duty towards his tenants.'

'Quite so.' He lifted an eyebrow. 'And I am here to see my buildings. Please judge me on my own merits, Miss Clare.'

'And have you? Have you seen what needs to be done—the holes in the roofs and the smoking chimneys?' Diana asked quickly before her courage failed. She had seen the conditions that the people lived in. Concern for other people and their welfare had been her salvation. She knew that.

'I have never shirked my responsibilities, Miss Clare.' He held up his hand, preventing her from saying anything more. 'Sir Cuthbert was not overly concerned with his estate and his manager was incompetent. We can agree on that. It is in far worse shape than he led me to believe. Give me time to put things right and I am certain you will be pleasantly pleased with the situation.'

'Are you saying that you would not have taken the estate if you had known?' Diana shifted the basket to her other hip. A shiver ran down her back. She was not sure why the thought alarmed her.

'I always enjoy a challenge, Miss Clare. It saves me from getting bored.'

'And boredom is undesirable?'

'You are only leading a half-life, if you have a safe existence.' His eyes flashed steel. 'In order to live, you need to take risks.'

'Ah, does that mean you will be leaving soon?'

'I believe that Ladywell Park offers me enough challenges for the present.' Lord Coltonby stopped by an apple tree. He picked two apples off the branch hanging over the road, and offered one to her. Diana took the fruit with trembling fingers and held it while he took a large bite of his. 'I dislike predicting the future. It can change in an instant.'

Diana rapidly placed the apple in her basket, resisting the temptation. 'Sir Cuthbert always hated being here after he had had a taste of London. The attractions of the city can exert a strong pull.'

'Sir Cuthbert and I are not alike.' He took another large bite of his apple. 'My primary interest is racing, Miss Clare, the breeding and the running of horses. It is how I earn my crust of bread. Northumberland grass is sweet. The air is clean. The purses and plates are rich because the local landowners have the coin from coal. It is a simple equation.'

'Everyone in the village will be glad that something is being made of Ladywell Park. It was once a prosperous estate.'

'It will be again. Better than before. I intend to build a new house overlooking the Tyne. I have had plans for such a house drawn for a very long time.' Brett finished his apple and tossed away the core. 'I made a vow once.'

'Which is why you wish my brother to sell you the land?' Diana inclined her head. The reason for Lord Coltonby's attention was now clear. He thought she could exert some influence over Simon. She should have guessed. The knowledge made her both relieved and vaguely disappointed. 'I am very sorry, Lord Coltonby, but I have no say over what my brother does.'

His eyes widened slightly. 'How did you know I was going to ask you?'

'It stands to reason. Simon was in a frightful temper when he returned home last night.'

'I would consider it a great personal favour if you would at least speak to him.' He paused. 'We shared a landing at Cambridge and it was not successful. I fear he holds my youthful indiscretions against me.'

'My brother keeps his personal feelings out of business.'

'Does he?' Lord Coltonby's lips twisted upwards. 'I wonder if that is a good thing, or not.'

'He never consults me on such things.' Diana tightened her grip on the basket. The conversation was meandering down an unexpected path and she had no wish to repeat the High Street incident. 'Now tell me, is the grass really that much sweeter than Warwickshire? Does the location give you that much advantage? Everyone in Ladywell will want to know.'

'Much.' His eyes grew grave. 'Racing horses is my passion. When I race, I race to win. And I want to be where the biggest purses are.'

'I will remember that.' She gave an uneasy laugh. 'I doubt we will have the occasion to race or even to pit our wits against each other.'

'You never know. You might enjoy it.' The words poured out of him, smooth as velvet. She could almost feel them stroking her skin. 'Are you issuing challenges now, Miss Clare?'

'No.' Diana forced her chin to rise and refused to let him see her discomfort. He was trying to unsettle her, that was all. She tried to ignore how silent the track had become and how the sounds of the children playing were now quite distant. 'If nothing else, London taught me caution. I found it hard to credit how many inappropriate suggestions were put to me before Algernon was cold in the ground. Good day to you, Lord Coltonby.'

She took several steps and then felt his hand on her elbow, preventing her from leaving. His breath fanned her cheek, warming it. Diana kept her body still and concentrated on a stone in the road. 'Let me go.'

'I can only apologise for the crassness of

Songbird's brethren, but you mistook my meaning.' His voice became clipped, his eyes chilled. 'I would never use such a stratagem to force a woman to do anything that she did not want to do. You have nothing to fear from me, Miss Clare, with or without your spinster's cap.'

She knew the combination of her current gown and cap made her look bilious and forty. Even Simon had remarked on its ugliness. She had been pleased with this before, but suddenly she wanted Lord Coltonby to look at her in a different way. A faint tremor went through her. It was as if she had opened Pandora's box and all thoughts and desires she had tried to suppress or hide rushed out in one fell swoop. Maybe she was wonton after all. Maybe all this attraction was coming from her. Maybe her cap no longer protected her. Maybe it never had. No, it had to. It was just further back on her head than she would wish.

Diana jerked the ribbons of her cap hard. The right-hand ribbon and half the cap came away in her hand. Her insides turned over and the stain of humiliation flooded on to her cheeks as she saw the gleam in his eyes.

'It still does not suit you. Heed my advice, Miss Clare—get rid of the cap. Better yet, burn it. A truly determined suitor would take no notice in any case. It only gives the illusion of protection.'

The man was insupportable. How dare he say such things! Her cap was important. It kept her safe. It showed the world that she was a lady, that she was not in the market for a husband. She would have to repair the cap immediately. 'Illusion of protection?'

'I once knew a man who swore that a certain rabbit's foot would keep him from illness and ruinous debts. He paid a tremendous amount for it. He even cajoled me into returning to a nest of thieves and cut-throats to retrieve it after he had been injured in a fight and could not leave his bed. I tried once and was beaten back, but the pleas of the man only increased as he begged me to help him. Bagshott had suggested caution and to forget it, but I opted for the bold approach and retrieved the item. I had promised, you see.'

'And what happened to the man after…?'

'My brother died of typhoid with the rabbit's foot clutched tightly between his fingers. And he was in the process of removing to the Continent to escape his creditors.'

'I am so sorry.'

'Don't be. I merely sought to illustrate what happens when one puts one's faith in objects. Actions are what counts, not objects, Miss Clare.'

'Good day to you, Lord Coltonby.'

'And you, Miss Clare.'

Brett watched her go—her skirts swung about her legs, revealing a well-turned ankle. The encounter had gone better than he had dared hope.

A light suggestion. Friendly banter. Nothing too overt. Miss Clare in the end would do as he wished.

He smiled. And there was very little Simon Clare could do about it, except fume and fret. He looked forward to seeing Clare's face, but mostly he wanted to see what *Miss* Clare would do next. The chase in many ways was far more satisfying than the final surrender.

'I had expected you to be at home.' Simon's annoyed tone greeted Diana before she had even had time to put the basket away.

'I was out visiting the colliers' families. Mrs Dalton is confined with her third child and the Widow Tyrwhitt has taken to her bed.' She paused and removed her bonnet. 'It is my afternoon for making the rounds. You agreed on the importance of this. It is our duty to make sure they are looked after.'

'Yes, yes, you do a fine job. God knows that I cannot see the point. People always have complaints and they fail to understand the virtues of business.'

'Simon.' Diana pressed her lips together. They had had this argument several times over the past few years. It bothered her that Simon appeared to care more about the machinery rather than the people who made it work.

'Later, sister. There is something you need to see.'

'What have you done, Simon?' Diana's corset suddenly felt too tight as she looked at her brother. He was swaying back and forth like Robert did when he'd found a new bird's nest. He was up to something.

'You need to come with me to the colliery. Straight away. There is no time to change.'

'To the colliery? Now?' Diana glanced out of the window at the lengthening shadows. 'It will be nearly dark by the time we get there. Can't this wait until morning? I can then take a basket to the Widow Bosworth. You know how she likes company now that her boys are working down the mine.'

'There is something I want you to see.' He put his hand on hers. 'Please, Diana, say you will come? For me.'

When he looked like that with his dark green eyes, Diana was forcibly reminded of how her brother had been before he had married Jayne, before he had become obsessed with order and control. Before business had ruled his life. Whatever new thing he wanted to show her, it would take her mind off Lord Coltonby and that could only be a good thing. 'I will come.'

'Behold the future!' Simon proclaimed when they arrived at the colliery.

Diana stared at the huge black machine on wheels. A gigantic smokestack was at one end and at the other, a place for someone to stand. Her mouth went dry. 'What is it?'

'A travelling engine based on adhesion rather than pulling or ratchet.'

A travelling engine. The holy grail of every coal owner in the district. Besides William Hedley at Wylam and the viewer at Killingworth, she doubted another man in the whole of England could make a travelling engine work.

'Where did you get it?' she asked, coming to stand by Simon. 'Who drew up the plans?'

'I acted decisively.' Simon's expression was that of a rapt schoolboy. 'Isn't it a thing of beauty?'

'But how did you get it? Only last week, you said that you could not find one. Or even obtain the plans for one.'

'I have ways and means, Diana.' Simon hooked his thumbs into his waistcoat. For the first time in months, Diana saw him smile, a genuine smile instead of the tight-lipped one that did not reach his eyes. 'I had to take the opportunity. All the other masters would have given their eye teeth. Once it is up and running, whole vistas will open out in front of us. I can start up Little Ladywell again, run wagons along the disused wagon-way. Then no one can claim that the land is worthless and redundant.'

Diana sucked in her breath. The disused wagon-way. The land Lord Coltonby wanted to purchase. While she did not doubt Simon's dedication, she wondered how much he was being spurred on by his desire to antagonise his old rival. 'And you discussed this with Lord Coltonby?'

'They delivered it today. I could hardly discuss it before I had the engine.' Simon advanced towards the big black machine, and ran his hand down its side. 'Hedley is right. The only way an engine will work is to be free running, not on a ratchet system.'

'And how much will it cost? Who are the other investors? You have to be practical, Simon.' Diana crossed her arms, and refused to let her brother divert her attention.

'Not if I run it along the old wagon-way. I worked it all out in my mind. It can be done. The old staith can be reopened. And I will have no over-privileged aristocrat telling me how to run my business.'

'Simon!' Diana said through gritted teeth. 'You are behaving in a high-handed fashion. You will antagonise him. I remember the quarrels you had with Sir Cuthbert.'

'But he had learnt the errors of his way. Common sense prevailed.'

'Only because he needed money.' Diana drew a breath. She would have to explain about her encounter earlier and what she had seen. 'Lord Coltonby is different. He isn't intent on drinking the port cellar dry and gambling away his inheritance.'

'What on earth are you talking about Diana? I knew Coltonby at university. Gaming and drinking are the man's life. He was a seven-bottle man. And I could not count the number of card tables he graced, how many brawls he was involved in.'

'University was a long time ago. It strikes me that he is someone who you would want to have as an ally, not as an enemy.'

'He was the over-privileged son of an earl. He threw his weight around. Humiliated me. And I refuse to bow to his wishes and desires. He is not getting one inch of my ground until he has sweated blood for it.'

Diana stared at the large black machine. She had never realised how deeply Simon's experiences at university had affected him. But she had also heard the passion in Lord Coltonby's voice when he spoke of his estate and his desire to do something with it. There was more to the man, if only Simon would see it.

'Simon, you need to grow up and think beyond what happened to you all those years ago.'

Brother and sister glared at each other. Finally, Simon looked away. He loosened his stock. 'Once I get The Duke to run properly, I will see whether I need that strip of land. If not, I will sell it to him for the going rate, not some paltry sum. I only offered it as a sop to Biddlestone when he said he might invest in the engine. Does that satisfy you?'

'It will have to.' Her stays seemed to pinch more tightly than before and a pain developed behind the back of Diana's eyes. Simon had decided to set himself on a collision course with Lord Coltonby and that did not bode well for anyone. She concentrated on the engine. 'But why are you calling it The Duke? After the Duke of Northumberland? One of the royal Dukes? Are you hoping for investment?'

'No, because it is noisy and belches quite frequently.' Simon gave a brilliant smile. 'The steam pressure needs to be high. Nearly to the breaking point of the boiler.'

Diana watched her brother with a sinking heart. Stubborn and unwilling to listen to reason. There were times when she wanted to shake him. He thought he could ride roughshod over everyone and everything in his path. He did not mind the enemies he made as long as the business prospered. Some day, he would realise that there was more to life than proving his business acumen. 'Simon, there are those who doubt that anyone can make a reliable travelling engine.'

'I will do it. When have I ever failed with machines?' He caught both her hands. Simon gave a lightning quick smile, transforming his features and making him more like the boy she remembered from childhood, rather than the embittered man she'd discovered when she returned from London. 'Trust me to do the right thing. It will work, Diana. I know it will. Have faith in me.'

'I do have faith, Simon. How could you ask that of me?' A shiver went down Diana's back. 'I hope you are right. I don't think Lord Coltonby is a good man to cross.'

'Neither am I, Diana, neither am I.'

Diana offered up a silent prayer that it would not come that. She glanced one last time at The Duke, sitting there black and brooding. How much was bravado on Simon's part?

Chapter Five

'Is it true what Miranda Bolt says?' Charlotte Ortner asked Diana, leaning over her tea cup, her face alight with excitement.

'What does Miss Bolt say now?' Diana regarded the candlesticks on the Ortners' mantelpiece. Her weekly round of visiting had proved more tedious than she'd thought possible. Everywhere she went hummed with whispers of Lord Coltonby and his arrival in the neighbourhood, endless questions and speculations. One would be forgiven for thinking nothing else had happened recently in Ladywell or the Tyne Valley. She had only a few minutes left before she could make her excuses and leave. She always stayed precisely a quarter of an hour—no more, no less. 'What new entertainment for the ball has she devised?'

'Miranda says that Lord Coltonby singled her

out for special attention and it is merely a question of time. She said you were a witness and saw his preferential treatment at close quarters.'

'Charlotte!' her mother called. 'Modulation!'

Charlotte lowered her tone and glanced over her shoulder, but, seeing her mother was actively greeting new arrivals, she continued in a low voice, 'I thought I could ask you as you weren't in the running, so to speak. Mama will be livid if Lady Bolt beats her in this marriage stake. And you are the only person who knows the truth. Does he have a penchant for Miranda Bolt?'

'I am really not able to indulge in idle speculation or gossip.' Diana folded her hands on her lap. Trust Miranda Bolt to twist the encounter. There had to be some way of rectifying the situation without calling attention to her own part.

'But Miranda said you were there and would confirm everything.' Charlotte's eyes danced and her mouth quirked upwards. 'Mama's eye is very firmly fixed on Lord Coltonby at the moment. Miranda is planning a stratagem for the ball, and so naturally I wanted to know. Does Miranda tell a tale that is too good to be true?'

Diana shifted on her seat. She needed to stop Miranda Bolt. If she continued in this fashion, the result would be heartache—or worse. Everyone appeared to have little understanding of a London rake's methods. Lord Coltonby would only be caught when he chose to be and not before. 'I have no reason to believe any wedding bells will be ringing for Lord Coltonby in the near future.'

'Wait until I tell Mama.' Charlotte placed her tea cup down with a bang. 'Miss Clare has made one of her pronouncements: Lord Coltonby is destined to remain a bachelor.'

'Please, don't say anything… My acquaintance with Lord Coltonby dates from London. I know what he is like.' Diana's cheeks burnt with a sudden heat. Why did people insist on reading too much into things? She had merely wanted to protect Miranda and ensure her reputation was kept safe, not begin an *on dit* of her own. Her hands went to straighten her cap, but instead encountered her hair. Hurriedly Diana placed them in her lap and made her face assume a beatific expression.

Charlotte's eyes narrowed. 'Why, Miss Clare, I do believe you have abandoned your cap. I cannot see it peeking out from your bonnet.'

'It…it did not suit the dress.' Diana stood up, hoping against hope that her meaning would not be twisted. The rent in the cap had been too great to be quickly repaired and she had hoped no one would remark on it as her status as an ape-leader was widely known. And how could she begin to explain the circumstances in which it had been ruined?

'But Lord Coltonby remembered the acquaintance and he sought you out, practically the day he arrived in the neighbourhood.'

'There are reasons for it.' Diana shifted from one foot to the other. She wanted to avoid mentioning the encounter in the lane. It would only add fuel to the fire. 'Simple reasons. Reasons that have nothing to do with Lord Coltonby.'

Charlotte leant forward. Her eyes gleamed. 'He is the most excitingly attractive man to come into the neighbourhood for ages. Not only titled, single and pleasing to the eye, but with sufficient income to support a wife. Is it any wonder you are tempted?'

'I have no plans to marry. Ever.' Diana pasted a smile on her face. 'I have no wish to join the circling hordes. Your mama's matrimonial plans are safe.'

'Oh, is that how it is?' Charlotte gave a coy little smile. 'You are full of secrets, Miss Clare. I shall have to tell Miranda that she has a rival. You are planning on going to the ball, aren't you?'

'I believe, Miss Ortner, that my time here is at an end. It would be impolite to stay longer.'

However, Diana noticed with a sinking heart that Charlotte had already turned from their conversation and was whispering in excited tones to one of her newly arrived friends.

'And will that be all, Miss Clare?' The shop-keeper stood with his quill poised.

'I believe it will be sufficient.' Diana gave her head a shake. She should have behaved more rationally at the Ortners. The sensible thing would have been to nod and exclaim about the audacity of Miss Bolt. She should never have tried to put the story right. Miranda didn't need Diana's protection.

It was most disconcerting. Normally, she had more control. She did not add to the gossip. But today it seemed to her that everyone was staring and whispering behind their hands. She had made a fool of herself. Their gazes remained friendly, but she knew how quickly such looks narrowed in disapproval…

'Miss Clare?' the shopkeeper said again, bringing her back to the present. Her cheeks burnt slightly. 'I need to know how much of the green velvet you want. Sufficient is a very expansive word.'

'Two lengths will be more than enough.'

'Very well, Miss Clare.' The shopkeeper retrieved his scissors and began cutting the material.

Diana breathed more easily, and studiously ignored the slight jangle of the bell behind her. She refused to turn around and see who had entered the shop. Refused to see if it was him. Life would return to normal now. This instant. She was a mature sensible woman, not given to flights of fancy. She behaved with decorum at all times. She had learnt the value of restraint.

'Here you go, Miss Clare.' The shopkeeper held out her packages.

She gathered up her brown-paper parcels and narrowly missed colliding with Lord Coltonby. His face appeared as black as thunder. His large hands reached out and steadied her, closing around her forearms. A tide of heat washed through her body and her fingers grew lax on the parcels. She forced them to curl back around them, and her body began to regain its composure. She stepped away from Lord Coltonby and nearly tumbled over a bucket. His fingers came very firmly under her elbow.

'You appear flustered, Miss Clare,' he said as he led her out of the shop. His eyes twinkled down at her. 'Something I have done, I hope?'

'No, not flustered, Lord Coltonby, merely in a hurry.' Diana reached up one hand to straighten her bonnet. She longed to ask him why he had gone into the haberdashery. It was not the sort of place she assumed he would frequent. French modistes maybe, if he was outfitting a mistress, but a simple haberdashery, never. 'It is one of the worst of my faults. I spent far too long at the Greys'. And the Ortners'.'

'One can be so busy noticing one's faults that one forgets to notice one's virtues, Miss Clare.'

She tilted her head to one side and prepared to sweep out of the shop with dignity. 'You turn a phrase very charmingly.'

'Sometimes, the truth is charming.'

'I prefer my truth to be unvarnished, without adornment. It is an irritating habit, I am told, but it has held me in good stead these past five years.'

'Or merely prevented you from living?' His eyes slowly assessed her. 'I see you have abandoned your cap. It makes you look years younger. I must congratulate you. Now, perhaps, you will consider wearing a more becoming colour.'

'My life is quite full enough, Lord Coltonby, and I have not yet had the time to repair my cap. I have no need to be made into an enthusiasm, a project to amuse your days. A pleasant attempt, but I know how quickly enthusiasms fade.'

'You truly do not believe in the veracity of that statement.'

'It is what keeps the *ton* fashionable and exclusive. You have to know which is the right tailor, or the correct box at the theatre, which authors to read and which are beyond mentioning. The dances and figures change constantly.'

He blocked her way. 'I ask to be judged on my own merit, Miss Clare, not some poor unfortunate's. It is a small request.'

Diana's cheeks grew hot. It pained her that he was correct. She had been judging him based on someone else. 'There are books waiting for me at the library. I received a note this morning.'

'Minerva Press? Another novel by the author of *Pride and Prejudice?* What excites your fancy today, Miss Clare?'

'Improving tomes on agriculture and crop rotation,' Diana replied in a crushing tone.

'Why do you feel the need to avoid novels? To keep from driving off the road?' He arched a brow. 'I would have thought putting them in a basket behind you would have sufficed.'

'You are an aggravating man.'

'I do but try.' He inclined his head. 'You pique my interest, Miss Clare. Will you truly take out an improving tome?'

She started towards the library and he fitted his steps with hers. Rather than create more of a scene, Diana ignored him. The librarian gave a nod as Diana headed for the stacks. Randomly she picked up a manual on agriculture and the need for efficient crop rotation. 'You see—an improving tome.'

'I never doubted it, and that one is particularly dry.'

'You have read it?' She stared at him. 'Crop rotation?'

'I do my research. It makes for an easier life.' He took the book from her and placed it back in the stacks, standing so close she could see the precise folds of his neckcloth.

She nodded to several library patrons who stopped to acknowledge her. She had thought that Lord Coltonby would make his excuses and depart, but he continued to stand at her elbow, surveying the variety of books. A silent sentinel. 'Are you going to the Bolts' ball? Or do such things frighten you?'

The unexpectedness of the question made her blink and nearly drop the book of sermons. 'I think it is best if I choose my books now. We are beginning to be remarked upon.'

'Clearly something you wish to avoid—which is why you made remarks while visiting this morning.'

'How did you know?' Diana closed her eyes and the full horror washed over her. How people—and Lord Coltonby—must be laughing at her and her pretensions. 'I had forgotten how quickly rumours can pass from lip to lip. Can I assure you, Lord

Coltonby, that I merely wanted to protect an innocent. You are not and never have been the marrying kind. Women who wish to marry should be wary of you.'

'But you have no wish to marry. Does this mean you are not wary of me?' His eyes gleamed. 'What an interesting proposition, Miss Clare.'

'That is not what I meant, and you know it,' Diana said in a furious undertone. 'Certain things have been taken out of context. I merely sought to put a stop to gossip. I do prefer the truth.'

'The truth has many guises, Miss Clare.'

'It was wrong of me.' Diana swallowed hard. 'But I simply had to say something. Otherwise certain women might have given your words and actions a different connotation. I have no wish to see any young girl ruined for the sake of a few pie-crust promises.'

She kept her head high and hoped he would understand.

'You appear to have already made your decision, Miss Clare.' He moved a step closer to her, reaching behind her to pluck a volume from the shelf, his hand skimming her bonnet. 'I am only trying to understand our positions, and to make sure that the rules of engagement are precise.'

'You make it seem like a battle.'

'Oh, it bears some similarities.' His eyes became hooded. 'Certain campaigns must be planned strategically and all eventualities considered.'

'I know your reputation, Lord Coltonby. Your many seductions. I am simply trying to avoid having innocents seduced.' She gave a little laugh and moved away from him.

'You do me a great honour, but I assure you I am human. My exploits have been exaggerated. I have never dallied with an unwilling lady.'

She stared at him in astonishment. She found that she wanted to believe him, that his exploits were not as bad as they had been painted. She wanted to trust her instincts, but they had failed her so miserably before. She could not risk it.

'This is hardly the sort of the conversation one has in a library.'

'I am always open to suggestions, Miss Clare.' His voice was as smooth as silk, reasonable, as if it were she who had proposed something outrageous. The cheek of the man!

'Lord Coltonby, you are being outrageous. Deliberately!'

'No, I am enjoying our conversation and wish to prolong it.' He lifted his eyebrow. 'Would you please explain your objections to this? We are near neighbours.'

Diana tapped a finger against a book of sermons on the shelf. 'And when I do, will you leave me alone?'

'If I consider them valid, of course. I am a reasonable man.'

Diana gestured about her as the rational objections seemed to have completely drained from her mind and the only thing she could think about was the way his long fingers held the books he had chosen. 'For one we are in a library.'

'That can be remedied, presuming you have discovered all the improving books on agriculture that you need. Reading should be a pleasurable experience, Miss Clare. Why do you close yourself off to such things? If you cannot enjoy your reading, why read?'

'The sort of easy words I'd expect from a member of the Jehu club.' Diana shook her head slightly; it seemed to be growing lighter with every breath she took. The only thing that appeared to be keeping her on the ground was the book of sermons currently pressed against her chest.

'And it does not matter how tightly you hug that book, or how many times you repair your cap, life will still happen to you.'

'I am not afraid of life.' Her voice rose sharply. 'Can I help it if I am wary of your reputation?'

'And if I promise to be on my best behaviour?' His voice lapped at her being. 'Will you then continue this conversation? I did so want to hear more of your views on my estate and what actions I should take.'

Diana glared at him. He was insensible to reason. But it also seemed like life had taken a sudden unexpected turn. A little voice in the back of her mind warned about the dangers of becoming involved, however briefly, with a known rake, but she quashed it. But Lord Coltonby's interest was surely only neighbourly. A tiny tug of disappointment wavered within her.

'As it appears that I cannot get rid of you, you may escort me back to my gig.'

'I am delighted that you have seen sense, Miss Clare.'

'Miss Bolt and I were admiring your curricle the other day,' she said firmly, directing the conversation towards more impersonal topics as they started down the High Street towards the livery stables. For once she would indulge in speaking about horses to an expert. 'Or rather *she* was, and I was looking at your horses. Are they from Tattersalls?'

Brett regarded Miss Clare. Her long eyelashes had swept down over her ivory skin. Her dark gown with its high neckline hinted at her curves rather than revealed them. Had he not held her in his arms, he would have been tempted to say that the curves did not exist. But he had, and his body knew they were there. Each tiny step she took was a victory. Slowly. Slowly he'd lead her where she needed to go. She was like a frightened bird and he looked forward to gentling her. However, it was not proving to be as easy as he had first considered. How to get under her defences? That was the question.

'Do you like horses?' he asked, tucking the books she had chosen under his arm and guiding her progress along the street.

'My brother despairs of me. He swears I will break my neck one of these days. With him, they are an imperfect mode of transportation only.'

'Your brother is not fond of horses? That makes sense. I never trust a man who does not have a passion for horses.' He forced his voice to remain smooth. 'A man who has no time for horses has no time for life's pleasure.'

'He has his reasons. Valid ones.' Miss Clare waved a vague hand. 'I understand it, but I disagree. I have loved driving ever since my father first let me hold the ribbons. It was his first proper carriage and I was about four.'

'Ah, that explains a great deal.' Brett gave a short laugh, remembering her indignation at being caught in the mud. His shoulders relaxed. He would use his new-found knowledge to his advantage.

'Does it?' She tilted her head to one side. The shadow of her bonnet brim pointed directly to the fullness of her bottom lip.

'Your annoyance when we first encountered each other.' Brett tucked her arm in his and began to stroll towards his curricle. Not too fast. She gave him a startled look, but he noted with inward pleasure that she did not draw away or find an excuse to depart. He would break down these barriers she had erected. 'I thought it was directed at my rescuing you, but in reality it was directed at the situation. You hated being caught out, not being perfect. And when you are, you retreat.'

'It was arrogance rather than inexperience that led me into that mud pool.'

Brett watched the sunlight kiss her cheeks. There was a passion within this woman, as much as she tried to hide it. He could sense it. But she had repressed it, hidden it even from herself. He would reawaken it and see if the woman she was now bore any relation to the quicksilver girl he had met in London. A memory of her laughing and pointing at the fireworks in Vauxhall Gardens suddenly surfaced and he knew he wanted to hear her laugh like that again. 'Your eyes were spitting mad that day by the mud pool. They shone brighter than the fireworks at Vauxhall. Surely you remember those.'

Miss Clare's face became clouded as the life drained from it.

'I try to forget London.' Her long lashes swept down over her cheeks, hiding her eyes and her shoulders hunched ever so slightly. It was as if she expected to be beaten for it. An impotent rage coursed through Brett at his simple error. She had been at Vauxhall with Finch. He longed to have Finch in front of him, so the man could see what havoc his carelessness had wrought. Brett had disliked his superficial charm and easy manner years ago. He had seen the way the man whipped his horses and his careless disregard for their welfare after outings. No matter what the weather, or the time, horses had to come first.

'Do not judge all men by the failings of one.'

He waited. A breeze blew a tendril of hair across her face. With impatient fingers she brushed it away, but still she said nothing. He willed her to understand.

'I thought it was my love of horses that made him notice me.' Her voice was low and her fingers toyed with the string of her parcel. 'I thought… that we had something in common. Rather, my money and his need for ready cash.'

She gave a hiccupping laugh, as if she had practised the words a thousand times.

'I am sure there were other reasons why he was interested in your hand.'

'That is a backhanded compliment.'

'But sincerely meant,' Brett said gently. 'Take a chance. Trust me to be different.'

Her eyes twinkled, transforming her face, back to the woman of the mud pool. He relaxed slightly. The mood had passed. He could reach her. Somehow he wanted to transform her back to the woman who had been delighted by Vauxhall's fireworks. If he could do that, he would be well pleased.

'Sincerity is always to be welcomed.'

'Shall my horses meet you? However briefly?'

'I would like that. I would like that very much.'

As they approached the curricle, Brett signalled to his tiger. The bays arched their necks and pawed the ground. Brett half-expected Miss Clare to behave like other women and clutch at his arm. Or possibly to turn her lips down in disapproval. Instead, she gave a delighted smile, one that reached her eyes, and advanced towards the horses. She reached up and touched their necks, speaking to them in a soft crooning voice. His tiger nodded his approval.

'It is good to see that you are fearless, Miss Clare.'

She gave the bays one last pat and then stepped away from them. 'They are high-stepping beauties. I would love to be able to sit behind them…' she finished whistfully.

'Now, come driving with me now.'

A strange light flickered in her eyes and he wondered if he had lost her. He willed her to say yes.

'To drive or to watch you drive?'

'You would have to prove your worth before I would allow you to handle the ribbons.' Brett gazed into her eyes. They were changing again.

'Many more people claim to be able to drive to the inch, than can actually achieve the feat.' Brett shrugged.

'And how does one prove this, if you refuse to let them drive?'

He regarded Miss Clare's gloved hands. They looked strong and capable, but small. He shuddered to think what could happen if the horses bolted. The bays took all of his strength to control. 'Before I allow my horses to be driven by anyone—man, woman or child—I make sure that I know the driver is up to the mark.'

'Caution? Hardly a word I would have associated with you.'

'Practical. It prevents accidents.' He touched his hand to his hat.

'Why? How difficult are they to handle?'

'They are a challenge. I enjoy challenges. They fly when I let them, but in the hands of an inexperienced driver, I would not like to be responsible for the consequences. Are you tempted, Miss Clare?'

She gave the brim of her bonnet a tug, shading her face, deliberately hiding it from him.

'I came to town in the gig.'

'My tiger can return it.' He held up his hand and took a deep breath. It felt as if he were playing a very high-stakes game of whist. One final try, then he would be forced to resort to another gambit. But he would win. She wanted this. He could sense it in his bones. 'I promise to be on my best behaviour. Are you prepared to take a ride behind the horses? To feel the wind against your face? They have a turn of speed that is almost unequalled. Of course, if you prefer to return home in the company of your staid mare, I understand completely. Do not complain you were never asked.'

'I am no coward.' Diana fiddled with a button on her glove, weighing her options. Did she dare take the risk? Lord Coltonby had already made it abundantly clear that any attraction was on her part and her part alone. She was not risking her reputation. She was simply going for a drive with a neighbour, an entirely different thing. 'I should like to feel the wind against my face.'

'A drive home, nothing more.' A faint smile played on his lips. His eyes held a distinct gleam. 'I wish to be neighbourly, Miss Clare.'

Diana wet her lips, took once last glance down the High Street and nodded.

Chapter Six

Brett concentrated on the horses and the taut reins, rather than on the slim woman sitting next to him, but every so often he glanced over to where she sat, face entranced, watching the horses' every move. He had half-expected her to cling to his arm, the instant he allowed the horses to leap forward, but her back remained resolutely straight and her hands folded. She showed no inkling of screaming, but every aspect of enjoying the ride.

Colour had flooded back into her cheeks and her eyes shone with a blue-green intensity. She leant forwards slightly as if she was urging the horses to go even faster. The wind caught her bonnet and sent it flying backwards.

'I had quite forgotten what it was like to have the wind blow throw my hair,' she said with a laugh as she struggled to replace the bonnet, holding on to it with one hand.

'And do you like it?'

'I like it very much. It is exhilarating.'

'Good, I am glad. If I have made you remember joy, then it pleases me.'

'Oh, yes, joy.' She leant forward. 'Can you make them go faster?'

Brett flicked the reins and the horses sped away. He knew in that instant that he had never seen a woman more alive. Her love of carriages and fast horses shone from her—but it also made her dangerous.

He pulled on the ribbons and the horses came to an abrupt halt.

'Why have you stopped here?' A furrow appeared between her brows as she turned in her seat, looking up and down the deserted road. Her hand clutched the side of the curricle and the bright colour faded from her face, draining all the life from her features. 'Have I been foolish in the extreme? You gave your word, Lord Coltonby. Straight home.'

'We are going back to your house, but I wanted to stop here for a moment. I wanted privacy for our conversation. We need to get the parameters in order.'

'Take me back,' she squeaked. 'Now! I command you! I beg you! Do as I ask.'

Brett resisted the urge to curse. He had misjudged the moment. He had to gain her trust, but certain things needed to be said before they went further. He always conducted his romances in this manner. It made things less messy when the time came to part. He wanted Diana Clare to have no false expectations, no excuse to claim breach of understanding.

'I have my code, Miss Clare. You are as safe here as you were in the library. I merely wanted to speak with you privately. Forgive the slight deception.'

'Privately?' Her eyes widened, much as a horse's did when it was spooked.

'To make sure you understand that I have no intention of marrying.' Brett made sure his words were said very slowly and unhurriedly, almost singsong. 'My attention is not to be perceived as a courtship. Marriage does not figure on my horizon.'

'Am I supposed to swoon at this earth-shattering news, Lord Coltonby? You are not telling me anything that I don't already know.' She gestured frantically towards the road. 'You may drive on, having said your pretty piece. Allow me to reassure your vanity by saying that I have no intention of marrying you.'

'It is well we understand each other. I would hate for a miscommunication.'

'As would I.' She turned her face away.

He reached out and his hand covered hers. Brett felt it tremble slightly and let it go. He would accept the strictures of their relationship for now, but he intended to have more. There was a passionate woman under her frosty exterior. He was certain of it. Brett silently cursed all who had made her this way. She was like some nervous wild thing, intent on camouflaging herself so that she could escape unnoticed. London gossip had badly scorched her, but he could see the woman inside trying to escape. 'You are a welcome distraction from the necessary business of sorting out the estate, and I value your friendship. I enjoy getting your perspective on the problems I face. Biddlestone nearly ran it into the ground.'

'It was lucky you acquired it, then. It is an estate that begs to be loved.'

'But seems unlovable to the casual observer.'

'And are you a casual observer?'

'I pride myself on my keen eye, Miss Clare.'

Diana shifted uneasily on the curricle seat, increasing the space between her and Lord Coltonby. With his thigh pressed against her leg, she found it difficult to concentrate on anything but his physique. He was speaking of more than the estate. It terrified her that he might be speaking of her. 'I need none of your flummery, Lord Coltonby. If you are going to persist in this sort of behaviour, we will have to return to being the barest of acquaintances. We need to decide which of the cottages you should…'

'Brett.' His voice positively purred. And the look he gave her was pure male. A look that sent her pulse racing. The look of a rake, a practised seducer, she reminded her heart. 'I really must insist you call me by my Christian name, if we are to be *intimate.*'

Intimate. Diana felt her cheeks grow hot at the picture it conjured up in her mind. She banished it, locked the thought away in that little part of her mind where she never permitted herself to go. Forced herself to remember the pain and humiliation she had suffered and to silence the little voice which protested that Brett was different. Diana took a deep breath and regained control. She would hold true to her promise. She would never be seduced again. She had learnt her lesson.

'Acquaintances implies no intimacy.' She tilted her chin in the air and focused on the horses' ears. 'Lord Coltonby or Coltonby will surely suffice. I cannot address you by your Christian name. Think of the scandal.'

'I must disagree with you. The word said in

private will have no effect.' His eyes danced with an unholy mischief and Diana began to wonder what precisely she had agreed to. She should never have behaved impulsively and agreed to the drive. She should have contained her temper. When would she learn not to give in to temptation? Reason was what was important. Brett's hand slid down her shoulder and his fingers curled around hers, held them in a light but gentle grasp. Diana resisted the urge to tighten her fingers about his. 'Try it. Once. Here and now. No one but me will listen.'

'But I…' Her tongue became thick in her mouth and she turned her head away. It seemed there were two of her—the lady she had promised over and over again to be on her journey from London to Newcastle, and then her true self, the one who could not resist temptation. She had thought the latter gone, but she had only been slumbering, waiting her chance. But was Diana ready for heartache? For the pain, for the scandal?

'Give it a try. You will find it quite simple. Allow my name to flow from your lips.'

'Brett,' she whispered, her voice barely audible. Her lips ached as if they had been brushed by his. She touched her fingertips to her mouth. Concentrated hard. 'There, I have said it. Are you satisfied?'

'Say it like you mean it. Roll the R's.'

'Brett!' Diana said, through gritted teeth. 'And I never roll my words.'

'I would have preferred honey-sweet seduction, but I will take the tartness of vinegar for now.' He clicked his tongue and the curricle began to move. Diana felt a sigh escape her throat. Of regret? Of disappointment? She refused to ponder the emotion.

'You are incorrigible.'

'So my nurses used to tell me.' His laughter rang out, startling the wood pigeons in the trees.

'You had more than one nurse?'

'My brother and I had a succession of nurses. It depended on whether my father was in funds. My mother used to despair. The worst was that the roof leaked. In many ways, I was pleased to be rid of the Abbey after my brother died. Constant repairs and a house so riddled with damp that one should start anew.'

Diana absorbed the knowledge. 'But your father was an earl. Surely he had the money to fix the roof and to keep the damp out.'

'My father was also a poor gambler. He gave in to impulse and failed to do his research properly. Inclined to rush his fences. Neglected to ensure the settlement before his death.'

'You are wealthy now. Or is that something else Lady Bolt has mistaken?'

'My wealth is my own, Miss Clare. In that I have proved more adept than my brother or my father. The title I share with my forebears. There is a difference.' He clicked his tongue and the horses stirred, obeying every flick of his ribbons. There could be no doubt that the beasts knew who their master was. *Their* master, but not hers. She refused ever to have a master.

'Stop! Stop!' A young girl stepped out in to the road and waved her arms wildly. 'Please stop, I beg you.'

Brett pulled hard on the horses and brought the curricle safely to a halt.

'Jenny Satterwaite, what sort of mischief is this?' Diana asked before the girl had the chance to say another word. 'I know about the tricks you and your brother played on Widow Tyrwhitt.'

'No trick, Miss Diana.' Jenny drew a line in the dust with her toe. 'And I did clean out her house, like. Mam said it were proper, like.'

'Then what is the difficulty? Is it your father again?'

'No, Miss Diana. He's back at the mine.'

'Is some hazard up ahead?' Brett asked smoothly.

Jenny shook her head. 'It's me mam. She's

stuck. Stuck in the stairwell and there ain't none that can help. Me and Jimmy have pulled and pulled, but she ain't moving.'

'How did it happen?'

'The stair boards were loose, but no one has fixed them. We've been waiting for the new lord to come. Me mam said he would put it right.'

Diana shifted uncomfortably, not daring to look at Brett. She could not bear it if he refused this child.

'He is here and he will help if he is able.' Brett leapt from the curricle. 'Do you have someone who can hold the horses?'

Jenny's brow puckered. Then she nodded. 'Jimmy can. He loves horses. Da is hoping to get him a job at the mine as soon as there's an opening.'

She ran off back in to the house, shouting. Diana stared at Brett in astonishment. What did he plan on doing? 'Shall we send somebody out?'

'Forgive me, Miss Clare but you will be slightly delayed. I believe this woman has the greater need.'

A small boy, a year or so younger than her nephew Robert, came out of the house. His eyes widened when he saw the horses. 'I thought Jenny was funning me.'

'If I give you a penny, can you hold these horse? Tight, mind, and don't let them move.'

'I will do it, sir.' The boy stood straighter.

Brett held out his hand to Diana. 'Right, shall we see about this woman in distress?'

They followed Jenny into the cottage and immediately were greeted by a series of moans. Diana's heart twisted. She had half-expected it to be another one of Jenny's tall tales, but Mrs Satterwaite was lying half in and half out of the stairwell, her face creased in pain.

Without hesitation, Brett went over and lifted her out. There was a great cracking as the board gave way, but the woman emerged to great squeals of delight from Jenny.

'Thank you, sir.' Mrs Satterwaite gave a tired smile. 'I had no idea how I'd have kept going till them that lives next door came home.'

'Is there somewhere you can rest?' Diana asked. The cottage with its narrow stairs was even darker and danker than she remembered from her visits.

'Bed's upstairs. We had to let the downstairs room go and move upstairs now that money's tight.'

'Look after this.' Brett took off his coat and handed it to Diana. Her fingers curled around the warm cloth and held it close. 'I believe I can fix this—temporarily. Boards, nails and a hammer, if you please, young Jenny Satterwaite.'

The girl ran off and quickly produced them. Diana watched as Brett nailed the boards in place, covering the rotten patches. Then he tested each of the other stairs. 'Not perfect, but it will suffice for now. I will send the workmen to fix it properly tomorrow.'

'Yes, my lord.' Mrs Satterwaite's eyes grew big. 'If you please, my lord, I've been telling me man about those boards for an age. He is a good man, Miss Diana. It were just the accident that turned his head.'

'It will be sorted now. I intend to look after my tenants properly.' The words echoed in the small cottage. Before, she had thought his words were easy, but now she could see that he meant them. He cared about these people. 'I trust you have no objections, Miss Clare.'

He took his coat from her unresisting fingers and they returned outside. Jimmy Satterwaite held the horses. His face was screwed up into an intense look of concentration. At Brett's approach, the horses pawed the ground but Jimmy clung on with dogged determination, preventing the curricle from moving.

'I doubt my tiger could have done better.' Brett handed the boy a coin. 'Come to my stables. I can always find a job for a boy who's good with horses.'

Diana watched the boy run back into the cottage, shouting the news. 'You are not what I expected.'

'Neither are you,' he murmured as the curricle

started moving once again. 'And do I have your leave? May I call you Miss Diana like the Satterwaites do?'

'If you must.' She took a deep steadying breath and willed the ride to last a little longer, but already the gates to the Park were looming ahead.

'Diana, named after the huntress goddess of the moon.' His voice purred her name, doing strange things to her stomach. 'Have you been to Italy or Greece, Miss Diana? Have you seen how large and yellow the moon can be as it rises over the sea?'

'I have only once been away from Northumberland—to London.'

'A pity. Italy is beautiful, but with the war, Greece is more accessible.' He slowed the horses to a steady walk. His arm came over the back. 'I should like you to see Greece with its hidden glades and moonlit beaches.'

Diana ignored the slight tremor inside her. Words flowed from him as easily as water slipped down the Tyne.

'I doubt that will be possible. I have too many responsibilities here.'

'Will you go to the ball?'

Diana hesitated for a heartbeat. She could readily imagine dancing a cotillion with him. It would be so easy...then she shook her head decisively. 'My mind is made up there as well. Balls and I are not a happy combination.'

He reached out and touched her cheek. It took all of Diana's willpower not to turn her face into it, to press her lips against his palm. Her being shivered. 'But attempting to change it could be amusing.'

'I am not here to provide you with amusement.' Diana moved her face away from the delicious torment.

'Ah, the proper Diana Clare.' His hand fell to his side.

'You did promise—friendship.' Diana kept her back ram-rod straight. 'Surely you are not going to break your word? Or was it simply a rake's promise, one designed to lull me into a false sense of security?'

'It is you who holds the reins. We will proceed at your pace.' He put his hand over his heart. 'On my honour as a gentleman.'

'And your honour as a renowned whip?'

He sighed and rolled his eyes heavenwards. 'That as well. You are perfectly safe with me, Diana, even if you persist in challenging me. Confirmed ape-leader that you are.'

'Should I be flattered with your assessment?' Diana asked in a tight voice.

'That is a matter for you to decide.' His face

betrayed no emotion and he appeared utterly absorbed in handling the reins.

Diana breathed easier when she arrived back at the Lodge. Brett had obeyed her wishes. He helped her down and his touch was impersonal rather than the searing one of earlier. A vague disappointment washed over her body. She realized she had wanted more.

A wisp of hair blew across her face, reminding her how the wind had felt in her hair and she brushed it away with thoughtful fingers. Diana knew in that moment that she could never wear her caps again. She had remembered the joy that came with experiencing life.

Another spray of roses needed to go in the garland, Diana decided as she regarded her sketch with a practised eye. She had spent the afternoon sketching out a new mural for the summer house.

She had begun decorating it five years ago when she'd needed to forget Algernon, pouring out every passionate impulse until it seemed like her soul was on the walls and her body was only an empty shell. It had seemed complete six months later, but now she realised it could do with another garland or two of painted flowers. It had worked once. It would work again.

'I understand you made an exhibition of yourself this morning,' Simon said, glowering in the doorway of the dining room. 'I would have thought you'd be the one person I could trust not to invite scandal.'

Diana looked up from her sketch. Simon's face bore traces of grease and the stock at his neck was askew. Her hand trembled slightly. She had considered that there might be some talk, but not that Simon would hear it—not so quickly, at any rate. Nor be upset about it. He had to realise that she was a grown woman and could be trusted to behave sensibly.

'Hardly an exhibition, Simon. Lord Coltonby offered me a lift in his curricle. It would have been churlish to refuse.' She tucked a stray lock of hair behind her ear and made her voice sound firm. 'It has been a long time since I have ridden in a racing curricle. The bays flew down the road with their heads held high and the wind whipping all around us. Truly magic.'

'I know how they flew.' Simon's frown increased. 'Maurice Bolt challenged Coltonby to a race this afternoon. He wagered his best mare against Coltonby's boot-blacking receipt.'

'What happened?' Diana pressed her hands against her thighs, and silently prayed that Brett had done nothing foolish. Maurice was the apple of Lady Bolt's eye and thoroughly spoilt. According to Mrs Sarsfield, he had been sent down from Oxford last term for some unspecified misdemeanour. And Rose had decreed that no maid ever wanted to be caught in a corridor with him. Diana knew she ought to be neutral, but she did hope Brett had won and won decisively.

'Coltonby won by a length. He is a menace. What sort of man claims a horse when he has only wagered a receipt?'

'Maurice should not wager what he can ill afford to lose. And for that matter, what sort of man wagers his horse against a receipt?'

Simon's face turned beet red and his mouth opened and closed several times. Diana forced her hands to remain in her lap and her back to stay straight. Surely her brother was not so blind to reason that he could not see whose fault it had been?

'I only speak the truth, Simon. And Maurice probably only challenged Lord Coltonby because he thought the bays were tired. He deserved everything that he received.' She leant forward, and was relieved to see an answering smile on Simon's face. Crisis averted. She searched her mind for a more appropriate topic, one that would not include Brett Farnham and his exploits.

'But why did you need a lift?' Simon asked before she had fixed on a good subject. 'You took the gig in. I distinctly remember you saying at breakfast that you were taking the gig.'

'Lord Coltonby's tiger returned it. Jester is in the stables, munching away at her manger of hay.'

'That is by the by.'

'Do you really think I would pass up the chance to go behind a team like that? The speed, Simon.' Diana clasped her hands together. Willed him to understand. 'You know that I liked to drive curricles once upon a time.'

'But Lord Coltonby…' Simon's mouth turned down at the corners. 'He has a certain reputation with women. I worry, Diana.'

'I hardly think he would be interested in me, Simon. Ever since we renewed our acquaintance, he has behaved perfectly properly,' Diana replied, looking her brother steadily in the eye. 'Are you saying that you don't trust your sister?'

She picked up her drawing pencil and sketched another leaf.

'He won't marry you, Diana.'

'Good. I have no intention of marrying him either, Simon.' Diana tightened her grip on her pencil. 'I am quite resolved on the subject.'

'You are not considering…' He cleared his throat.

'Simon! What you are suggesting is infamous.'

Simon's face brightened. 'I was worried. It was the talk of the reading room this afternoon. How my sister had brazenly wangled a ride with the notorious Lord Coltonby and then how he'd triumphed over poor Maurice Bolt.'

'Who has spread the rumour?' Diana saw the confirmation in his eyes. Her stomach churned. She had failed to consider that Lady Bolt might act out of spite. 'Since when have you put any credence in her pronouncements about me?'

'Women sometimes take strange notions into their heads. I have no wish for this aristocrat to break your heart. I know what that Finch fellow did.' Simon slammed his fist on to the table. 'Dammit, you deserve better than that, Diana. When Coltonby was at university, I lost count of the number of women he sneaked into his rooms. My sister will not share that fate.'

'Simon, stop it. You are spinning fancy.'

'Diana, you must be careful. The man has deliberately singled you out. There will be more to it than meets the eye. He will want something in return.'

Diana held back her words. She knew all too clearly that Simon's late wife had had her heart broken and had married on the rebound. Simon, blinded by her beauty, had not realised what was happening until it had been too late. It was one of the reasons Diana had been pleased to escape to London. Jayne had faded over the years, becoming a pale shadow. Diana knew that even now Simon refused to believe that Robert was his, refused to accept the evidence of his own eyes.

'I learnt my lessons years ago.'

'But you are no longer wearing your cap,' Simon protested. 'It suits you, but I wondered why. Are you seeking to enter the marriage market again?'

'I may have little interest in marrying, but I do not have to conduct myself as a dowd.' Diana carefully sketched a rosebud. 'The two are unconnected. I grew tired of the caps. They made me feel old.'

She bent her head and redoubled her efforts at drawing the rosebud as Simon's eyes bore into her neck. He had to believe her. 'Diana, I will trust you, but may I ask you a favour, a little trifle?'

Diana's hand stilled and she regarded her brother's suddenly intent face. 'A favour. What sort of favour, Simon?'

'I want no distractions, Diana. I do not want to be worrying about you making a spectacle of yourself again. Let me concentrate on my engine.'

Diana pressed her lips together. He was not concerned about her or her reputation—or her protection—rather the distraction it represented. All her brother wanted to do was to work on that engine. 'I have no plans to make a spectacle of myself, as you put it. I am not even planning on going to the ball. You may go alone.'

'You know what I mean—today. You and him. No more fodder for the gossips.'

Diana fought to keep her voice calm. 'Nothing happened, Simon. Nothing at all. He is our neighbour. I hardly wish to start a feud with a neighbour.'

'Diana, be reasonable. I need to concentrate on the engine. How can I if you will persist in parading down the High Street with Lord Coltonby? It is distracting.'

'I did not parade, brother, but I will assure you I have no intention of doing anything of that nature again. As you know, I only went to town because you insist I socialise with the local gentry. I am far happier here—painting and reading, visiting our workers' families and the sick.'

'I will have to accept that.' Simon stuck his thumbs into his waistcoat, every inch the superior brother.

'You will.' Diana jabbed her pencil down and broke the point. How dare he put strictures on her as if she had no more brains than a feather duster? 'You may find that you have much in common with Lord Coltonby. You should take the time to be neighbourly yourself.'

'I have nothing in common with that...that arrogant fop. I have worked for every penny we have, Diana.'

'I only meant that you were both men of intelligence. I am well aware of the sacrifices you have made, Simon. You do not need to detail them for me.'

'Then you will understand.' Simon leant forwards, so that his face was level with hers. His green eyes burnt with a fierce intensity. 'I will do what is necessary to make sure Ladywell Colliery not only survives, but thrives. The travelling engine will be my legacy to the world. And no one is going to stop me.'

Chapter Seven

Diana looked back over her shoulder at the line of painted flowers and leaves. The morning's work had sped by and she now could see the outline of the garland taking shape. It would work, this plan of hers. It had worked five years ago when she had done the first few. Her mind needed a focus, an outlet for her creativity, rather than sitting there, dreaming about things that could never happen.

A leaf was slightly off centre on the first sequence of roses. She wrinkled her nose and stared at it, the mistake in the shading growing more obvious by the breath. Diana bit her lip, considered her options. Did she really want to reposition the heavy ladder for one bit of shading? She could reach it, if she stretched. She glanced down at Titch. The little terrier wagged her tail and shook her head before giving a low bark and covering her nose with her paws.

'I will be careful, I promise.'

She dipped her brush in the paint and began, balancing precariously. Her knees trembled slightly as she reached out a little bit further. Her mind circled back to the problem. Brett Farnham with his money and title had his pick of women. He always had. She didn't need Simon's university tales to tell her that—she had the evidence of her own eyes from London. Why would he be interested in her, an acknowledged spinster? She sighed as she added one final line of dark green. Eventually if she repeated it to herself enough times, maybe her heart would believe it. Maybe she would stop listening for the scrunch of carriage wheels on the gravel.

'Do you always take risks like that?' Brett's low voice resounded in the room.

She turned quickly and the ladder rocked violently. A small shriek escaped her throat. She made a wild grab for the top rung. Missed. Her body fell backwards through the air. Slowly. Strong arms closed around her, and held her.

The stillness of the air was shattered with the thump of the ladder hitting the ground and the splintering of glass. She shivered and tried not to think about what could have been. Looking up, she noticed the dark lashes that fringed Brett's grey eyes. Short, perfect for a man.

'You are safe.' His voice caressed her ear. Their breaths mingled, more intimate than a kiss. His mouth was mere inches from hers. All she had to do was lift her head the merest fraction.

She swallowed hard and resolutely turned her face away. 'Let me go, please.'

'You should take more care. You could have been hurt.'

His arms loosened and her body slid down his, his hand on her back guiding her descent. Soft curves met the hard muscular planes of his chest and thighs. Slow. Sensuous. Creating a burning ache within her. She stood there within the circle of his arms, her body arching closer, seeking him. His hand tightened slightly, burning through the thin cloth of her muslin gown.

Then reality intruded. She realised what she was doing—practically begging for his kiss. She stepped away from him, filled her lungs with air and determinedly changed the subject. 'How… how did you find me?'

'I happened across your maid, sewing in the garden. She thought you might be here.' His voice was silk across her jangled nerves.

Silently Diana cursed the perfidy of Rose and her matchmaking tendencies. She would have to speak to her maid. She gestured towards the fallen ladder, and spilt paint. 'If you had knocked first, all this might have been prevented.'

'What were you doing, risking life and limb like that?'

'I was painting.' Diana rocked back on her heels and peered up at him over her shoulder. Her pulse raced as the shifting colours in his eyes mesmerised her. She had forgotten the exact curve of his lips and the way he had faint smile lines about his eyes. She pressed her fingertips together. Strove for a normal tone. 'It is one of my pastimes. An enthusiasm. An important one.'

'The ladder was not steady. It was an accident waiting to happen. You could have been seriously injured.'

Diana regarded the wreckage. Water and paint mingled with broken glass and crockery. The ladder, which had seemed sturdy, was now on its side, a pile of sticks. A shudder went through her. She tucked a stray lock of hair behind her ear, a small act, but one which steadied her. 'I had missed the green shading on a leaf. It seemed the easiest way.'

'You ought to have taken the time to move the

ladder. You could have overbalanced at any time. If you are going to take risks, you should have someone watching over you.'

'Titch is here.' She gestured towards where the traitorous terrier wagged her tail.

He reached down and gave the dog a pat. Titch wagged her tail furiously at the attention. 'As sweet as the dog might be, she does not inspire confidence.'

'I am fine, truly fine. Nothing untoward happened.' She clenched her jaw. 'I have no need for a protector.'

'Allow me to be the judge of that.' His eyes darkened again, becoming deep pools.

She forced her gaze away and stumbled over to the small table where the teapot and cups sat, waiting for her to take a break from her painting. She concentrated on the fine porcelain and tried to regain control of her pulse.

When she decided she could risk it, she turned, half-expecting him to have followed her. But he stood where she had left him. A large solid presence that had invaded her sanctorum. She knew she would not find the peace she had craved here, that the image of him standing there would be for ever engraved on her mind. Her way of banishing him had failed. She picked up a porcelain cup, but her hand trembled and she set it down with a bang. All she felt capable of doing was staring blankly at the table.

'Did you do all of this?' Brett walked over to the far wall and examined the earlier garlands. His voice was calm, soothing, as if he were speaking to a skittish horse. 'The flowers are very intricate. At first glance, one would almost believe them to be real.'

'It is something to occupy my days. I try to avoid going into the village.' Diana crossed her arms over her breasts, and stared stubbornly at the wall. 'It amuses me to get it correct. I have recently returned to these murals. It needs another garland around the walls. Around the ceiling as well as at chair level. I can't think why I had not realised before.'

'You should be more careful. Your maid should keep you company.'

'I generally am, but I also require solitude when I am painting. Ask anyone. Miss Diana Clare is exceedingly sensible, they will say. An uninteresting life.'

'Except when she drives into mud pools and falls off ladders.' A faint smile played on his lips as he took a step closer. The tiny room appeared to shrink. Diana's hand wanted to stretch out and touch his white shirt front. Instead, she twisted it around her apron. 'It was providence that I arrived when I did.'

'I understand you won a race yesterday.' Diana gestured about her, tried to retake control of the conversation as her heart thudded in her ears. 'When I first heard that you had raced, I was worried that the horses might have been tired out.'

'I wanted Bolt to think that. He was mad to think I would even consider racing if my horses were not up to the job.'

'You tricked him. You wagered your blacking receipt against a mare.'

'He made the challenge. I accepted. There are many who wish to discover the secret of my black boots. My valet has been offered numerous bribes, but, thus far, he has proved a loyal servant.' He gave a short laugh and put a boot on the chair. 'My boots remain as black as ever and now I possess a decent brood mare. I really must go driving down the High Street with you more often.'

Diana resolutely ignored the sudden flush of warmth that went through her. The words flowed naturally. Smooth. Elegant. And all the more deadly for it.

'I can offer you a cup of tea.' She picked up the pot and held it in front of her like a shield. 'Rose only left it a little while ago. I covered it with a towel.'

He pulled out his fob watch, checked it. 'We have no time to spare. We are going driving and I hardly think you want to be seen with paint flecks in your hair.'

'And you think I will go driving with you? Down the High Street again? My brother was livid.'

'In the country.' His eyes danced and his voice became a low purr. 'Your brother can have no objection to my current scheme.'

'Why would I want to do that?'

'I thought you might want to take a basket of food to Mrs Satterwaite. You appeared concerned about their welfare.' He paused. Each word became slower and more seductive. 'Think of the possibilities, Diana.'

'I can easily drive the gig. I will have the cook pack some calves'-foot jelly. It is a quick journey. You really must not think about troubling yourself.'

Brett took a step closer. His smile became more enticing. 'The offer to drive my curricle may not come again for some time. And my cook has already made a meat jelly and a rice pudding.'

'You mean to let me drive?' A shiver of delight ran through her. The bays! And the curricle! 'As reckless and foolhardy as I am?'

'I wanted to see if you can handle the ribbons. However, it is your choice. We can stay in the summer house if that is your desire.' He reached out and covered her hand with his for a heartbeat.

A brief touch, but one that promised much… 'Is that what you want? To remain here in the summer house with me discussing the weather?'

Diana withdrew her hand as she gazed up into his eyes. It was strange how quickly the planes of his face had become familiar. Even his scar seemed pleasant, rather than foreboding as she had first considered it. The walls of the summer house seemed to push inwards, making the space between them shrink. Diana swallowed hard. 'We could have a cup of tea.'

'I am quite amenable to taking tea in whatever form you care to offer it.' His voice dropped on the word—*tea*—lengthening it, giving it a connotation she had not considered before.

Silently she cursed her wayward imagination. She forced her breath in and out several times and willed her shoulders to relax.

His eyes sparkled. 'But I think you would prefer the drive. Think of it. The wind rushing past you, the ribbons taut under your hands, the road opening out in front of you.'

The words curled around her insides, causing tingles to run through her.

'You mean to torment me until I give into your request?' She tilted her head to one side, trying to assess his mood.

'To remind you and, I will admit it, to bribe you. I thought you would enjoy showing me your skills.'

'You mean I am to drive the bays?' Diana clapped her hands together. 'They are not nearly as difficult as you made them out to be.'

Brett shook his head. 'I want to be sure you can handle the ribbons. The bays may come in time, but for now the black gelding is harnessed to my curricle. He is steady, but not for the novice. Then I will know…if we should *progress* further.'

Diana bit her lip. He was offering an olive branch to a neighbour. He was willing to give her a chance to prove she could handle the ribbons. And a chance to observe Mrs Satterwaite's condition, to do her duty, rather than simply drive for pleasure. Temptation shimmered in front of her. She could do this. She had given Simon her promise not to go to town, but the proposed drive in the country was an entirely different matter.

She glanced down at the enormous apron that covered her round gown. It was paint splattered and all enveloping. Hardly clothes suited for being seen in public. It would give her a chance to regain her reserve, to forget what it was like to be in his arms. 'If you will allow me a moment to change, I would be delighted to show that I can handle the curricle.'

'Diana.' His hand reached out, held her as she attempted to move past. Her feet skittered into each other as his scent enveloped her.

'Yes?' she breathed. Her mouth ached and she barely recognised her voice.

He brought his finger to his mouth and then touched her cheek. 'You have green paint, just there.'

A little impersonal touch, but one that made her insides turn over. A warmth grew within her but she resisted the urge to explore where his hand had made contact. 'I do?'

He nodded. 'It is gone now.'

All she could do was to stare at his forefinger. Surely he would kiss her. Her tongue wet her lips and she waited, but he merely arched an eyebrow. 'The curricle awaits its driver.'

'I will make sure I scrub my face, then. Make sure every piece of paint goes.'

'It looked quite sweet.'

'I have no wish to disgrace you when we are out on the drive.'

'I doubt you will do that.'

'But I must be properly dressed.' Diana hated the way her voice caught. But she knew once she was in her most severe riding habit, she would feel less off balance, less tempted to make a spectacle of herself. She had spent five years going over the mistakes she had made, and the lessons she had learnt and she refused to throw that all away. Brett Farnham was dangerous. She had to remember that.

'In your own time.' His voice floated after her as she hurried away from the summer house. 'I am a patient man.'

Brett was prepared to admit that Diana could handle the ribbons as well as most men by the time they left the Satterwaites. Mrs Satterwaite was recovering from her ordeal nicely and had asked if her Jimmy's tale was true, would Lord Coltonby be prepared to employ him? When he confirmed it was, she'd called on all the angels to bless and keep him. Brett had smiled. The day was turning out to be far more enjoyable than he had thought possible.

Under hooded eyes, he watched Diana's profile and saw the intent but happy expression on her face. She had changed out of her paint-splattered clothes into a very severe riding habit. But rather than hiding her charms, it only enhanced them. After holding her in his arms earlier, he knew what must lie under the high-necked collar and artfully placed lace at the base of her throat. His fingers itched to unwrap her and lay siege to her hidden desires.

She reminded him of one of his more nervous horses, one which had been badly abused by a former owner and was disinclined to trust. He would handle her reins very carefully; gently but firmly he would lead her in the direction he wanted to go. He would teach her and she would trust him. Each step towards intimacy had to come from her. If he gave the slightest indication that he desired more, she would shy away as she had done yesterday.

'Does your brother let you drive?' he asked to distract his thoughts from the agreeable way her bosom filled out her dress.

'Simon considers horses to be a means of transportation rather than a way of life. He grumbles about the cost. And how if horses could eat coal, we would save a great deal of money.'

'For me, horses are a way of life.'

'That does not surprise me.' Her merry laugh rang out. 'You appear to have a way with them. I had despaired of ever getting Jester out of that mud pool.'

'Is the piebald your only horse?' Brett kept his voice carefully neutral, but watched her face for any sign of hesitation. She might not want to go into the village with him, but she *would* go to the ball. It would be the final act to push Simon Clare over the edge. Clare would learn a very important lesson. The best part was that Brett was having a far more enjoyable time than he had presumed possible. Miss Diana Clare was entirely unexpected.

'Jester is good for generally driving about the country. Simon keeps a pair for the carriage, and I have a chestnut for riding. Robert, of course, is still on ponies. He keeps begging for a proper horse and I hope to convince Simon that he is old enough. But all that will have to wait until he returns from school.'

'How old is Robert?'

'Nine.'

'Surely he could move on to proper horses? What is your brother thinking about?'

'My sister-in-law was thrown from a horse. She took too high a jump because my brother had dared her and spent the last few years of her life in pain.' Diana's face became shadowed. 'She eventually caught lung fever and died, but Simon has hated horses ever since.'

Brett regarded the horse's ears. He had no wish to feel sorry for Clare. But for the first time, he had a small glimpse of what the tragedy must have done to him. For a long time, the only sound was the steady turn of the wheels and the clomping of the horses.

'I had wondered about riding,' Brett said into the stillness. 'Do you feel the same way as your brother?'

The torment of sitting next to her was growing

with every breath he took. She was not his usual sort of fare, but there was something about her. He kept finding reasons why he had to see her, and couldn't help but think about the way she held her head or her hands.

He would make her want him, would make her forget about everything but her desire for him. She would come to him.

'I generally ride out every morning. Early. Sir Cuthbert's father used to let me use the Park's grounds as well as our own, but now…' She made a little gesture with her hands. 'I had not wanted to disturb you. Or for you to feel that I was taking advantage.'

'Please do not let the change of ownership stop you.' He put his hands over hers on the reins, and they quivered beneath his. 'You do take someone with you?'

'Generally, I have a groom, but really, if I am riding on the Lodge's grounds, there is no point.'

'Is there anywhere in particular you recommend for riding in the neighbourhood?' His eyes were intent on her mouth. 'What is your favourite ride? Where is the best place to exercise a horse?'

Her fingers curled tighter around the ribbons and for an instant he was sure he had gone too quickly. 'If you ride up the hill and past the spinney, the view over the Tyne is very good, particularly in the morning when the mist hangs and it has an otherworldly look. It always makes me feel as if life is worth living.'

'It is a good view to know about.'

'Yes it is. You should go up there sometime.'

'I intend to.'

Her eyes had turned a deep turquoise. Brett fought against the temptation to cup her face in his hands. They would meet there, one day, he promised himself, but not yet. She had to want it first.

'Tell me about your nephew, the one you left London for.'

'He goes to Dr Allen's Academy in Newcastle. He boards there.' Diana paused. How could she explain Robert? He wanted his father's attention, but Simon refused to pay any notice. 'He gets into scrapes, but he means well.'

'I should like to meet him. I enjoy speaking with children.'

Diana started and the horse began to move more swiftly. She grasped the ribbons and rapidly brought him under control. Brett raised an eyebrow.

'Now there is something unexpected,' she said with a laugh. 'It will teach me not to be surprised when I am driving a curricle.'

'The horse—or the fact I enjoy other people's children.'

'You and children.' Diana gave a smile.

'Why?'

'I would have thought as a founder member of the Jehu, you would be immune to the joys of such things. Drinking, gambling and debauchery—wasn't that the creed?'

'People change and grow.' His eyes became hooded. 'Children provide a respite from the strictures of the society. Some day, I should like my own. I like to think I will do a better job of it than my father. I swore I would on his deathbed.'

'And I wish you well with it.' Diana disliked the slight quaver in her voice. No doubt, he would marry some Diamond of the Season. She had to remember that theirs was an acquaintance, a friendship, not one destined for the altar. She refused to even consider dreams of what that might be like. And yet, it refused to go away.

'You seem perturbed, Diana.'

'I think the paint fumes were rather stronger than I expected.' She gave her head a shake and banished the image of Brett holding a baby. 'But driving has revived me.'

His fingers closed over hers, a warm firm grip,

but one that did not allow for refusal. 'Then would you care for another challenge and a wager?'

'What sort of wager?'

'A simple one. I will wager you driving the bays whenever you want against a dance at the Bolts' ball.'

'But I am not going to the ball,' Diana replied quickly before she could give into the temptation. Wagering with him could only be dangerous. How could she even be contemplating such a thing?

Brett raised one eyebrow. 'Are you not confident of winning, Miss Diana?'

'In order to dance with you at the ball, I would have to be going to the ball. I am not.' She clenched her fists. 'In any case, I do not make a habit of wagering.'

'And the thought of going to a ball is so dreadful that you are not prepared to risk it for the pleasure of driving my bays... whenever you want to.' He rubbed his hand across his chin. 'It appears to me that you do not consider yourself an expert driver, and this is why you have no wish to take up the challenge. It has nothing to do with wagering and everything to do with you not feeling confident.'

Diana bristled. Not confident? She could tackle anything. 'What do you want me to do?'

'I have set up a little obstacle course. Something

to test my reflexes. It occurs to me that if you can complete a clear round, you will prove to my satisfaction that you can drive…unless you are afraid of losing.'

'I am not afraid.' Diana drew a deep breath and ignored the sudden warning voice in her mind. This was not a wager per se. It was about proving him wrong. But she had to think strategically. 'I have doubts that you can complete this course.'

He pursed his lips and she thought for a moment he would refuse.

'How sensible you are, Miss Diana.' As he took the reins from her, his voice became liquid honey. 'The rules of the course are that you do it as quickly as possible and the curricle does not hit any of the hurdles. I shall demonstrate.'

The curricle went through a gate into a harvested field. Bits of stubble and gleanings still lay about, but the ground was firm. Five sets of hurdles were placed at odd angles to each other, providing a series of quick turns.

Diana wrinkled her nose 'The hurdles seem to be set awfully close together.'

'It can be completed…if you know what you are doing.'

Brett clicked his tongue and the black gelding set off at a fast pace. Once the curricle tipped on to one wheel and bounced back down, but he managed to make it through all the openings.

'Well done.' Diana clapped her hands.

Brett gave a boyish smile. 'It is your turn, Miss Diana. At a trot, if you dare…'

'Of course I dare.' Diana spat on her gloves and took the ribbons. She regarded the first opening, went over the course in her mind, trying to remember how Brett had done it. It was the fourth set of hurdles that was the most difficult. Once she got past them, everything would be straightforward.

'Whenever you are ready.'

She flicked the reins and the horse set off. The first set of hurdles flew by. The second and the third. Diana reined in tightly and felt the curricle slip a little. She corrected her grip and aimed for the fourth set, held her breath and heard the carriage wheels slide through.

She let out a breath. Risking a glance up at Brett's face, Diana could see it had become set.

The last hurdles loomed in front of her. An easy set, slightly narrower than the others, but her line was true. She would do this. She could imagine the bays in front of her, responding to her every moment. She would drive out every day. She flicked the ribbons, urged the horse forwards, to complete the final obstacle.

The curricle started to go through. Diana winced as she heard the slightest crunch of the wheel against the left hurdle. She pulled back, trying desperately to change the angle as the hurdle seemed to hold. The curricle went through and she pulled the horse to a stop and prayed.

She released a breath.

'I have done it! I have done it!' She raised her hand in triumph.

Behind her, a distinct thump resounded. She glanced back and saw the hurdle down on the ground. 'I...I...'

Brett lifted one eyebrow and his lips twisted upwards in a sardonic smile. 'I believe you will be going to the ball after all, Miss Diana, but a solid attempt all the same.'

Chapter Eight

Of all the idiotic things she had done in her life, yesterday's wager with Brett Farnham was one of the worst. She should have known that the course would not be easy. She should have yielded to caution. She'd made her rules for a purpose, not to be bent or disregarded. But it was done and she would abide by the terms of the wager. The next time, she would turn a deaf ear to his blandishments.

Luckily she still had the very modest ball gown from two years ago when Simon had forced her to go the Grand Allies rout at the Assembly Rooms in Newcastle. Rose had reluctantly agreed to alter it slightly, grumbling that either the blue-green or the deep rose pink would have been a better choice. After insisting on the brown, Diana retired to the summer house and painted furiously.

'I thought I might discover you here,' Brett's low voice slid over her skin. 'I am pleased to see that you took my advice and your feet are solidly on the ground.'

'The garlands are nearly completed.'

'Hopefully they give the effect you want.'

'Not entirely,' Diana admitted. 'There is something missing.'

'A perfectionist. Is this the only summer house that you have painted?'

'I painted the Bolts' summer house four summers ago when the Dowager was still alive.' Diana kept her gaze on the flowers. 'She insisted that no one else would do.'

'You did those murals?' His eyes widened. 'Now I am impressed. Sir Norman showed me them the other day when I picked up my winnings.'

'Thank you.' Diana bowed her head as warmth infused her body. 'In the end, I was very pleased with them, but the Dowager was a hard task master—always changing her mind.'

'Of course, you have completely ruined my stratagem for getting you out into the garden during the ball.'

Diana looked up at him and saw a small smile tugging at his lips. 'I never go into gardens during balls.'

'A wise policy, but you will go to the ball and you will dance with me.'

'I have not danced for years.' Diana gave a strangled laugh. 'Some of the newer dances were nearly beyond me. All the twists and turns. It was a nightmare at the Grand Allies ball. I was so nervous that I would be asked to dance, but thankfully only Simon bothered and that was only out of duty, so I excused him.'

'Your steps might be slightly rusty but you have natural rhythm. I can see it in the way you move, the way you walk.'

'Thank you.' Diana took a quick glance up at him. The sunlight from the door gave him a halo, darkening his face, but highlighting his broad shoulders and well-formed legs. What would it be like to be in his arms? She quickly dropped her gaze and studied her hands. A paint blotch marred the right one. Something real and solid to cling on to. He was being kind.

'I do mean it. I seem to recall you dancing beautifully in London.'

'You will find me a poor partner unless it is the Roger de Coverley at the end. The last time I took lessons was five years ago and I am certain the figures will have changed.'

'I have a plan to deal with your lack of knowledge.'

'You do?' Diana started to rearrange the brushes in the water pot—smallest on the left, largest to the right. Everything correct and in its place. Simply because she had abandoned her caps did not mean she had abandoned her reason or her rules.

'I shall teach you to waltz. You and I are going to dance a waltz together at the ball.'

'A waltz?' Diana swallowed hard and concentrated very hard on the middle brush, the one she had used for the red of the final rose. 'I have no idea how to waltz.'

'I suspected that. It is why I am here.' He held out his hands. 'I plan to educate you on the finer points of the waltz.'

'You must be joking. I won't waltz.'

'But you agreed, Miss Diana. You agreed to dance with me at the ball.' His voice was smooth, but there was a steely determination. 'Unless you want me to choose another forfeit, a forfeit more suited to a wager between a man and a woman. You were the one who lost the wager. It is up to me to name the terms.'

'You wouldn't dare.'

'Try me.'

Diana backed away, looking about her. 'But where are you going to teach me to dance?'

'Here will prove adequate for my purposes.' He

held out his hands. 'My expertise is at your disposal. You do not want to look foolish in front of the Honourable Miranda and the Ladywell gentry, do you?'

Diana put her hand to her throat. 'With you? Alone? In the summer house? There will not be space for more than a few steps.'

'A few steps will be all you need.' He quickly moved the table out of the centre of the room before placing his coat, hat, gloves and cane on it. 'There, you see—lots of space.'

'There must be a thousand reasons why I should refuse. It is a highly improper suggestion.' Diana squared her shoulders and took a deep breath of air. Tried to think something else besides how Brett looked clad only in his shirtsleeves. 'I would be dancing unchaperoned.'

'And one reason to do it.' Brett's voice became the merest whisper.

'What is that reason?'

'The very best.' He paused. His bare hand touched her shoulder. A shiver went down her back at its warmth. 'Because you want to. Because you desire it.'

'I think it is probably the worst reason.' She backed away.

'It will be perfectly acceptable. Have I done

anything untoward? Behaved improperly?' He inclined his head. 'Come with me, take a risk.'

Diana kept her hand firmly at her side, concentrated on filling her lungs with air and then releasing it. The action appeared to steady the muzzy feeling in her head. 'I fail to see when I would need to know how to dance the waltz. It is a pointless exercise.'

'The dance is all the rage on the Continent.'

'Napoleon is all the rage there as well,' she returned quickly, ignoring the tingling that ran through her body. 'Does this mean we shall have him here as well?'

His face sobered. 'He will lose. His reign will come to an end—sooner or later. But I speak of dancing, not politics—an infinitely preferable subject when conversing with ladies. You will not get around me that easily. To the matter at hand— your waltzing lesson.'

'Sometimes, dancing and politics appear to be the same thing.'

He laughed, a rich deep laugh that circled around her and lapped at her senses. '*Touché*, Diana Clare, I know why I like you. You always argue your corner and counsel the sensible action. You are…unexpected.'

'And this is a bad thing?' Diana tilted her head,

trying to assess his mood. He seemed intent on teasing, rather than seducing. She breathed slightly easier.

'When taken to extremes, but I think there is hope for you yet.'

'I shall take it as a compliment.'

'Will you take your lesson like a well-brought-up lady?' He leant towards her and lowered his voice. 'Or do you wish to display your ignorance in front of Miss Bolt and her mother? I overheard Miss Bolt proclaiming that there would be a waltz at the ball. She seeks to prove a point, I believe.'

Diana pressed her lips together. The scheme sounded like one of Miranda Bolt's. And no doubt she and her cronies would be the only women on the floor who could actually dance it correctly. She could hear the giggles and the small pitying sighs. He was right. It would be fun to wipe the smirks off their faces.

'I have trusted you this far. I will trust that you waltz like a gentleman.'

Brett looked down at the pale oval of Diana's face and willed her to stay. It was not deception. He would not do anything that she did not want to, but she *would* waltz with him at the ball and he was determined that she would not make a fool out of herself. Then he would take her out into the garden. And when the kiss happened, it would seem to come from her. He would simply give her the opportunity. And there would be nothing Simon Clare could do about it, except give him the land. A perfect, fool-proof plan.

'Shall I demonstrate the steps first?' he asked, moving away from her and her teasing scent—a hint of vanilla, lavender and something else. It lingered in his mind and he found himself thinking about it at odd times, wondering about her and what she was doing.

'It is probably best. How long can learning to waltz take? A few basic steps. Once around the summer house?'

She moved away from him, crossed her arms and watched him with a sceptical expression. It would be easy to capture her and to tilt her face towards his and make it change. He took a step forward, stopped and regained control.

'Oh, it will take several turns. I think the tea can wait until we are finished. You don't want the servants gossiping.'

'I suppose you are right.'

Brett heard the slight tremor in her voice. Silently, he cursed Finch and all those who had harmed her with careless actions or words. He could see flashes of the woman behind the mask she wore.

'Solid preparation is always the foundation of a good campaign.'

'Ah, yes, a campaign, I can see that.' Diana clasped her hands in front of her, lacing the fingers together. In another moment, she would find an excuse and flee. The moment would be lost for ever. Brett was certain of that. He willed her to stay. To trust him and her instincts. His plan required her to dance the waltz beautifully.

'I generally get my way in the end,' he said softly, watching the way a curl of hair kissed her cheek.

'Your way?' She put her hand to her throat and took a step backwards as her eyes darted about the small room. 'Are you certain of that?'

'Which is why I am going to teach you to waltz. Now pay attention.' Brett picked up a chair, held it in front of him. 'Pretend you are this chair. Keep your eyes on my feet. You will be following my footsteps in reverse. It is terribly bad manners to step on your partner's toes.'

He quickly executed a few steps. A burst of laughter came from behind him. He stopped. Frowned. 'What is wrong with my dancing?'

'You look…ridiculous. Waltzing with a chair.'

'Then dance with me.' He placed the chair down and turned to face his quarry. 'It is easier if I have a woman in my arms.'

Brett waited as her tongue flicked over her lips turning them a deep red. He held his body still. Suddenly, like the sun breaking out from the clouds, her face transformed and she held out her hands. Brett released his breath.

'You have convinced me. What do I do?'

He stepped closer, allowed her perfume to envelope him, savoured it. Then he forced his mind to attend to business. 'Place one hand on my shoulder.'

'Like this?' She raised her hand and grabbed. 'Do I have it right?'

'Lightly. A caress. Not a death grip.'

She gave a nervous laugh and loosened her grip. 'I am not used to such things. Perhaps we should forget it. There must another dance, an easier dance, you could teach me. What else is fashionable in London?'

He placed his hand on her waist, lightly. Held her there. 'No, I want to teach you to waltz. I came here today for that purpose. Now allow me to help you.'

She trembled slightly at his touch, but did not move away. He concentrated hard as his fingers itched to draw her close and to feel the way her soft curves met his body. Suddenly he longed to undo the tiny buttons that held up her dress and to reveal more of her creamy flesh, but he pushed the thought aside, wondering where it had come from. And why it seemed to block out any other thought.

'You only have yourself to blame if I step on your toes.' She smiled up at him.

'You won't.' He allowed his hand to increase the pressure. He started to hum slowly. 'It is one, two, three and turn. Listen to the tune.'

He began to hum a waltz. She stood rigid in his arms, head cocked to one side.

'Very pretty, but I doubt that Lady Bolt will allow such scandalous behaviour in her ballroom.'

'The Honourable Miranda has her dear papa wrapped around her little finger. It will happen. Now stop trying to find excuses and start moving your feet.'

He forced his feet to move, stepping carefully, keeping the proper distance, resisting the temptation to pull her closer and to breathe in her scent. Hesitantly she followed his steps, but rapidly grew in confidence. He moved faster, feeling her limbs move in time with his.

'I keep thinking I will stumble or fall. Are you sure it is the right tune?' She looked up at him with a tiny frown between her brows. 'We seem to be moving awfully quickly.'

'I know what I am doing.' He took a step and

changed direction. Her skirt swirled out, grazing his shins. She gave a breathless laugh and he spun them around the narrow confines of the summer house again. 'Follow my lead. You are doing well. We shall make you an expert at the waltz in no time, and then no dance shall hold any fears. All will say what an up-to-the-minute miss you are.'

Her footsteps slowed and he cursed his wayward tongue. She started to pull away, but Brett tightened his hold on her waist.

'I doubt I shall ever be able to dance this in front of others. I have no idea what folly possessed me to agree.'

'Relax your shoulders. It is not folly to learn new things.' Brett smoothly turned her again, her skirts billowing out again. He wanted to keep on dancing with her, around and around.

'Sometimes, it is. I learnt the hard way. I know what I am doing now. The lesson should end.'

'Stay.' He kept hold of her hand. 'Please. You are nearly perfect. Once more around the room. I wish to be certain.'

Her footsteps faltered, slowed. He sucked in his breath. His body felt as if wave after wave of molten heat had hit it. His control began to slip as her lips were inches from his…

'Please,' she breathed.

Brett took it for an entreaty and gave into his desire. He lowered his lips to hers, sliding across their lush softness. He pressed his hand against her back, drew her closer, drank from her lips. A moment suspended in time and space, having no beginning or end, just the sweet temptation of her mouth. His tongue traced the outline of her lips and then the tiny parting, a gentle persuasion.

His arms went around her waist, pulled her closer, felt the melting warmth of her. He adjusted her body to his and his lips moved against hers—asked rather than demanded.

There was an innocence about her kiss as if she did not fully understand the passion that could exist between a man and a woman, the passion that threatened to overwhelm him. Brett couldn't resist deepening the kiss, flicking his tongue against hers, teasing her. She gave a little moan in the back of her throat and then she stiffened, pulling away. With his last ounce of self-control, Brett allowed her to go. Forced his body to take a step backwards and his ragged breathing to slow. It was harder to do than he imagined, but necessary. He would not force her.

The lesson was over.

This was not the time, nor the place. When she came to him, he wanted to be able to take his time and savour every inch of her. She would come to him, he was certain of that. It was only a matter of time.

'I believe that is enough for now.'

'For now?' Her fingers explored her mouth and her sea-green eyes were dilated, wide and alluring, surrounded by dark spiky lashes. He gazed up at the ceiling, trying to concentrate.

His hand reached out and lifted a curl from her shoulder, tucking it back into place. 'A lesson in waltzing was all I promised. One new thing a day.'

'I think you ought to go.'

'I believe that would be a good idea.'

Every particle of him longed to pull her back and kiss her, make her beg him to stay, but it would cause more problems than it would solve. She was far too tempting a morsel for something rushed. And they had been lucky. It was only a matter of time before her maid came searching or one of the servants found a reason to visit the summer house. No, the situation was far from ideal. Right now, right now, he needed to think, to clear his head.

He ran his thumb over her lips. 'So beautiful, so beautiful.'

Brett turned on his heel and strode out of the house and away from temptation.

* * *

Diana sat, regarding the toast and tea on the breakfast table with a distinctly jaundiced eye. This morning, she had taken pains, dressed in her best blue riding habit and had gone for a gallop, fully expecting to see Brett as she reached the top of the hill. Nothing. It bothered her that she had succumbed, that she had eagerly anticipated seeing him. Bother Brett Farnham and his flirtation!

'Mind where you put that.' Diana moved Simon's plans away from her coffee cup.

'The answer is in here, Diana. A bit more steam, a bit more pressure, and the engine will go.'

'But will the boiler be strong enough?' she asked, turning her mind forcibly away from Brett and his lips. 'I heard one blew recently at Wylam.'

'You know nothing about engines, Diana. Don't even start.' Simon snatched up the drawings, knocking over his tea cup. He gave a low curse and then apologised.

Diana spied several letters as well as Simon's copy of the *Newcastle Courant,* half-buried under his massed papers, pens and ink. 'You should have said something.'

'I am very busy with the engine.'

Diana reached for the letters. She had recognised Robert's childish scrawl, but frowned at the bold masculine hand of the second letter. With impatient fingers she broke the seal. Her heart dropped further. 'Lord Coltonby has had to depart for a few days. He hopes to be back soon, but makes no guarantees.'

'Why would Coltonby be writing to you?' Simon's green gaze narrowed.

'He and I have become friends, after a fashion. I told you that we both like driving.' Diana opened Robert's letter. 'Robert has written from Dr Allen's. He is doing Tacitus and Cicero this term. Hates them both.'

'I refuse to be distracted with Robert's news. Did Coltonby say why he was departing or where he was going?'

'Is it important, Simon?' Diana regarded her brother and willed the sudden hollow feeling inside her to go. 'He has left the neighbourhood.'

'It means that I have the measure of the man. Lord Coltonby will be no threat to us. He is much the same as Biddlestone.' Simon bent his head and made a few more notations on the plans. 'And it was far easier than I dared hoped it would be. If you will excuse me, sister, I have work to do.'

'But don't you want to read Robert's letter?' Diana held the missive out. 'He has mentioned

Henry again, the lad who gave him so much trouble last term.'

A pained look crossed Simon's face. 'Later, when I have time to answer it. Or, better yet, you answer it. You know what he wants to hear. I am no good at such things.'

Diana stared after her brother. A great feeling of hopelessness swept over her. There had to be something she could do to help Simon and Robert, but the one person she felt instinctively would give her some advice had gone away. It bothered her that within a few short days she should come to value his opinion. She tapped the letter against her mouth, pondering.

She had to go to the ball, even if Brett was not there. She was tired of hiding in the house. Tired of wearing browns. Tired of running from life.

'I have changed my mind about the brown silk, Rose,' she said when the maid came in answer to the bell.

'Yes, miss?'

'You were right after all. It is only fit for the rag-and-bone man.'

'You are not going to the ball?'

'Do you remember the gown that I was going to wear to Vauxhall Gardens, but decided against? The deep rose silk?'

'Yes, miss, it complimented the colouring in your cheeks.'

'It came home with me, didn't it?'

'Yes, miss. It is in the attic.' Rose's eyes widened and she clapped her hands. 'You want to wear that.'

'It is a bit out of fashion, I know, but I think it will suffice.'

'It could be altered...' The maid screwed her face up. 'I mean, the ball is less than a week away, miss, but it could be done.'

'Do it, Rose.' Diana caught Rose's hand. 'Do it for me. I am through being overlooked and disregarded.'

The white waistcoat he wore for Almack's or the patterned one he wore for other balls? Brett checked his appearance for the fourth time. The white one. He wanted everything to be perfection. Diana Clare would keep her part of the bargain and dance with him. To waltz in anything but his best would not do.

Over the past few days as he had travelled to the various stock markets in Northumberland conducting business, Brett had found it difficult to banish Diana from his mind. The temptation to taste her lips again nearly overpowered him and his mind had wandered. In Rothbury, he had ended up missing the one horse that he had wished to acquire. Not a fatal error, but disturbing neverthe-less. Normally distance made him forget, but it had only increased his longing. Her eyes and her mouth had invaded his dreams.

Brett fumbled with his neckcloth, swearing at his own incompetence. He then took up another piece of starched linen and began to do the intri-cate folds. Concentrated. This time, the neck-cloth fell into its accustomed shape. All was right with the world.

Tonight he would put the final pieces of his scheme into place, and he would strike. It would be the end of it. A pang of something went through him. Regret? Sorrow? Brett did not stop to analyse. He had enjoyed Diana Clare's company. That was all. Her wit and her refreshing conversation. He frowned. The neckcloth was slightly skewed to the right and looked as if he was still at Eton. His hands went to straighten it. Spoilt it. He tore it off and began again.

'The neckcloths appear not to be holding their shape this evening, sir, as well as they normally do. Shall I ask for more starch next time?'

'They are fine as they are.' Brett ignored the growing pile on the ground. Seven at the last count. 'I was…attempting a new fold.'

'And, my lord, if you do not mind me saying, a

woman is not worth fretting over. Fickle, they are. Changeable.'

'I have never fretted over a woman, Vrionis.' Brett lifted his chin, and completed the last precise folds. He stepped back, slipped on the black tail coat. 'Ever. Remember that.'

'I know that, sir. I was just saying, like…in case you had forgotten it. The air up here in Northumberland.' His valet brushed a speck of dirt from the coat. 'Only the other day, I caught myself looking at a piece of skirt, wondering, like, what it would be to have little ones with her. Nearly frightened me out of my breeches. I have given the woman in question a wide berth since then. A very wide berth.'

'The air has nothing to do with it. I know what I want. I know why I am going to this ball.' Brett closed his eyes. His first glimpse of Miss Clare at Vauxhall Gardens all those years ago rose before him. A vision in white, her eyes sparkling as she looked around her with great eagerness. Her laughter as the fireworks had sparkled overhead. A woman in love with life. Innocent but with promise. He shook his head, willed the image to be gone. 'I am only going tonight to ensure Miss Clare carries out the terms of our wager. She failed to negotiate the last set of hurdles. I will not have her going back on her word.'

'As you say, sir, you never fret about a woman.'

Chapter Nine

Everyone who was anyone in the Tyne Valley and Newcastle—from the Grand Allies who owned the coal mines and ran the north of England to the various serving officers and their wives—appeared to be at the Bolts' that evening. From joining the queue of carriages to reaching the Bolts' door had taken the Clares' carriage a half-hour, a journey that normally took but a few moments.

Diana adjusted the neckline of the deep rose ballgown. Thankfully her figure remained unaltered from London and Rose had been able to work miracles with her needle and thread.

Lady Bolt's mouth visibly tightened when she and Simon greeted her. However, as Diana took her customary place at the side of the dance floor, she knew that it would take more than an elegant dress to make her the belle of the ball. The men's eyes slid over her and she became invisible as time after time she saw the bright goldenness of the Honourable Miranda being led out on to the dance floor. It was foolish to even hope that Brett might be attracted to her. He had merely sought her out as a distraction from the boredom of being buried in the country. Simon had been correct. She had been foolish even to hope and even more foolish to allow that kiss to happen.

Obviously he had removed himself in order to allow the situation time to resolve. Sensible but ultimately disappointing.

Diana forced her mind to concentrate on exchanging pleasantries with various neighbours. Hopefully, after tonight's disappointment, he would stop invading her dreams, filling her with an intense longing, a longing so great that when she woke, her lips ached and her body burnt. It was an affliction, but one from which she would recover in time.

Diana clenched her hand and redoubled her efforts to listen intently to Mrs Sarsfield's explanation of how she had managed to cure her grandchildren's fever with little more than a cold compress. Mrs Sarsfield's cap with its many ribbons positively quivered as she related each detail with increasing animation. Diana felt her eyelids begin to slide shut and struggled to contain her yawn. It would be hours before Simon would want to leave.

A shadow fell across her face and her nerves instantly became awake. Without even looking, she knew who approached. Even Mrs Sarsfield fell silent and her withered cheeks pinkened.

'Miss Clare, how delightful to see you again.' The purr of Brett's voice flowed over her. 'I had wondered if you would be here.'

Diana turned her head. She had forgotten how devastating he looked in evening clothes. His broad shoulders neatly filled out the black tail coat, his pristine white neckcloth was tied to perfection and his black breeches clung to his thighs.

She remembered when Algernon had once pointed Brett out at the masquerade they had attended the evening after they had become engaged. He had been surrounded by a bevy of beauties, but had lifted a glass of something in her direction and she had looked away, cheeks glowing with heat, desperately confused by her reaction. The same sort of nervous anticipation filled her now. Only this time, she knew it for what it was—desire—and knew what it was like to be held in his arms.

'Lord Coltonby.' She kept her voice cool, but

tightened her grip on her fan and forced her gaze upwards to where the many crystals of Lady Bolt's imported chandelier twinkled. When she felt she had regained her sense, she looked directly into his ever-changing grey eyes and discovered that she had forgotten the multitude of colours therein. She swallowed hard and strove for a normal voice. 'I see you have returned from your journey? Did you discover everything you desired?'

'Most things, but I hurried back for the dance. The evening festivities have been on my mind constantly.'

'Constantly?' She ignored the sudden fluttering of the butterflies in her stomach.

'I even let several farmers believe they had got the better of me in order to be here.'

'Hopefully, that does not mean you made any mistakes in purchasing your horses.' Diana attempted to keep her voice light, to remember that this conversation was purely for show, but she wanted to believe that he had returned to see her. 'I would hate to think that, in your haste, you had mistaken the horses' form.'

'My eye for line and form remains undiminished, even when attempts are made to disguise them.' His eyes travelled slowly down her face and came to rest on her neckline. 'Definitely undiminished.'

Diana forgot to breathe as she resisted the urge to pull her lace higher up. She should never have let Rose alter the bodice this low. Her only hope was that he would think the pink of her cheeks was down to the warmth of the room.

'Are you two acquainted?' Mrs Sarsfield enquired, raising her quizzing glass. 'I am not sure I have had the pleasure…'

'Lord Coltonby,' Diana said quickly in an undertone. 'He has recently acquired the Park.'

'Oh, I have heard about him. And you. Old friends, Miss Ortner said. And I said that there was more to it than that, but my daughter-in-law refused to believe it.' Mrs Sarsfield gave a distinct nod and smacked her lips together as if she had chanced upon a particularly juicy piece of gossip. 'Wait until I tell her I have actually met the man in question.'

'But Mrs Sarsfield…' Diana began.

'The introductions, if you please, Miss *Diana,*' Brett commanded.

Diana swiftly made the introductions as Mrs Sarsfield beamed and her ribbons quivered. The elderly woman gave a little titter as Brett bent over her hand, treating Mrs Sarsfield as if she was the most important personage in the room. Two bright spots appeared on her cheeks.

'I had the pleasure of meeting Miss Clare in London many years ago and made it a point to renew our friendship when I moved up here,' Brett said smoothly as Mrs Sarsfield's effusive greeting died away.

'My daughter-in-law dismissed my notion out of hand as fanciful. She swore that you two could not possibly have met. And that…well… never you mind.' Mrs Sarsfield stood up. 'If you will excuse me, I am going to enjoy this.'

Without giving Diana a chance to protest, Mrs Sarsfield hurried away, moving more quickly than Diana had thought possible in a woman of her stature, pausing only to hurriedly whisper to another group of elderly ladies.

'I believe you have made a stir,' Diana commented. 'One smile from you and she melted.'

Brett merely lifted one eyebrow. 'It is you have made the stir in that dress. All I hear is the men asking themselves who the vision in deep rose is and how can they beg an introduction. I came over to stake my claim before there was an insurmountable queue.'

'And pray, when will this queue develop?' Diana gestured at the empty space in front of her. 'I have yet to see any sign.'

'After we dance.' He held out his arm. 'Shall we? One small cotillion?'

Diana let out a little breath. So it would not be a waltz after all. It was probably safer this way, but she had wanted to feel his arms about her again, however briefly. She refused to let idle compliments turn her head. She was the sensible Diana Clare. The débutante who lived for parties and who had hoped to make a splash in the *ton* had vanished long ago. Her dreams had turned into a nightmare and it was only her rules that now kept her safe.

'I might step on your feet.'

'No one will be watching my feet. All eyes will be on my partner.'

'I had not realised that you had returned,' she said. In another moment, she would follow Mrs Sarsfield's example and melt under his gaze. 'I had wondered if your business would keep you out of town.'

'My note said I would appear. Trust me when I say that I keep my promises.'

'I would have understood.' Her hands curled tighter around her fan, waiting for the signal that they should go out on the dance floor. 'I would have understood if you'd thought better of our rash arrangement. It seems foolish now that I think about it. This dance will certainly fulfil the terms of our wager.'

Brett's jaw tightened and he slowly looked her up and down. 'You only think you understand, Miss Diana, but I wonder if you actually do.'

'Like you, I keep my promises, but I am glad that I came.' Diana dropped her voice. 'Miranda Bolt gave me black-daggered looks as I entered, but she soon cheered when it became apparent that I was in my customary place, speaking with Mrs Sarsfield.'

'There is to be a change to your customary place.'

'You need not worry about that.' Diana made a little gesture with her fan. 'Simon will look after me once he has finished speaking with Mr Hedley and some of the other Grand Allies. They are discussing the merits of engines.'

'I promised you a dance. I have come to claim it.' He held out his gloved hand, beckoned to her as the orchestra struck the first notes. 'A waltz. I did guess correctly after all.'

'Mrs Sarsfield considers the waltz to be immoral,' Diana said quickly to banish the thoughts of Brett's hand on her shoulder and their bodies moving in time together. 'She predicts it will never be accepted by society. Her daughters-in-law all agree. She has been most vocal on the subject.'

'And I predict that it will be danced at Almack's

in the very near future. Its popularity is growing on the Continent.' His fingers curled around hers, pulled her towards the dance floor. 'The time for speaking has ended. Now you can show me how you practised in my absence.'

'I know the theory from our lesson.'

'But as in life, the practice is very different. Relax and let the music be your guide. I shall go wherever you wish. Even out into the moonlight, if that is your fancy.'

'I believe I shall decline at present.' Diana drew a deep breath. This was flirtation for the benefit of others. She had to remain calm and offhand, no matter how much the feeling of warmth was enveloping her.

'When the opportune moment arises, you must try it.' His hand tightened on her waist, burnt against the silk. 'I believe you will find the experience quite rewarding.'

A warm shiver went down her spine. Ruthlessly, Diana suppressed it. She was never going to dance with Brett in the moonlight.

'Shall we concentrate on this dance, rather than speculate on others?' Diana nodded towards the dance floor where several couples, led by Miranda Bolt and a red-coated officer, were assembling. At the sight of Diana, Miss Bolt's face took on a petulant expression. 'Miss Bolt does not appear at all pleased with the turn of events.'

'Wait until she sees how you dance.' The corners of his mouth twitched. Diana swallowed hard and attempted to remember the intricate steps as she placed her hand on his shoulder. Her whole being was aware of him.

She managed to get through the first few steps without treading on Brett's toes. Gradually her feet appeared to remember the steps he had taught her and she grew in confidence. His hand seemed to burn a brand on her waist and his fingers gently held hers. Their limbs moved together in time to the music.

'Your mastery surprises me, Miss Diana,' Brett said as they slowly circled the room. 'I fear your days warming a chair will have ended with this dance. Already I see several soldiers lining up to usurp my place. You will have to be careful to keep your feet on the ground.'

'Not all of my life was spent as a wallflower, Lord Coltonby.' Diana kept her chin up. 'I know the perils of giving credence to compliments.'

'We agreed—Brett.'

'But Lord Coltonby feels safer,' Diana returned, and concentrated on a point over his left shoulder rather than the intent expression in his eyes.

'Does he?' Brett expertly spun her around so she was once again forced to look him in the face. An unholy light danced in his eyes. 'Would you care to wager on this, Miss Clare?'

Before Diana could think of a suitably crushing reply, the music stopped. Diana breathed deeply and smiled. Before she could escape from the floor, a queue of officers had formed, all begging for the favour of a dance. Diana found she had little option but to accept. And all the joy and pleasure she had once had in music and ballrooms came back to her. Once or twice as she circled the ballroom floor, she was certain Brett's eyes were on her, but each time that she looked, he appeared deep in conversation with someone else.

'Ah, Lord Coltonby, you are here. My sister thought you had departed from the district.' Simon Clare blocked Brett's view of the dance floor. 'But I knew you would not miss this dance.'

'Clare, it is good to see you again.' Brett kept his eyes on Diana, who was dancing yet another cotillion, laughing up into the face of some red-coated soldier for a moment longer than was strictly necessary. A surge of white-hot anger coursed through him. 'The ball is very pleasant.'

'Quite a change from the fare you are used to in London, I would imagine.'

'A welcome change.'

'As you may have heard, I have been working on a travelling engine. It is showing real promise. But it is an investment that I cannot miss.' Simon Clare pulled a tightly folded sheaf of papers from the inside pocket of his coat. 'I have some papers here, if you wish to glance at them. A number of the others have expressed an interest. Of course, Sir Norman proclaims that his will go better, but I fear he is mistaken. It will never run.'

'In the middle of a ball? Are you mad, man?' Brett swung around to face Diana's brother. The man would never change. Business, always business. 'You may send the papers over in the morning.'

'If that is what you wish…if you think you cannot make sense of them tonight.' Clare returned the papers to his pocket. 'I naturally bow to your wishes.'

Brett regarded him through narrowed eyes. Exactly what was his game? Was he simply inept at social conversation or was there something more sinister? He would give Clare the benefit of the doubt. 'My head is perfectly clear.'

Clare's cheeks flushed slightly. 'Sir Cuthbert always encouraged me to bring the papers to any function we might be attending. It saved time. He preferred the hurdy-gurdy of the dance for pushing the pen.'

Brett thinned his lips. The look in Clare's eyes said it all. He considered Brett to be a fop, a macaroni like Sir Cuthbert. It was time that he learnt they were different. Very different. He looked forward to delivering the final blow tomorrow, to seeing Clare crawl.

'I conduct my business in the proper venue. Balls are for pleasure, not negotiation.'

'Never let it be said that I didn't offer. I thought we could discuss the land at the same time.'

'See to it that you do not make the same mistake again.' Brett turned on his heel, shaking with anger.

'My sister appears to be enjoying herself on the dance floor,' Clare called after him.

Brett halted. What new game was Clare playing? Why was he bringing his sister into this? 'She does, rather. I was lucky to discover her sitting amongst the widows. It would appear I have inadvertently brought her to the attention of some others.'

'I know and I wanted to thank you for it. She took the notion somehow to wear a new ballgown. Dressed up. More fancy than I have seen her for…for years. I had thought it was going to go wrong and then you stepped in and danced with her.'

Brett stared at the man, astonished. He was actually thanking him. His shoulders tensed and the muscles in his arms clenched—the same reactions he always had before the start of a race or a high-stakes game of cards. He should say something, start the process of explaining to Clare what he had done and why. But the words refused to come. 'I was pleased to help. We are friends.'

'There is now a queue twenty deep for the honour of dancing with her. Some of them have come to me, begging to hear about the engine. I do worry that it will go to her head, but she does deserve some happiness.' Clare pointed towards where Diana was laughing at some sally a red-coated officer made. Brett forced his shoulders to relax. 'I trust her implicitly, of course, but as one Cantabrigian to another, I do worry.'

'Your sister is most assuredly a lady, Clare. I believe we can agree on that point.'

'Quite.' Clare blinked at him, and he looked surprised. 'I am so glad you agree.'

'I will endeavour to ensure that no harm comes to her,' Brett said as he watched Diana start out once more for the dance floor. He wanted to rip the officer's head from his body for even daring to put his gloved hand on her bare shoulder.

'Thank you, Coltonby. I appreciate it.'

Brett's mouth thinned as he watched Simon Clare disappear into the throng. He knew then that he could not use Diana in the way he had planned. He wanted her. He would have her, but he would not use her. He wanted to protect her. And the thought scared him far more than facing a team of runaway horses.

Cheeks flushed and feet throbbing, Diana was forced to admit defeat and retired to a chair. It had been so long since she'd properly danced that she was determined to enjoy every moment. Seeing the Honourable Miranda's slightly shocked countenance as she had realized that Diana was not a wallflower was the added spur she had needed.

The major with whom she had been partnered for a quadrille left to get her some refreshment. Diana stared ruefully at her dancing slippers. In her excitement at dancing again, she had forgotten how much they could pinch. She had also forgotten the sharp burning sensation when drops of wax fell on to the back of her neck. It was a hazard of dancing under chandeliers, but as far she could tell none of the wax had landed on her gown. She craned her neck and tried to inspect the point where her sleeve joined the back of the bodice.

'It is good that you are sitting down,' Brett

purred. 'You appear to have danced without a break since our waltz.'

'I have had years to catch up on.' Diana blinked up at Brett. She had spent the better part of the last six dances trying to forget that he was in the room and failing. She had finally managed to convince her wayward mind that he would not speak to her again tonight, but then he had appeared, glowering. His brow was darker than Simon's. She clutched her fan tighter. That was it—Brett had decided to play an older brother. The thought should have brought a feeling of relief, but she knew he meant more to her than that. She would get over it. 'It is interesting how much of the excitement and the sheer thrill of dancing that one forgets. Have you enjoyed the cotillions and quadrilles? I noticed you led Mrs Sarsfield out. It was thoughtful of you.'

'I have danced enough, but your cheeks are over-bright. Are you sickening?'

'Hardly.' Diana waved her fan in front of her, carefully hiding her expression from Brett. He had noticed. It would be far too easy to develop a *tendre* for him. It frightened her that her body became more alive when he was near. 'Merely tired from my exertion.'

'Shall I get you a cup of punch?'

'Major Spence has gone to fetch me some punch.'

'How good it is to know that Spence is looking after you.'

'Like you, he seemed concerned. He suggested a turn in the garden, but I explained a sip of punch would be enough.'

Brett's face looked as if he had swallowed something distasteful. 'And you believe the punch will revive you?'

'Lady Bolt's punch is considered to be the finest in Northumberland. She keeps the receipt a closely guarded secret, but it is reputed to have wonderful restorative powers. Mrs Sarsfield thinks it is to do with the amount of rum and gin Lady Bolt adds.'

'I shall have to try it…but later. Is there anything else you require? Shall I take you into supper?'

'A cup of punch and a sit down is all that is necessary at the moment.' Diana rearranged her skirts. 'Lieutenant McGowan has already requested the honour of accompanying me into supper.'

'He is not here now. I believe he is dancing with Charlotte Ortner.'

'But I agreed.'

'Do I detect a certain mulishness to your tone?'

'A certain decidedness, yes.'

'It is something to be admired, but not necessarily welcomed.' He held out his arm. 'Shall we stop this silly quarrel before it begins? Come have a stroll with me around the room.'

'I did promise Major Spence that I would wait here. Like you, I keep my promises.' Diana saw the man in question advancing behind Brett. She had to admit there was no comparing the two. Major Spence was weak chinned and possessed a nervous tic in his eye whenever she asked him about when he was going to join his regiment in the Peninsula. 'And he has gone to the trouble of getting me a cup of punch. A gentleman by all accounts. Lady Bolt assures me on this point.'

'Jeremy Spence is not to be trusted.' Brett's voice held more than a hint of menace. 'Not even with a glass of punch. Remember that.'

'He was involved in a gallant action in the Peninsula. Apparently he is noted for his gallantry. It was something to do with a convent, but he refuses to say. It appears to me to be more than natural modesty, but Mrs Ortner and Lady Bolt find him charming.'

'There is gallant and there is *gallant,* Diana, as I am sure you know.' Brett lifted one eyebrow. 'You did, after all, keep company with one of the Jehu. You know the language we use. Spence drove with the crowd as well.'

Diana's cheeks burnt with an even greater intensity. She had forgotten the *double entendre* of gallant. A gallant action was one involving a mistress. Her hand began to tremble and she concentrated on not snapping the slender ivory leaves of her fan. 'In a convent?'

'Nuns are women as well. And it involved more than one convent, or so Spence boasts in male company.'

'I bow to your expertise.' Diana shifted uneasily. She had thought Major Spence safe despite her slight unease. All her rules told her he should be, but now it seemed that she had no compass to guide her. She had to trust in luck. She swallowed hard. Not luck. Brett. She had to trust Brett. And surprisingly the thought brought her comfort.

'Thank you for allowing me to handle this.' Brett smoothly took both cups of punch from Major Spence. 'It was so kind of you to fetch Miss Diana and me some punch.'

'There are to be three of us?' The major's pale blue eyes blinked rapidly and his prominent Adam's apple bobbed up and down. 'I had hoped for a quiet word with Miss Clare, Coltonby. You do understand my meaning.'

'Miss Clare explained that you would be giving details of your gallant action and I do so love tales of heroics.' Brett smoothly took the cups of punch from the major. 'She did urge me to take a sip of Lady Bolt's punch. I trust you won't mind. After all, I should hate for you to be accused of anything underhanded.'

'No, no, not at all. I will fetch another cup.' Major Spence's lip curled slightly. 'After all, one never likes to upset an earl and particularly not one with a reputation like Lord Coltonby's.'

Diana glanced quickly from the major to Brett. Brett merely straightened his cuffs and took a sip of the punch. 'An excellent concoction. I do believe Lady Bolt is to be complimented. You must try some, Major Spence, before it is all gone,' she said.

'I shall, dear lady.'

'Have this one.' Brett held out the other cup. 'Miss Clare will be going into supper shortly in any case. I believe Lieutenant McGowan has that honour.'

Diana gritted her teeth. Brett was behaving far worse than her brother. He was truly insupportable. 'I did ask Major Spence for a cup of punch.'

'I will get another one for myself, dear lady.' The major handed her the cup. 'I am used to making sacrifices for the ladies.'

Diana took a sip and nearly choked. The punch

appeared to have twice the alcohol that it normally did. Brett lifted an eyebrow.

'Precisely how many convents were involved in your gallant action, Spence?' Brett said, drawling the word gallant. 'I am very interested in learning the unembellished truth.'

'Well, naturally I hesitate to give the full details because of Miss Clare's sensibilities. War is not for the ladies.'

Diana regarded Major Spence over the rim of her glass. His cheek was flushed. Brett's surmise had been correct. His gallant action was Jehu gallant. 'I must assure you, Major, that I do not give way easily to fainting.'

The major tugged at his collar and his florid face grew even redder. 'I wish to state…' he began, but then stopped. His eyes darted from Diana to Brett and back again and his Adam's apple bobbed up and down several times 'The fireworks are about to begin in the garden, Miss Clare. I over- heard Maurice Bolt telling another lady. If you would be so good as to join me on the terrace, we can find a good place to watch the display.'

Diana froze. Her hand trembled slightly and the punch threatened to spill. Brett's fingers took the cup from her as she struggled to regain her com- posure. Fireworks. Gardens. Darkness.

A black hole opened inside her and threatened to swallow all her happiness and joy, sucking her into the past and its nightmare.

How could she have forgotten, even for one instant?

'I believe Miss Clare is very comfortable here. She and I are looking forward to your tale of derring-do.' Brett's voice appeared to come from a long way away, calling her back to the present.

Diana smiled up at him and he nodded slightly.

'We are waiting, Spence.' Brett tapped his fingernail against the rim of his glass. 'Indulge us.'

'I see Sir Norman quizzing Simon Clare on his new engine. I believe Sir Norman is keen to acquire one of his own. If you will excuse me. I truly must hear more.' The major rapidly retreated.

Diana forced her shoulders to relax and her breath to come naturally. She was not in London, but Northumberland. The events of five years ago were in the past. She was safe in the light. With people. Nobody knew. Nobody guessed. Everything was behind her.

'If you wish to go and hear about the travelling engine, I won't keep you. It is Simon's pride and joy.'

'There are other things to interest me.' He raised a casual shoulder. 'I am not overly enamoured of machines—filthy necessary evils that thankfully stay still. My horses always shy around pumping stations and wheel houses.'

'Then you have not caught the infamous Loco Motive fever?'

'Thankfully, no.'

'Perhaps you have not been in the north-east long enough, then. Everyone from the Duke of Northumberland on down seems obsessed with the idea.'

He curled his fingers around hers and drew her to her feet. 'Now, most everyone has gone to see the fireworks. I seem to recall that you enjoyed them. The punch of Spence's has done you no good, perhaps the cool air will help.'

The faint screams and the whistles of the rockets penetrated the room, but they were far away. Bearable. Slowly she shook her head and pulled away. 'I find they are not to my taste. They… they…that is to say, I dislike the bangs.'

His eyes grew troubled. 'But I have a clear memory of you laughing up at them. Once at Vauxhall Gardens.'

'It must have been some other girl,' Diana said firmly. 'I have never liked them.'

Silently she prayed he would accept her lie.

'Shall I remain here with you?'

'No, you go. I will go and keep Mrs Sarsfield company.'

He made a bow. 'As you wish.'

Diana's shoulders sagged. She had done it. All would be well. She had survived.

Chapter Ten

The morning sun shone directly in Diana's eyes as she lay in her bed, gazing at the curtains. Every time she'd closed her eyes, Brett's face had appeared and her body had relived the waltz and the pressure of his hand against her waist again and again. Her body had ached with an intense longing. Finally as the first cocks had begun to crow, she had fallen into a dreamless sleep.

'Your brother left hours ago, up at the crack of dawn, muttering about the impertinence of the aristocrats, or so his valet proclaimed.' Rose said, bustling in with fresh tea and toast. Titch followed at her heels, looking hopefully for a dropped crust. 'I took it to mean that he did not have a pleasant time at the ball. Did you have a good time? Was the gown remarked on? You never really said last night.'

'Your gown made me the belle of the ball, Rose,

but I had forgotten how tiring they can be.' Diana reached under the counterpane and gave the base of her foot a rub. 'And how much they can make your feet ache. Luckily I remembered to put on that cream—you know, the one the stableman uses to keep horses' hooves soft—and do not have blisters.'

'The master appeared quite surprised at the amount of time you spent dancing.' Rose gave a loud sniff. 'Why he should be surprised, I have no idea. You looked a picture in that dress.'

'My brother was his usual early-morning self, then.' Diana pulled the covers up and snuggled further down into the bed. 'I am pleased I slept in.'

'You are avoiding my question, Miss Diana. There has been talk. Who played you court? Your dress was fit for a princess. How many soldiers? How many titles? And what about your Lord Coltonby?'

'Has anyone paid me court for the past five years, Rose? Stop teasing me.' Diana kept her gaze resolutely on the bed curtains, but at Rose's clucking she turned over on her side. 'Out with it, what news have you heard? What am I supposed to confirm?'

'There is talk about Lord Coltonby and he did come to call.'

Diana's hand paused. Her feelings about Brett were too new and fragile. She had no idea what she wanted to do. The only thing she did know was that marriage was not possible. For either of them. He seemed to have only brotherly concern for her. He had left after they'd kissed and only returned because he had promised to dance with her at the ball.

When he did marry, he would undoubtedly go back down to London and find a suitable wife, a Diamond, rather than a Disgraced Has-Been with a modest fortune.

'Rose, Lord Coltonby is an old acquaintance. He was a friend of my former fiancé. He took me under his wing and re-introduced me to society. He has done so, and there it ends.'

'If you say so, Miss Diana, but why has he sent this note? First thing, by special messenger?' Rose produced a missive from her apron pocket. 'It is the second time in under a week that I have seen that handwriting. And the under-housemaid had it from the stable hand who had it from the Bolts' footman that…'

Diana resisted the urge to snatch the missive from Rose's hand. Instead she leant down and fed Titch some toast. The terrier gave a soft snuffling bark. 'The servants' network never ceases to amaze me.'

'It is a good thing we have it, too, since certain people will not bother to inform other people of what's happening.'

'Rose dear, there is nothing to say. You would be the first to know. Have I ever kept secrets from you?' Diana kept her eyes firmly on Titch's ears. There was one secret that she had kept from Rose. They had never spoken of that night more than five years ago. She had often thought it providence that Rose had left to visit relatives before Diana had returned from Vauxhall.

'Humph. I do worry about you, Miss Diana. I want to see you settled.'

Diana stared at the heavy cream-coloured paper and resisted the temptation to immediately break open the seal. 'Has any other post arrived?'

'A letter from Master Robert's headmaster. The master glanced at the handwriting and then said that you would handle it as you were so good with the headmaster last time.' Rose shook her head. 'The lad doesn't mean any harm. It is a bit of fun. Boys will be boys. My younger brothers were always trying to put handfuls of beetles and spiders down my back. One is a clerk in a shipping office now and the other's joined the navy.'

'He does it to get Simon's attention.'

'You know that. I know that. The man in the moon knows it, but will the master listen?'

Diana drew in a breath. Perhaps Robert and his troubles at school were the distraction she needed.

Another way to remind her of her duty. Her time was better spent on this rather than on thinking about castles in the air and things that could never be. Her treacherous mind kept returning to Brett's kiss and ways in which it could be repeated.

'Any guess on what he has done this time? I only hope it is spiders down some poor boy's back.' She opened the letter and quickly read the complaint. The corners of her mouth twitched. 'Robert has let off a stink bomb in the headmaster's study. Doctor Allen quite rightly points out that he cannot tolerate this sort of behaviour. Simon will have to contact him and persuade him otherwise, if Robert is to stay at that school.'

'Are you going to tell him about the last time? You know what he was like.'

'Robert must learn that he has to obey rules.' Diana tapped the letter against the table. 'I will write to Robert and explain. If he is expelled, his father will never let him have a horse.'

'Young master Robert will not take any notice of the threat. The times I have told him not to take the softening cream off your dressing table... horses have their own, I said.'

'You are right, Rose, I shall have to write to the headmaster and beg him to reconsider his threat. Robert takes such threats as a challenge.' Diana put a hand to her head. 'With Simon in his current mood, the combination of the two would stretch my nerves unbearably. They may deserve each other, but do I deserve them?'

'He has a good heart, Robert does. He picked me a bunch of daisies before he left.'

'Both of them do, Rose. However, I do get tired of being the one to enforce discipline, of being the sensible one, while my brother immerses himself in his work.'

'If Robert is thrown out of this school, where will he go? The master won't have him here. Remember the ink incident.'

'We solve that problem if it arises, Rose.' Diana put the letter to one side and reached for the tea pot. She became aware that Rose still stood there, regarding her with a strange expression. 'Is something amiss?'

'There's a letter from Lord Coltonby and you are seeking to distract me with tales of young master Robert,' Rose said. 'I heard from Lady Bolt's house-keeper you danced a waltz with him. A waltz, Miss Diana. Where did you ever learn such a thing?'

'Yet more gossip, Rose?' Diana lifted her cup to her lips and hoped Rose would ignore the sudden flaming of her cheeks. 'The tongues have clearly been busy this morning. When shall I be informed of the engagement?'

'There is something between you two. Why write to you? And come calling? Twice. And all this fuss to get the ball dress altered. A body wants to be prepared.'

'You may put the patterns away, Rose.' Diana swirled the tea in her cup. 'There is no wedding in my future.'

'But, miss…'

'He has become a friend. He is being kind. He sees me as no more than a younger sister.'

'Then your *friend* has sent you a note. One which you refuse to open. You should read it immediately.' Rose crossed her arms. 'He is unmarried and an earl. He will be looking for a wife, it stands to reason. You should stop doing yourself down, Miss Diana.'

Diana's throat closed. She refused to explain the how and the why, not after all these years. 'I have sworn never to marry. There is Robert to think of. Stop attempting to matchmake, Rose.'

'You get the strangest notions in your head, Miss Diana. Not marry? The women who say such things do not have an earl as a suitor. Nor a sizeable fortune. You are not thinking straight, Miss Diana.'

'I enjoy my independence. Once I was delivered from a disastrous alliance, and I do not want to risk it again.' At the sound of Rose's disgusted noise,

Titch began howling. Diana gave a sigh. 'I suppose you will not give me any peace until I do open the note and respond to it.'

'What do you have against the man?'

'He had a certain reputation five years ago,' Diana said slowly, drawing out each word. She bent down and picked Titch up, placated him with a corner of toast. 'He would pursue anything in a skirt. I am a challenge to him. He finds me an amusement. He will soon tire of the chase and find other prey. It is what men do.'

'Who are you trying to convince—me or you? I looked through my magazines. You know, the ones Mrs Sarsfield sends me. They go on about his horses and the purses that he was won, but he hasn't been involved in the Crim. Con.'

'He is infinitely discreet.'

'Or maybe you underestimate your charms.'

'I know what my charms are, Rose.' Diana buried her face in Titch's soft fur. The little dog gave her a disgusted look and leapt off the bed.

'I know what they are as well, Miss Diana. And you are doing yourself a disservice. You are frightened of living. Any time a man comes sniffing around your skirts, you put up shields and blocks. Excuses.'

'There is no need to be vulgar.'

'But I am right.' Rose gave a decided nod. 'You have piqued his interest. You should capitalise on it. You never know where such friendship might lead.'

'I am being realistic, Rose.' Diana knew her cheeks were glowing as the maid's beam increased. 'Try to understand.'

'Oh, Miss Diana, you can be such fun to tease. Think nothing of me. I am so pleased you have decided to wear pretty clothes again.'

Diana broke open the seal and read the note. A few words leapt out at her and her breath stopped.

A matter of urgency has arisen.

'Is there a problem, Miss Diana? You have gone ashen.'

'I think I will be going out after all.'

'And you are still positive that he wants nothing to do with you?'

Diana brushed the crumbs from the bed. 'Ask Jenkins to get the gig ready.'

'I am coming with you.' Rose moved her ample bulk in front of Diana. 'You are not without friends, Miss Diana—should you need them. You are far from being alone. This isn't London. You have a certain standing in this community. People know and respect you.'

Diana reached out and clutched Rose's hand,

relief flooding over her. She had dreaded the thought of travelling there on her own. This way it was somehow more respectable. But she kept wondering—what had Simon done now? Why did Brett need to see her? 'Thank you.'

'You wished to see me urgently?' Diana held the crumpled note aloft when Brett entered his drawing room. She had spent an uncomfortable few moments alone after the butler had shown her into the room.

Annoyingly, Brett appeared remarkably unruffled in his black morning coat and buckskin breeches. Even his neckcloth was impeccably tied. He gave no sign that he was under mental distress or that anything untowards had happened. She was aware that her bonnet was slightly at an angle and that her old burgundy gown and pelisse had been the first ones to hand. And her hair was pulled back in a simple knot. Now she wished that she had taken more time, rather than starting out like some mad thing.

'You are later than I'd thought you would be,' he said finally. 'I had expected you before noon. It is a shame, but there we have it. A few hours of daylight remain.'

'You expected me to come here?' Diana's

fingers curled around the note, twisting it beyond recognition.

'Why else would I have sent the note?' He tilted his head to one side as his eyes assessed her. 'Asking you to visit.'

'Demanding.'

'Definitely asking.'

'A polite note would have sufficed. The whole tone was alarming in the extreme.' Diana swallowed hard. Since the moment she had first read the note, various possibilities had gone through her brain, each more dreadful than the last. 'What has happened?'

'I had no wish to alarm you. A situation has risen and I would like some advice.'

'You have a funny way of going about it. I was certain some terrible disaster had befallen you, that something was dreadfully wrong.' Diana crossed her arms.

'Nothing is wrong. There are things I wanted to discuss with you. Reasons to have you visit.' Brett gave an unrepentant smile.

'But I thought…Simon had been and there was trouble.' Diana stumbled over the last few words.

The corners of Brett's lips twitched. 'Can I help it if people choose to leap to illogical conclusions?'

'You knew I would think that!' Diana gritted

her teeth, refused to give in to his increasingly engaging smile. 'You are insufferable! I care about my reputation, even if you do not.'

'Have no fear. I will not use it as some sort of bargaining counter. What has passed between us, stays between us.' His face sobered and a muscle twitched in his cheek. 'Harm comes to reputations when people are indiscreet. No one has ever accused me of being indiscreet.'

'I know the value of discretion.' She pressed her hands together. She wished she knew exactly what was in his mind—but how to ask the questions when she feared the answers? 'I know how the world works. One may do much, if it is not flaunted before the censorious eyes of society. Men have far more licence than women. Hypocrisy reigns.'

'An advocate of Mary Wollstonecraft?'

'The scales had dropped from my eyes before I read her work, but, yes, I see much to admire in it.' She waited to hear his mocking rebuttal.

'It is the way of the world. However much we might hope to change it.' He lifted an eyebrow. 'I, personally, loathe hypocrisy.'

'I…I am pleased you feel that way.'

'Sit. Please sit.'

'I would prefer to remain standing.'

'The sofa will be more comfortable than your dance-worn feet, but if it is your pleasure…'

Diana concentrated on the room rather than on his mouth or his hands. The furniture had changed very little since the Biddlestones' occupancy, but Diana noted the other changes. Silver cups from various horse races now lined the tables and, instead of the long line of Biddlestone family portraits, the drawing room was full of portraits of horses, each labelled with the rider and winning races. A few simple changes but enough to exude a masculine rather than feminine touch. Diana waited for him to begin speaking.

'Why did you summon me here? I have a right to know,' she asked in a small voice when she could bear the silence no longer.

'Are you interested in another commission?'

'Commission?' Diana tilted her head to see if she could detect a hint of laughter in his eyes, but he appeared serious. 'What sort of commission?'

'I need your help, your painterly eye, and it struck me that given today's beautiful autumn weather, why wait? A man can achieve much if he acts. We are friends after all.'

Friends? Eyes? He was about to say his goodbyes. A great lump rose in Diana's throat. She did not want to say goodbye. With the greatest effort, she kept her face as neutral as she could.

'I do value your friendship, Brett,' Diana said quickly before she had a chance to regret it. 'I shall be disappointed of course to see you quit the neighbourhood. Your being here has added a certain colour to my life.'

Diana found she had no desire to think about what might happen when this friendship came to an end. That was all it was, she told herself firmly—an unlikely pairing that must inevitably come to an end and one that she would treasure.

What had happened in the summer house was solely her fault. It had been a light kiss that had meant nothing in the grand scheme of things. He must have bestowed a thousand such kisses in his lifetime. She would not let him know what it had meant to her. What dancing in his arms last night had meant. And how the hours in front of her seemed to stretch out unceasingly.

'Diana, are you attending me? You have a faraway expression in your eyes.'

Dimly she realised that he had been speaking, gesturing with his hands, an excited expression on his face. 'Yes, yes, I agree. It will be the best thing.'

'You miss the point entirely, Diana. Are you quite the thing?'

She put a hand to her head and sank down on the sofa. 'I fear last night's unaccustomed festivities made my head throb this morning.'

'Too much of Lady Bolt's punch?' He stopped and reached for the bell. 'I can remedy that. Lightly browned toast and copious amounts of tea. I was hoping for a stroll in the gardens, but your health is far more important. We shall have to do this the next fine day.'

'You were explaining about your commission. What do you want me to do? I will pay attention now, I promise.'

'There is a folly—a grotto—on the estate. It is rather plain and unadorned.' He leant forward, his eyes shone silver grey. 'I think it could be more. It should be more.'

'I know the one you mean.' Diana glanced at the wall behind him, which boasted a stain from a leaking roof. The grotto. Of course the grotto. He had seen her work and knew she had done the painting for the Bolts' summer house. It had nothing to do with his imminent departure. She placed her reticule carefully in her lap and berated her mind for leaping to inappropriate conclusions.

'How long has the grotto been there? Do you know?'

'The late Sir John Biddlestone, Sir Cuthbert's

grandfather, had it put in.' Diana breathed easier. It was a topic they could discuss and the strain would become easier. She wanted to get back to their easy friendship, the one they had had before the kiss, before her mind became filled with him. 'He wanted pleasure gardens to ramble in and for his wife to paint, as she was a keen water colourist. Unfortunately she died a few years later and not much more was done. I suspect it has not been cleaned out properly for years. Sir Cuthbert was not overly fond of the estate, but neither did he want to let it out.'

'I intend to change that. This estate is to be my principal seat. It must have a garden worthy of an earl.'

Diana stared at him. How was she going to go on facing him, meeting up with him when their liaison had ended? She was like an addict, craving more. 'Why is it to be your principal seat? Surely you must have more estates down in Warwickshire.'

'My father and brother did not manage their affairs correctly and neglected to ensure a settlement. All the historic Coltonby lands were sold to pay my brother's debts.' Brett's face became shadowed. 'It has fallen to me to restore the family fortune. And luckily, I proved adept at making money. I want a new beginning. The shadows of the past can be long and inharmonious.'

'And you want me to paint the grotto?' Diana bit her lip. Painting the grotto would be fun. She could already see the shells and pictures that she wanted to put on the walls. She knew she could do an excellent job. It would give her an outlet for her passion. 'My painting is…well…floral and I think the grotto would need shells, something in keeping with the water.'

'I agree.' A sardonic smile twisted his lips. 'Stop throwing up obstacles where there are none. Let me judge your work on its merits. Indulge me.'

'I indulged you with the waltz lessons and I know where that led.' Diana kept her voice steady. She had said the unmentionable. She had brought it out in the open, but it had needed saying. 'We are both adults, Lord Coltonby.'

'Nothing happened that you didn't desire.' His grey eyes seemed to pierce her soul. 'Or do you seek to deny what happened when you were in my arms? Do you need reminding?'

Diana tightened her grip on the letter as images danced in front of her. Her lips ached at the merest thought, the faintest look. She wiped a hand across her mouth and concentrated on the various pictures of horses and their jockeys.

'What happened in the summer house is best forgotten and never spoken of again. Ever.' Her voice sounded high and strained to her ears. She prayed he'd understand. 'I trust you will heed my wishes on that. It is the most sensible course of action.'

He snapped his fingers. 'Consider it in the past as it is the most sensible course of action. Far be it from me to ever suggest that you act in a reckless manner.'

'You are laughing at me now.'

'Not at all. I am very serious. I do want you to see the grotto, Diana.' His fingers reached out and took hold of her elbow, caressed her there. A warmth seared through her. She moved her arm and he let her go. She put her hand over where his fingers had been.

She took a deep breath, plunged onwards. He had to understand what she was saying, why she could not allow such a thing to happen again. 'What could have happened doesn't bear thinking about. And it would have been entirely my fault, I asked you to kiss me.'

'Are you quite through with being noble?' His cold voice cut through her, chilling her to the bone.

'Yes,' she said steadily. 'Although I consider it to be practical, rather than noble.'

'Nobody will ever force me into marriage.'

'Nor I. I promise you that.' She lifted her chin and ignored the knots in her stomach.

'You?' His eyes widened at her words. 'Whatever are you speaking of, Miss Clare? Why would you be against marriage?'

'I plan never to marry.' She kept her head up and refused to flinch despite his incredulous expression. 'I made that vow after Algernon Finch died. Nothing has ever happened to make me change my mind.'

'Was that because you buried your heart with him?' His voice was barely a breath, so low that Diana wondered if he had even spoken.

'Nothing so melodramatic. He was after my money.' She waved a hand and tried to make her voice sound calm and reasoned. How could she begin to explain about the perfidy of the man? Of the letters she had discovered, mocking her? Of that last horrible night when he had ensured that she could never break the engagement? Of the hours she had spent scrubbing his touch from her skin? 'I realised how close I came to losing everything. A woman's property is only her own if she is unmarried.'

'If she is a widow, she has control of her property. You are not a widow unless the Northumbrian definition is different from the rest of England's,' Brett corrected after a long silence.

'Your brother or your guardian must control your estate as you have never married.'

'I trust my brother. He has looked after my money well. The colliery and the other businesses thrive. He has built on the solid foundation that my father left.'

'Yes, no one could ever accuse your brother of not being devoted to his business interests.'

Diana released a breath and resisted the temptation to crumple Coltonby's note further. Simon had sent the papers to Brett. They were much alike, her brother and this earl, possibly too much alike. Both were determined. 'Simon does keep his word. At the moment, the colliery consumes the vast proportion of his time. He worries about it failing to keep pace with the other Grand Allies, particularly now that Mr Hedley has developed a travelling engine for Wylam Colliery.'

'Mr Hedley guards his secrets well, and it is unlikely that your brother will be able to get one for the Ladywell.'

'My brother can be very resourceful when the occasion demands. He searches for more investors.'

'I saw an example of his resourcefulness last evening.' Brett's level gaze met hers. 'Does he often do business at balls?'

Diana regarded her hands. 'My brother swears

the age of the travelling engine will arrive sooner than people expect. He wants to convince people his ideas are right.'

'If it does, I shall make a proper assessment of the risk. But enough of this talk about Loco Motion and collieries.' He inclined his head and reached out to take the paper from her hands. 'The grotto awaits if you feel capable of walking. I am most anxious to hear your thoughts on its possibilities.'

'We could discuss it here.' Diana met his level gaze with hers.

'But the possibilities are there, out in the grounds. How can you begin to advise if you have not actually seen what needs to be done?'

She picked at the button of her glove. 'I will call Rose. She can accompany us.'

'You hardly need a maid to go walking with you. I am sure she is quite safe in the kitchen conversing with staff. Allow her to have a good long gossip and a chance to rest her feet. I asked the cook to prepare a picnic for beside the grotto.' His eyes became hooded. 'I thought after walking out there, we might need a little light refreshment while we discussed my requirements.'

'Surely it will not take that long.' Diana looked at her reticule as her insides trembled and a flood of warmth went through her. Out there. Alone. This time, she would not behave irresponsibly.

'I wish to go over my scheme in depth. We are friends, Diana. I value your opinion. You may think of possibilities.' His voice was smooth. Diana glanced up, but his expression was bland. However, she could not rid herself of the feeling of being caught up in a current that was heading for somewhere unknown. 'And remember, Diana, you are free to return to the house whenever you wish.'

'I know that.' She took a deep breath, concentrated. The only thing she knew was that she wanted to be with him. 'Shall we go?'

Chapter Eleven

Brett resisted the impulse to support Diana's arm or guide her hand as they walked along the overgrown path towards the grotto. The red pelisse with white lace at the collar complimented her bonnet as the skirt of her dress billowed out, slightly revealing her slim ankles. The colour suited her far more than the browns and greens he had seen her in before. But she was the very picture of demure femininity. It belied the woman who had danced with him last evening and who had once again invaded his dreams. He tightened his jaw and kept his steps moving towards the grotto.

Patience and careful planning were the keys to success. Her words about never marrying had been an unexpected blow. It had not occurred to Brett that Diana might not be seeking marriage, but it bothered him that she had rejected the notion out of hand.

Was it her polite way of rejecting him? Or just the institution?

His fingers curled around his cane. He would discover her reason in due course, but today's plans revolved around other pursuits. He wanted her to feel comfortable with him and to begin to understand that she and he were intimate friends. That her head was not to be turned by the red-coated officers who had pursued her at the ball.

'What are you planning for this area?' she asked, stopping suddenly and gesturing towards a heavily wooded area where scrub and brambles vied with a few good specimens of trees. Brett forced his thoughts back to the garden and away from his plans for the afternoon.

'It will have to be cleared. The cedar of Lebanon will be happier standing on its own. The pleasure gardens will be restored to their former glory.'

'That will take a long time.' Diana's head was turned resolutely away from him. Her shoulders were set. 'It takes years to make a garden. It is not a harum-scarum thing accomplished in a few weeks and then off to London.'

'Time I have. I intend to live here once the new house is built. There is an aspect overlooking the Tyne that I particularly favour.' He touched her elbow, supporting her over a rough patch of ground. 'It will be done properly. I want your advice about the grotto and which motifs should be painted on the inner walls.'

She gently moved her arm and her body away. He fought his instinct and allowed her to go. 'I think you will need to do more than slap paint on the rock to restore this garden. That is all.'

A small gasp came from Diana's throat as she scrambled over the last few remaining boulders to reveal the grotto. A small weed-choked stream emerged from the mouth of a substantial cave. Nettles and brambles formed a curtain over the entrance.

'It has possibilities. Surely you must see that.' Brett mentally cringed. He hated the pleading note that had escaped from his throat.

'Possibilities, hmmm.' She walked away from him, tilting her head from one side to the other. 'Certainly it does want love and attention. The whole estate is crying out for it.'

Brett regarded the tumbled stones and muddy stream. He wanted her to see it as he saw it—the possibilities, rather than the depressing reality. A test of sorts. Could she look beyond the practicalities? Could she taste the dream? Her blue-green eyes became even deeper pools that Brett wanted to drown in. He shook himself and forced his voice to remain bland.

'You have a talent and an artistic eye. I merely seek to use them for my own ends.'

'And I merely do it for the pleasure of it. I claim no expertise.'

She tiptoed closer to the edge and peered into the cave. The thin material of her dress clearly outlined her bottom—round, tight. Appetising. Brett allowed his eyes to wander over it, to linger as she peered first this way and that. 'You do yourself a disservice. What I have seen is entirely satisfactory.'

'You are right. It could do with painting, or maybe an actual shell border. I have heard of several houses with shell-patterned borders. Little shells, carefully placed.'

'It sounds time consuming.' Brett forced his mind from pondering the exact shape of her bottom and how it would feel in his hands. He had to remain casual. She seemed more nervous than ever today as her hand straightened and re-straightened her bonnet, an overblown confection of silk flowers and ribbons and straw. Fashionable, he supposed, but it hid her glorious dark hair.

'Time consuming? Yes, but it does have the most marvellous effect—a sort of jewel-like quality with the water and the light.' Diana waved a hand towards the grotto. 'Shells would make this spot very romantic.'

'Would you be placing the shells?' Brett kept his voice steady. Willed her to answer yes. Willed her to agree to having reasons to visit him.

She regarded the cave walls for a long time, her finger tapping against her mouth. He could almost see the pictures painting themselves in her mind. Waited with bated breath for her verdict.

'I could do it, but it would take some time,' she said finally, breaking the silence. 'Perhaps it would be better if you employed someone, someone who knew what they were doing.'

'I have faith in you. You can do anything you set your mind to. You waltzed beautifully last night.'

'Easy words.' Her laugh spilled from her throat.

'Perhaps you don't have faith in yourself.' His fingers closed around her upper arm and he breathed in her scent of lavender and soap. A far more intoxicating combination than other women's perfume. He willed her to remain there, close by his side. 'Trust your instincts.'

'I am not sure I can.' Diana's words were no more than a breath. 'Brett, help me, please.'

Diana felt his hand rest lightly upon her shoulder, the merest whisper of a caress, but she knew it was there. He stood inches from her. Waiting. The urge to turn around became a compulsion.

All her admonitions of last night and this morning, all her promises and resolutions faded like mere wisps of morning cloud. She needed this. She was born for this—out here next to this grotto with its impossibly choked stream and hidden romance. She was drawn to him like a moth to a flame despite the certainty of being singed. It only mattered that he was here and he wanted to kiss her. She wondered if she dared to take a risk. She knew she wanted to, knew that she could not live with the thought that it only might have been.

Abruptly and without warning, his hands turned her. She met his mouth full on. Warm, soft and seeking. His lips roamed over her face, pressing small kisses against her mouth and her eyes. Each touch sent a tremor along her body, stoking a fire within her.

Finally, his mouth returned to hers and his tongue traced the outline of her lips. First around the outside, delicately, and then along the crease, demanding entrance. A slow but thorough exploration. Her lips opened under the onslaught and she drank from his mouth, lifting her hand to curl around the back of his head to bring his lips and tongue closer. She needed them closer.

Cool, sweet languor filled her as his tongue penetrated her mouth. Slow and lazy, but then with an increased urgency. There was a difference from the last time. In the summer house, the kiss had a finite quality, but today, it promised secret glades along pathways of pleasure. Paths that beckoned and urged her forward. Unhurried and leisurely exploration.

Her body arched towards his, moulding itself against the hard muscles. His hand fastened on to her waist, crushed her to him. He pressed small kisses along the corners of her mouth, her eyes and her temple, small nibbles that sent little pulses leaping throughout her body, warming her, making her yearn for something more. His mouth recaptured hers, devoured her. This was what it was like to be thoroughly and utterly kissed.

Diana shifted as he fitted their bodies together. Pressed against her and ignited a fiery hail of sparks that leapt and danced. Her world had come down to this—his mouth touching hers, his hand, his body. Him. Only a few thin layers of material separated them. She shifted again and his hand slid over her backside, held it there. Firmly. The point of her meeting him.

She gasped and clung on to the one straw of sanity she had left, wrenching her mouth away from his.

'You see what you do to me,' he growled in her ear.

She drew back slightly and looked up into his hooded eyes. Slate grey, now alight with a fire burning deep within. And she could feel an answering fire build within her. 'We are friends. Friends.'

'We went past friendship days ago.' Brett's voice was ragged and his breath came fast. But he stepped away from her. 'I'd be lying if I said differently. You would be lying if you denied it. You knew what would happen if you came out here. You wanted this as much as I did.'

'And what do you want?' She brushed a hand across her mouth, tried to ignore the aching points of her breasts. Tried to ignore the burning inside and found the task too hard.

His hands reached for her again, pulled her against him, the apex of her thigh meeting him. 'You.'

The word sent a delicious shiver down her back. Diana discovered she could not think beyond the shape of his mouth or the pressure of his hand on her waist. Her limbs appeared incapable of moving. Her tongue flicked over her suddenly dry lips wetting them, anticipating another onslaught of his mouth. He lifted an eyebrow and blew a cool stream of air across her lips. The coolness contrasted with the fevered heat of her skin and made her yearn all the more.

She swallowed hard and tried to concentrate on something other than the growing tide of heat that built within her. She had to be sensible and consider what could happen. She forced her feet to move.

'And I have no say in this? You are simply going to take? To plunder like a pirate?' She barely recognised her voice. Husky, breathless.

He placed his finger under her chin and raised her head so she was staring into his deep grey gaze. 'We stop when you say stop. I wish to bring you pleasure. No force. Never force. But be warned, once you say stop, it ends. All this ends.'

He withdrew his hands from her. Her body howled in protest. A great longing grew within her. She needed to have his lips against hers again. She wanted him to kiss her with that hunger.

'I understand.' She forced her gaze to meet his. A peace settled over her. She could do this. She trusted him to keep his word. They would kiss and that would be all.

'We go at your pace, Diana. But once we stop, we stop. I do not play the tease.'

'But the servants...what if we are discovered?' Diana tried to step away but his fingers twisted around hers and held her still. Gently, but firmly. A hot molten surge coursed through her, far more potent than anything that had gone before. She willed him to understand. It was not simple for her.

'We won't be. I gave orders that we were not to be disturbed.' His voice was low and slid over her like velvet. She tried to tell herself that he was a master seducer, but her body paid no heed. His look was for her and her alone. It had to be.

'Rose will pay no attention to your orders.' She pulled her hand away and kept her head high. 'She will come soon, worried.'

'She will not trouble herself. She will be drinking and sitting with her feet up.' His hand caught hers, his thumb circling on her wrist, distracting her. 'If she disapproved, she would have never told me you were in the summer house that day. She has done her best to foster this.'

'She had no call to be so brazen.' Diana felt her cheeks begin to burn. 'I never asked her to be. You must believe that.'

'I thanked her for it.' His words stroked like silk over her skin. 'And I will thank her again if she remains tucked up in the kitchen.' He paused, tilting his head to one side. 'Or we could go back and ring for a cup of tea. My cook won't thank you for interrupting their gossip, though. After all the trouble she went to, to prepare the food. You could at least take a glimpse.'

'I…' Diana's voice trailed away. One by one he had demolished her arguments. The first time she had truly put her resolutions and rules to a test, and they had failed her. Maybe she hadn't wanted to try very hard. Maybe she was wicked and wanton and all those things that people had called her five years ago. But she worried that if she went back, she might never sample his lips again. 'I could stay for a while longer. Explore the cave. Measurements should be taken. I will have to know the approximate number of shells that will be needed and the types you might prefer.'

Brett waved a hand. 'The picnic is here and the servants set it up. They brought the table from storage and the under-housemaid raided the garden for the last of the Michaelmas daisies. I was most particular. Come and take a look and see if it does not whet your appetite.'

'You seem awfully certain that I would come out here.'

'Hopeful. There is a difference.'

Diana bit her lip. Reason warred with desire. She wanted to be with him.

'It would be a shame to waste it. The servants will talk if we don't eat. You should try the seed cake. One little taste.'

Diana attempted to think of a coherent answer,

but his fingers had recaptured her wrist. They swept tantalizingly along her skin, caressing the underside of her wrist. Soft, silky, sultry, but entirely innocent. The fire that his kisses had stoked seemed to leap up, but she knew if she said anything that he'd simply lift one eyebrow. She pulled her hand away, covered it with her other one. A small smile tugged at his lips.

Diana held back the words asking what precisely he hoped to gain from this. She knew he wouldn't lie. What he offered held no strings. As long as there were no consequences, no one would question. She understood how society rules operated in these cases.

She drew a deep breath, stood poised on the brink for a moment longer and then plunged. 'I should like to see the picnic.'

'You will not be disappointed. I asked Cook to prepare all of the delicacies—pork pies, potted cheese, salmagundi salad and even a rich seed cake.' Brett rubbed his hands together. 'And I must say Cook's seed cakes are delicious. I have become quite partial to them.'

It was a picnic. A real picnic. Not the wild seduction she had imagined. She wanted to laugh. Had she really expected anything different?

'You make it sound tempting.' Diana forced her

shoulders to relax. She could control her body and, for this one day, she wanted to be with him. Nothing would happen if she did not want it to. She trusted him. 'I have not had potted cheese since…since before London.'

'You will enjoy the picnic.' His eyes turned serious and his fingers gave hers one last squeeze, then let go. 'And, Diana, we return to the house when you say the word. You are in charge.'

She followed him around to the side of the grotto. There in a sunlit grass hollow, a table with chairs had been placed. A starched white linen cloth lay over the table protecting it. With a flourish, Brett lifted the cloth and revealed the picnic. As promised, cold meat pies vied with salads and little pots of shrimp. A bowl full of late season fruits sat in the very centre—blackberries, apples and pears. The seed cake stood on its own little pedestal. There was even a crystal pitcher full of lemonade with mint floating on the top. The sort of picnic one might serve a maiden aunt. She gave him a quick glance under her eyelashes. Her stays felt far too tight.

'Does the picnic not please you?'

'I had thought it would be more…' She looked at her hands. She could hardly confess to secretly hoping for a bottle of wine and a blanket on the ground. Maybe grapes. She had thought him the consummate rake, but nothing here screamed seduction. It was all so ordinary. 'It is lovely, Brett. Thank you for thinking of it. Every single detail has been looked after.'

'Everything is done properly.' He pulled out a chair. 'If you would care to take your seat, we can begin. I find walking works up an appetite.'

'It looks perfectly splendid, particularly the seed cake.' A lump grew in her throat. 'I can't think when anyone took so much trouble over my pleasure.'

'It is *my pleasure* to look after you.'

A lock of hair fell across his forehead. Without allowing her mind time to react, she reached forward and smoothed it away. His fingers curled over hers, held them there for an instant, then let go. He undid the ribbons of her bonnet and lowered it to the ground.

'I wouldn't want it to get crushed.' Then he pulled off her gloves, finger by finger. Repeated the gesture with his. 'Nor have these mussed.'

She started to speak, but he put his finger to her lips and drew her to him again.

'Bonnets are a nuisance. And gloves can get soiled.' His breath tickled her ear, sending a fresh wave of heat through her. 'You should not have to worry about the sun. The table is in the shade.'

His hands cupped the back of her head and he lowered his mouth. 'Good enough to eat.'

'Brett,' she whispered as his breath once more touched her lips, made her remember.

'Enough talking for now.'

Hot. Insistent. His lips plundered hers with a carnal desire. No longer seeking, but demanding. Demanding a response, a response her body was only too ready to give. Her arms went around him, held him there. Her body touching his.

His steady fingers undid her pelisse and pushed it off her shoulders. 'You looked warm in it.'

His lips travelled lower, nibbling at the column of her throat and then tracing a line down to her lace fichu. Grazing her skin. A wave of molten heat washed over her.

The lace fell to the ground unheeded as his mouth traced the neckline of her gown. Her breasts grew full and strained against the confines of her stays. He cupped them with his hands, gently rubbed his knuckles over the cloth and smiled as the nipples puckered. Her back arched, seeking his touch. Wave after wave of sensation racked her, leaving her knees weak. Her hands came up and buried themselves in his thick crisp hair. She held on for support. Her fingers traced the outline of his ear.

'May I?' he whispered. 'Please?'

Beyond speech, she inclined her head, wondering what she had agreed to. She only knew that she wanted him to continue. She could not bear it if he stopped. His hands slipped beneath the cloth, stroking her fevered skin. A feather-light touch. And the already tight nipples hardened further.

A gasp came from her throat and she teetered on the brink of an abyss. Teetered and then fell as his fingers explored the outlines of her breasts. Her hands clutched his shoulder for support. Her body sought the comfort of his.

'Do you like this?' She could only nod in agreement as her eyes watched how his hands moved over and under her breasts. He leant forwards. His breath fanned her ear. 'You will like this more. I promise.'

She wet her lips with her tongue and tried to think of a sensible answer as his fingers found her nipples again. Catching them between his thumb and forefinger, he rolled them. Pleasure thrummed through her. And she knew she was powerless to stop. She needed this. Everything. Here. Now.

'Yes,' she breathed and then her body convulsed.

'Shall I stop?' He deliberately withdrew his hands, held them hovering over her breast. Tantalisingly close. If she breathed deeply, they would rise, and graze his palm. She tried and his hands moved upwards. 'To touch or not to touch.'

She shook her head. 'Are you planning on tormenting me?'

'For as long as possible.' His lips traced a line down her throat, stopping where her bodice kissed her skin. They slipped under the cloth and touched her naked flesh. Warm. Hot. Sensuous touches. Slowly he repeated the manoeuvre. Her hands reached up and buried themselves in his crisp hair. Each tiny movement sent shooting sparks through her body.

'I…'

'Hush.'

With one swift movement, he pulled her bodice down and freed one breast from its confines. Nestled it in his palm. 'Perfect.'

His hot breath touched her tightly furled nipple and then his cool tongue traced its edges, sampling. Finally his mouth sucked, taking the whole of the dusky rose areola inside. Her whole body became infused with heat. Her knees gave way and she knew the only thing keeping her upright was his hands on her waist. The ache that had been growing inside her opened into a throb, became insistent and she knew she needed something more than this. And all the while his tongue swirled and suckled at her breast.

An inarticulate noise sounded in the back of her throat. He lifted his head. One hand smoothed an errant curl off her now bare shoulder. 'This is only the first course.'

'There is more than one course?'

'There is always more than one.' He scooped her up and deposited her on the linen cloth that had covered the table and now lay in the crisp grass. He knelt beside her. She lifted her hands and loosened his neck cloth. Her fingers fumbled slightly, but he allowed her to take it off.

'I want to give you pleasure. Always.' He kissed the side of her neck.

She tried not to think that *always* was a debatable term. 'I can't think beyond the next breath.'

His hands stroked down her side and caught the hem of her gown, revealing her white stockings and lace drawers. She was exposed to the cool afternoon sun. His eyes roamed down her body. 'Very prettily arranged. Remain still. I want to savour the feast.'

'Aren't you overdressed?' She hardly recognised her own voice.

'Only if my lady thinks so.' He shrugged out of his coat. The whiteness of his shirt contrasted with the darkness of his hair. He himself propped up on an elbow, regarding her with an amused expression. 'Anything else?'

Giving into instinct, she pressed her lips to the triangle at the base of his throat. Felt the tempo of his heartbeat with her tongue. She withdrew and then tasted again, sampling the sultry smooth skin.

Her hands pulled at his shirt, freeing it from his breeches. She lifted it and ran her fingers along his smooth skin and felt the power of his muscles tremble beneath her fingertips.

He rolled over, on top of her. It felt right, and she could feel the strength of his arousal moving against her hips. She lifted her body to meet the welcome weight of him. His lips reclaimed hers and her body rose to meet the force of his arousal as it hit the apex of her thighs. He nuzzled and suckled until her body was racked with need. Her head thrashed and her hands sought him, but he thrust them away.

'Patience has its own reward.'

His fingers continued inexorably downwards, pushing aside the thin folds of her drawers, weaving between the gap in the material and burying themselves in her nest of curls. She gasped as his finger slid inside her. He stroked one shuddering stroke. Withdrew. Returned again, deeper this time. Her hips lifted.

'Tight. You are so tight,' he murmured. 'I dreamt of this. You, innocent beneath me.'

'Brett…' Her hands pressed against his chest, intending to push him away, but she found her arms had not the strength. A sudden dark panic filled her. He would discover her secret. She should tell him first, but she couldn't bear the look in his eyes when he knew. And she wanted this. This was so very different from… She summoned all her courage. 'I…'

His fingers stilled, lifted. 'Shall I stop? Or do we go on to the next course.'

She wet her lips and tried once more. 'Brett…'

'Hush,' he whispered and his mouth returned to hers. His tongue mimicked the play of his fingers and she felt the hot need grow within her. Consume her.

Her hands slipped under his shirt and found the smooth muscles of his chest. She rubbed her fingers across his nipples and heard his breathing become ragged. He reached down, guided her hand to his erection. Instinctively she curled her hand around it. Hot. Hard but smooth. 'See what you are doing to me? I want to be inside you.'

Desire flooded through her. Was it so wrong of her to want this? She reached up and cradled his face between her hands, looking him directly in the eye. 'Yes.'

He raised his body up and positioned himself between her thighs. She felt a nudge and he slid in a little way. He stopped and his eyes flew to hers. He started to pull away, but she raised her hips, keeping him inside her. Slowly he went further. Then suddenly as if he could bear it no longer, he fully entered her.

She stiffened, remembering the previous horridness. The dark hole of her memory opened up and threatened to swallowed her. She waited for the pain, then noticed he had stopped moving.

'Did I hurt you?'

Silently she shook her head, hating the sudden rush of shame. He must have guessed. Did he know what she was? What had been done to her? She breathed again.

'It will get better. Relax, sweetheart.'

'I am trying.' Her laugh sounded halfway between a sob and a cry.

His lips brushed her temple. Softly. Beguilingly. Flooding her with warmth at his unexpected tenderness. 'All will be well. I want you too much to stop.'

He began to move within her and she forgot everything as the waves of pleasure increased. Increased and then crested. Her hips began to move in time with his. Inside her, she felt him slide, and knew she had to move faster. A cry was torn from her throat and she heard his answer.

* * *

Much later, Brett looked down at Diana. Her long lashes lay dark against the cream of her skin. She had fallen asleep in his arms. He had not known what to expect, but she had exceeded all his expectations.

He made a wry face. From her kisses, he'd expected a virgin, but her response showed she had been inexpertly taken. He could well imagine the lies she had been told. And her reaction to the truth. She had not worn the caps and the awful gowns to mourn the man, but to hide from men. Somehow, he had succeeded in breaking through her defences and unwrapping the passionate woman underneath.

His insides twisted and he hated the way he had seduced her. When she had kissed him by the grotto, his earlier plan of a light romance had vanished, buried beneath the overwhelming need to touch her and to possess her fully. Luckily, she had responded with passion. He wanted to think the passion was for him and him alone.

She would forget other men. He might not have been the first, but he *would be* the last.

Mentally, he rehearsed his speech. He had never been tempted to say the words before and he wanted them to be right. He imagined her joy when she discovered he was prepared to give up the habit of a lifetime to marry her. He would ask, but properly. He wanted her to know that his decision was not spur of the moment, that he had not sought to irrevocably bind her to him. Everything was going to be done properly. He would show her the absolute respect she deserved. He needed her in his life with an intensity that scared him. Earlier, when he planned this picnic, he had convinced himself that if this did happen, it would be enough to break the spell. He knew now that it would never be enough.

He stood up, dressed, planned every move, every word and then placed a kiss on her temple. 'Time to stir, sweetheart.'

Her eyes flew open. She stretched her arms above her head. The temptress personified. His body leapt in response. And he knew he wanted her again, that he would never tire of her.

'I thought perhaps it was a dream.'

'No dream. Reality. Very much a reality.'

'But it remains our secret. Never to be mentioned again.' She brought her knees up to her chest and peeped at him through a curtain of hair. Her voice held a faint wobble of sadness. Her eyes showed a bruised vulnerability, a wariness that had not been there before. They became wild with some emotion that he could not recognise. 'You must promise me that. Swear it, Brett! Swear on your horses and all your carriages!'

'I shall not be telling anyone. I would never treat you like that.' Brett looked at her, perplexed. She gave a sigh and her eyes turned to ice. He ran a hand through his hair. This was not how the conversation was supposed go. He swallowed hard and tried a different tack. 'That is to say, it should remain between us. A happy memory. Something to be cherished.'

'Good.' She scrambled up and began to rearrange her clothes. Rapidly she covered her long limbs, and retrieved her bonnet, tying it with expert fingers. 'No one interrupted us. No one knows. There is no need for anyone to know. We go on as before.'

Brett stared at her. He resisted the urge to run his hand through his hair. He wasn't quite sure what he had expected. Tears, maybe. Recriminations. But not this matter-of-fact attitude. He had no wish to go on as before. What had passed between them had changed everything. She had to understand. They had no choice. They would marry. She would be his wife.

'We shared something more than friendship. I am not adverse to this happening again.' He gave a half-smile and willed her to understand.

'And I agreed.' Her hands stilled on the ribbons of her bonnet. 'I am no green girl, Brett. We are both adults. You are past thirty and I gave up any expectation of marriage long ago. What is between us lasts for as long as it lasts.'

The gods must be laughing at him. For the first time in his life, he was prepared to do the decent thing and she had refused him even before he'd said the words. He narrowed his lips and silently cursed. To say anything now would be churlish. It would sound ungracious.

'What shall we tell the servants? The food is untouched.'

'It is none of their business.' She walked swiftly over to the picnic. With a few deft movements, she had scattered food. 'They will assume we had a pleasant repast. Now, shall we go? I have no wish to worry Rose.'

Brett resisted the impulse to sweep her into his arms. Patience. 'As you wish.'

'I do.'

'And, Diana, next time, it will be in a bed with white linen sheets. Properly and with all the time in the world.'

Myriad emotions crossed her face. Her mouth opened and closed several times. 'I sincerely doubt that.'

'Diana, wait. We need to talk. To plan.'

'To get the details of the story right? As you said, you are an expert at these sorts of picnics. You need not worry. I too know the value of silence and discretion.'

He watched her skirts swish as she walked quickly away, painfully aware that somehow, somewhere, he had lost control of the situation.

Chapter Twelve

What had she done? What had she done? Coward. Coward. Coward. With each turn of the wheel, the gig seemed to speak the words over and over. She had lied to Brett. Diana knew that. She did not want a hole-in-the-corner affair. She wanted something more, but, above that, she wanted him. She wanted him to look at her with favour.

Did that make her wicked and wanton?

She feared it did. But the alternative was too frightening—forcing Brett to marry her, even presuming he could be forced. She could not bear to think of his eyes looking at her with disgust.

She had tried to outrun her fate. She had made promises. She had confined her life to a set of rules, but it had not been life. Merely an existence. And she wanted to live. There was joy in being alive.

Diana laid her cheek against the cool leather and watched the changing leaves of the trees roll by.

'Are you going to tell me about the picnic Lord Coltonby had prepared for you?' Rose asked, settling her basket more firmly in her lap. 'Cook told me of the splendid delicacies she had prepared. Enough to tempt the most delicate appetite. I told her that my lady has a hardy appetite.'

Diana struggled to sit up, every nerve instantly alert. She had managed to keep her secret from Rose before. 'The picnic was wonderful. The cook excelled herself.'

'And you still want to deny that he is courting you?'

'He wanted advice on painting the grotto.' Diana kept her eyes on the passing landscape. The gig had reached the relative safety of the drive and she could see the tops of the chimneys. What happened back at Ladywell Park seemed remote and unconnected to the safety that her house always represented.

'The grotto? Why would he want that tumbled-down heap of rocks painted?' Rose made a tutting noise in the back of her throat. 'The ways of the gentry are a mystery to me.'

'Lord Coltonby wants to restore the pleasure garden. He plans on having Ladywell Park as his principal seat. He believes it perfect for a stud farm.'

'It sounds like a man whose thoughts have turned towards marriage and responsibility. I should wager that he has more on his mind than breeding horses.'

Diana delicately covered her mouth with her hand, deliberately hiding her expression. She did not even want to think about breeding. She had to assume that all would be well. And if there should be any consequences, then she would deal with them sensibly. She knew that coupling did not result in a child every time. She knew that from experience.

'Or perhaps he is simply a man tired for a brief time of London's delights.'

'And London's delights are not so great that they hold everyone. You returned to Northumberland. I remain here with you even though I was born with the sound of the great bell of Bow ringing in my ears.'

'No doubt the lure of London's fleshpots will re-exert their pull. He is a man, and has no family responsibilities.'

'You are being cynical, Miss Diana.'

'Am I?' Diana forced her lips to smile. She was not going to think about what had happened before. She wanted to believe that Brett was different from all the other rakes. Her heart whispered that he was, but she did not dare hope. 'Sir Cuthbert could not bear to be away from London.'

'Lord Coltonby is cut from a different cloth. I said as much to Mr Hunt earlier, I did. He should be grateful for such a good master, instead of grumbling about the extra work.'

'Sweet Rose. You are always quick to defend your favourites, even though I am not sure what Lord Coltonby has done to deserve your regard.' Diana reached out and clutched Rose's hand and gave it a squeeze.

Rose patted her hand. 'You were gone a long while. It stands to reason that Lord Coltonby is not simply wanting advice on where to put his bedding plants. Or painting.'

'We enjoyed the many dishes. Lord Coltonby swears by seed cake.' Diana forced a lightness into her voice. Prevarication would become easier in time.

'I had wondered what was keeping you. Lord Coltonby's valet kept me engaged in conversation. Every time I mentioned you, he had some little quip to tell, or told me that I had to try a little bit more of the seed cake.' Rose patted her stomach. 'He even gave me a glass of the port, the one Lord Coltonby saves for best. Mr Hunt did glower at us, but it was ever so pleasant.'

A trembling overtook Diana. The valet had clearly known what Brett was about. So Brett had enlisted his aid. The whole seduction had been planned down to the last detail! It was five years ago all over again.

She stared determinedly out the window, willing the carriage to arrive at the stables so she did not have to endure Rose's chatter. Then she paused and drew a deep calming breath. She refused to give way to panic. She would never again be the pathetic creature she had once turned into.

'Are you cold, Miss Diana? Perhaps having an outdoor picnic in the autumn was not the wisest of ideas. I will draw you a hot bath when we get to the house. That will soon put you to right.'

A bath. Diana glanced quickly at Rose and then back out at the parkland. A bath. Five years ago, it had been what she had needed. Scrubbing her skin until it was raw. She had felt soiled—inside and out.

This time, it was very different. That great un-yielding emptiness that had been part of her for such a long time had gone and in its place was a steady light, growing with each breath she took. For the first time since she had returned to Northumberland, the world appeared to be bathed in a radiant glow. Or was she simply looking at it with new eyes?

She reached over and gave Rose's hand a squeeze. 'Thank you for caring, and for being you.'

Rose gave a sniff. 'Can't see how I could be anyone else.'

'Oh, Rose, you are long suffering.' Diana laughed, loud and long.

'It is good to hear you laugh like that again, miss. I am fair certain that I can't remember the last time I heard that sound.'

'It was a while ago, Rose. A very long while ago.'

Diana listened to the hooves of her horse pound the earth. This morning, she had woken and known she had to ride. Fast. Furious. Away from the dreams that haunted her sleep. Away from the knowledge that Brett, having experienced her charms once, was in no rush to experience them again. It bothered her that she wanted him, that she had been woken by a nameless longing. It was not merely to touch him again, but to hear his voice and see his smile.

Her feelings went beyond mere attraction, and it frightened her, just as it exhilarated her. It was as if all her resolutions, all the tenets that she had lived by the last five years suddenly counted for nothing. The only thing she knew was that no man would ever hold her in his power again. She would be the mistress of her own fate. She would never be forced into a marriage of duty, or one-sided attraction. She was free.

She urged Merlin forwards, faster.

She had declined the use of a groom, intending to go no further than the ice house, but it had not been nearly far enough. Now, she allowed Merlin his head and they raced past the copse, the home pasture and on up to the hill towards the gap in the fence that led to Ladywell Park.

She turned Merlin's head and started up the long hill. At the top, the entire valley lay at her feet, with the Tyne snaking through like a silver rope. In the distance she could vaguely make out the buildings of the Ladywell Colliery. Familiar objects in a familiar, unchanging landscape. Diana breathed in the cool air, savouring the moment. It steadied her.

Another horse gave a soft whinny. Instantly her nerves stiffened. Was she ready for this? How would he react, seeing her again? All the pleasure in the ride vanished as if it had never been at all, leaving behind a tight feeling in her stomach.

'I wondered when you would make it up here.' Brett came from the spinney of trees, leading his stallion. He looped the reins about a slender branch and, leaving the horse, started towards her, catching Merlin's bridle with ease.

'How did you know I would come here?' she asked, her breath catching in her throat. Was she that painfully obvious?

'I saw you earlier, riding with your hair streaming behind you.' A faint smile touched his lips, giving him a saturnine look.

'I could have been riding anywhere. It was merely happenstance that I came up here.'

'You described this view to me. You wanted me to be here.' Brett's voice was low. 'It is even more magical than you described, watching the sunrise over the hills.'

'I am flattered that you remembered.' Diana attempted a haughty disdain. She could rebuild the walls around her heart. She could protect that vulnerable bit of her, and ignore the part that kept whispering about his sincerity.

'Some things are worth remembering. Views like the one I had this morning make life worth living. They provide a balm to the soul.'

'Does my soul need a balm?' She tilted her head and glanced up at him through her lashes.

'You were riding as if all the demons in the world were after you.' His face sobered. 'I promise you, Diana, you are safe with me. I am willing to be your champion. Trust me.'

'No, not demons,' Diana said slowly. 'I was revelling in the joy of being alive. It was like I had sleep-walked through my life for years and suddenly I had wakened to find this most marvellous world.'

A silence fell between them, unbroken except for Merlin's quiet chomping. She noticed that Brett's eyes had circles under them as if he had not slept. How long had he been here? Since before sunrise? Waiting for her? She wanted to reject the notion as fancy, but somehow it seemed to grow and take root, refusing to be suppressed.

'You came to see the view. But did you come also to see me?' She hated the way her voice trembled. Hated her need to hear him say the words. Men like Brett scorned ties or obligations.

'I was waiting to be asked.' His voice held an oddly humble note.

'You may consider yourself asked, then. I want to see you,' she whispered. Some day she would have to explain about the past, but not today. She wanted to enjoy this feeling for as long as it lasted.

He took the reins from her hands and looped them around the tree so that Merlin was tethered.

Fastening his hands around her waist, Brett lifted her down from Merlin. Her body slid against his. 'Aren't you going to kiss me good morning?'

He bent his head and Diana tasted his lips. It was

gentle and lingering. Her arms rose and fastened around his neck. The kiss rapidly deepened, calling to something deep within her. With all her heart, she wanted to be the girl she had been five years ago. She wanted yesterday to have been her first time. But it wasn't. And she had no idea how he'd react to the truth.

His lips trailed down the column of her throat, placing soft kisses that tantalised her. The embers within her body flared into life and she realised the fire she had thought doused had merely slumbered. Her body arched forward, seeking more contact with his. She attempted to hang on to sanity. The truth lay between them. If she never told him, it would hang there, making everything ugly. She prayed that the disgust would not be too terrible, but she had to say the words.

'Brett, what are you doing?'

'Your skin tastes like the morning dew,' he murmured, cupping her face between his hands. Delicately his tongue traced her lips. Lingered. 'No, I was wrong—sunshine mixed with dew.'

'You spout easy words.'

He moved his lips to her temple. 'What do you want? Shall I stop and go away?'

Go away? Her body protested at the thought.

She looked up into his eyes, saw the deep grey pools. 'What are you asking me?'

'I can feel a change in you, and it scares me…'

His breathing was ragged and he placed his hands on her shoulders. She looked up into his eyes. In another instant, he would put her away from him and would return to his horse. It was the last thing she wanted, and she was horrified at her reaction. Shaken to the core. And then, not horrified.

'Diana?'

Her answer was to pull his face back towards hers, her hands digging into his hair, holding him there. 'Kiss me, Brett. Kiss me like you did before.'

He groaned and lowered his mouth. Their tongues teased each other, tangling, touching and retreating only to tangle again. The fire within her flamed into carnal desire. Dark. Dangerous. All the more potent because she knew what would happen, out here with no one about. Knew and wanted it. Her body arched towards his again.

He lifted his head and stared down at her for a long time. This time, his hands pushed her from him, created a wall of air between them.

'Enough.'

'Enough?' she said, and something within her died. She ducked her head. Her lips tingled from the onslaught. She touched a hand to her lips and tried to ignore her aching swollen breasts. 'Enough? How can that be enough?'

'If we continue, I will have your skirts over your head and your back against the oak tree. And that won't do either of us any good.'

'It is a thought. Certainly.' She glanced over her shoulder at the tree. A curl of heat infused her. She knew he intended to make her pause, but pausing meant she would have to confess, would have to ruin this fragile new thing between them. She lifted her arms, held them out to him.

'You are a witch, you know that?'

'No, not a witch. A woman. A woman who has slumbered and now has come alive.'

'Very much alive.' He caught her about her waist and pulled her to him, moulding her body to his. Despite the heaviness of her riding habit, his hard arousal pressed against her thighs, making her wriggle. 'But you deserve more than that. You deserve better.'

She glanced at the oak. 'Would it be so bad, so terribly wicked?'

He gave a low husky laugh that sent ripples along her nerves. 'No, and some day, I promise you, we shall do that. Me filling you, with the rose-gold sunrise erupting all around us. My body worshipping yours.'

'But not today?' Diana bit her lip and tried to banish the pagan image his words had conjured. 'Is the sun too high in the sky?'

'I intend to make this right.' He turned his face away from the oak. 'I promised you a soft bed with linen sheets.'

Diana wrapped her arms about her waist. She knew she was not ready for a small house in some anonymous market town, giving up Robert and Simon. 'I thought we would be discreet.'

'What is indiscreet about a bed?' A smile tugged at his lips.

'That would be far too risky. People might discover us. There would be consequences. Not only for me or you, but for my family.' She forced the words from her throat. 'Servants talk, no matter what. Such things do not remain secrets for long.'

His fingers went under her chin and lifted it up. His eyes searched hers. Then he let her go. 'You don't trust me.'

'I know what happens. It is always the woman who falls.' She gave a little shrug. There were all sorts of trust. 'I desire you, but fear the scandal.'

'And if there was no scandal, what then?' He ran a hand down her back. 'The bed I am thinking of will have no one whispering or withdrawing their skirts.'

Her breath stopped in her throat. She could

almost believe that he was speaking of marriage. Her insides trembled and then she rejected the notion firmly. It was beyond the realms of possibility. She gave a small laugh. 'You mean the shepherd's hut in the spinney. I suppose it does have a pallet. I should have guessed.'

His lips thinned and his eyes grew hard. 'I mean the marriage bed, Diana. What happened yesterday may have consequences and I am no cad. It is my duty.'

She went ice cold. The marriage bed. He didn't want to marry, he hadn't professed undying love. Duty. He had made the offer because he felt an obligation. She had to tell him the truth. She steeled herself and searched for the right words.

'We agreed that marriage was not for either one of us,' she said in a small voice.

'Ideas can change.' He reached out and interlaced her fingers with his. 'What would be wrong with a marriage between us? We suit. I must marry at some point to produce an heir and why not you?'

Diana broke away. She crossed her arms about her waist. She had hated the thought of marriage to him when it would have been only duty on his part. Duty provided little comfort in the night. She could not bear it if she had to watch his desire turn to disgust once he saw the awful ugliness that resided deep within her. 'Let's speak no more of marriage in jest.'

His face grew dark. 'I am serious.'

'As was I, when I said that I would not marry.' With each syllable, her voice grew stronger and steadier. She was saying the right things, choosing the correct path. 'You did not coerce me into what passed between us. I knew what I was doing. I had no expectations of an offer. You may rest easy.'

'After what happened, it is my duty. You are a gently bred woman. Cosseted. Cared for. Protected.' Brett stood very straight and pronounced each word with care, as if they had been rehearsed and only emerged with great pain.

Diana winced. The gates of her mind broke open and memories of the other time flooded over her. The pawing hands. The heavy unwelcome breathing in her ear and the pain. All happening while her chaperon had sat, eating and drinking but a few hundred yards from her and the fireworks had burst overhead. She had cried out, but the explosion had swallowed her cries. She forced the gate of her mind closed. Breathed.

She wrapped her arms about her waist, shaking, unable to face the scorn he must have for her. Unable to show the ugliness that she knew must be in her face. 'I was not an innocent virgin.'

'Diana.' His voice was thick, almost unrecognisable. 'You are still an innocent. You possess little knowledge about what passes between a man and a woman. I can tell the difference.' He put his hand on her shoulder. 'Confide in me. Help me to understand.'

'It happened at Vauxhall Gardens,' she whispered. 'One time. I wanted to see the fireworks. I loved fireworks in those days. My chaperon stayed behind. She hadn't finished her supper. He had always been so polite, so correct. He had kissed me once on my cheek. I never thought. We had only gone a short way down a darkened path and a rocket went up, lighting the whole sky. I turned to see it. He kissed me, forced his tongue between my lips, called me a tease. His breath stank of drink. I broke free, but he caught me again with rougher hands. Told me I was a flirt.'

Her throat closed and a deep shudder went through her. She waited to see his disgust, but he squeezed her shoulder, warm steady fingers that somehow cut through the chill. She swallowed hard, regained her composure and then continued.

'His hands were hard. Roaming all over my body. Touching me where no one had ever touched me before. I begged and pleaded, but he seemed to like my fright. It made him more… He threw me to the ground and pinned me there with my skirts over my head. All the while, the rockets were going off. I could hear people's excited shouts and gasps. I yelled, but nobody came. It hurt such a lot.'

She put her hands to her face.

'What were you wearing that night? Your ivory dress?' His voice was cold, deadly. His hands clenched at his sides. 'Was it the night before you became engaged? Is that why your brother agreed to the marriage?'

She shook her head, unable to understand why he had asked. 'I wore my white dress with a lavender net. I cut it up into small bits and fed them to the fire when I returned home. All except one piece, which became the lining of my first cap. Why do you ask?'

He released a breath. 'I worried I might have been there. I could not have borne it to think that this happened to you and I could have stopped him. Did he do anything else, anything at all?'

'He said that I had led him on. That I was wicked and wanton and deserved everything that happened to me. That a true lady would never have behaved like that, and he could tell the difference. And he had only done that because I had wanted to. He said that he had changed his mind about marrying me and was going to end it that night.

But we would have to marry because of how I had acted and what we had done and he'd take great pleasure in spending my money. And my brother would pay dearly for it.' She gave a little shrug and tried to control the shaking of her body. 'Two days later he was dead. I prayed he would die and he did. It makes me very wicked, Brett.'

'It makes you human.'

She turned her face away. She was not going to mention the blood, or how Mrs Tanner had simply raised her glass and asked if she had enjoyed the fireworks when they had returned to the pavilion. How he had smirked. The hours she had spent scrubbing her skin, until it was raw and bleeding. The promises she made to God if only somehow she'd be released from her living hell. Then she had been. And she had tried to live her life as she had promised. Had worn the cap until it was rags to remind her. Only it had not been living, only surviving.

She screwed her eyes shut, refused to let the words tumble forth. Pity was the last thing she wanted. But it was vital that he understand that there was no need for his sacrifice.

'It is good the man is dead or I'd murder him with my bare hands for putting you through that. As it is, I wish Bagshott had not killed him so cleanly and instead that he suffered more.'

'They said that he didn't suffer. He looked peaceful. I wanted him to experience all the torments of hell.'

'Have you told anyone else your story? Your brother? Your maid? Who knows?'

'It was Rose's night off and she was visiting her family. I had the under-maid draw me a bath. And I have never told anyone. I have been too ashamed. And no one ever guessed.' A bitter laugh escaped her lips. 'They thought it was because he had died that I mourned him. How could I mourn a monster like that?'

'You should never have had to endure that alone.' He put his fingers under her chin and forced her to meet his gaze. 'He was wrong. He forced himself on you to ensure you would marry him. He was deep in debt.'

'But I—'

'You did nothing. Someone should have protected you and I will regret to my dying day that I wasn't there to answer your pleas. That nobody came.'

Hot tears ran down her face. 'You weren't to blame.'

'Neither were you, Diana Clare. Neither were you.'

'But I—'

'The offer stands. It is an honourable offer, Diana.

However you were mistreated has no bearing on your future. You are a lady. It is my duty.'

Honourable. Duty. With no words of love. She had no wish for that sort of marriage, even with Brett.

'You feel it your obligation to make an offer. I have refused. That is an end to it.' She forced her voice to become bright. 'Come, we shall say no more of it. You will thank me eventually.'

His cool eyes assessed her. Raked her up and down. 'That is your final word on the subject.'

'It is. I refuse to marry for some sense of misplaced duty. I refuse ever to marry.'

'Why are you standing here next to me?' His lips took on a cynical twist. 'What is it that you want?'

Diana took a long deep breath. Her whole body trembled. She knew she had to do it. She would change the subject and take control again. 'You.'

He swore loud and long, the words echoing across the valley. Words that made her want to curl up into a little ball and die.

'I thought you would have been pleased.' Diana forced the words out. 'A woman who is not looking for marriage. Who is only looking for the pleasure of the moment.'

'How little you know me.' Brett stared at her in disbelief as he struggled to control his temper. He wanted to reach out and shake her. She had to understand what he was offering. He loathed Finch with a passion, but he hated himself for having seduced her, for not having guessed. 'I make the offer for your own good.'

'I have no desire for that sort of marriage. I had a narrow escape from the sort of wedlock you are suggesting. I saw my brother's unhappiness at a loveless marriage. Why is it wrong for me to want a bit of pleasure? Why can't a woman behave like that and a man can?'

Brett was torn between kissing her into submission and shaking her until she saw reason. He took the safe option and did neither, running his hands through his hair. 'Will you listen to reason, Diana? Society will demand it or it will cast you out into oblivion if what passed between us the other day is discovered.'

'Society has no idea about what passed between us. And you are no cad, Brett Farnham. You will not drag a woman's name through the mud.'

He forced his lips to smile, but his insides twisted. He hated that he had been prepared to use her to get a piece of land. Some day, he would find a way of convincing her she was wrong. He might not love her, but he liked her. He desired her. And surely that was a better way to build a marriage than on some romantic folly. 'Then what do you suggest? I have no intention of giving you up.'

'At the start of our friendship, you made it abundantly clear marriage was an undesirable state.' Her chin tilted upwards and her defiant eyes blazed at him, challenging him to deny it. Brett winced, remembering his arrogant words. 'Some day you will thank me for saving you from this folly.'

Thank him? Brett stared at her blankly. She was refusing to marry him. Not refusing his bed, or to lie with him, but refusing to make it legal. The one woman he had ever offered for had just refused him.

He felt as if he had been punched in the stomach. The ring in his pocket weighed heavy. He had been certain—all he'd had to do was to offer. What woman would refuse an earl?

For a breath, he was tempted to walk away, but that would accomplish nothing. He wanted her. She wanted him. She would want to marry him. He would push her and she'd surrender. He would bind her to him. He would make her his. He would have no hesitation in using any means necessary.

'What more could I have asked for?' he said smoothly. 'You are a rare woman, Diana Clare.'

'Then you agree to my terms.' Her eyes showed a shimmer of uncertainty. 'No marriage and absolute discretion.'

'But of course.' Brett smiled inwardly. They were not finished yet. He would get his way in the end. 'You have agreed to be my mistress, and without preconditions.' He allowed his hand to travel down her arm. 'Some might call you foolish. I would prefer to use other words— generous, giving.'

'I have agreed to no such thing!'

'What other term should I use?' He drew her body to him, felt it mould against him. Soften. 'You know what it is like to be with me.'

He started to lower his mouth, his body already anticipating the sweet surrender to come. But she became rigid and her eyes were fixed on an object beyond his shoulder. Her hands, which an instant before had acquiesced to the onslaught, now fought against him. He allowed her to go. He stared at her, puzzled.

'There is someone there. Someone watching.'

Chapter Thirteen

Diana stepped away from Brett and tried to draw a breath but her stays constricted her. She pointed with a trembling finger. 'Someone is there. He moves in the shadows.'

Brett turned, stared for a moment, before turning back to her, hands reaching out. 'Your eyes are playing tricks. Who would be out here?'

Diana evaded his grasp. He had to see. He had to understand the potential for disaster. 'There was movement.'

'Most likely a weasel or stoat moving in the undergrowth. Think no more on it. If you wish to embark upon a life of sin, Diana, you cannot be perturbed at the slightest wood pigeon's wing clap.'

'No, it was bigger than that.' She shielded her eyes and her body stilled. A small figure moved along the trees, steadily but with great stealth.

'A child is there.' Brett held out his arm, blocking her way. 'Let me go and see. I will deal with the intruder.'

'I know that face!' She pushed against his arm, refusing to be held prisoner. 'I know it! Let me go!'

Diana picked up her skirts and ran towards the copse at the bottom of the hill. Behind her, the air echoed with Brett's oaths. 'Make up your mind, Diana!'

'Robert!' She reached the bedraggled creature within a breath and had gathered him to her. She kissed him, then held her nephew from her. 'Why, in the name of heaven, are you here? You should be at school.'

'Get off, Aunt Diana.' Robert scrambled away from her embrace and stood facing her. His breeches looked as if he had rolled around in a pigsty and he sported a great rent in his new jacket, the one she and Rose had sewed for hours to get it ready in time for school. A single tear trickled down his cheek. 'I am not a baby anymore. I am nine.'

Diana stared at her nephew, not sure whether she should throttle him or get down on her knees and thank him for being there. With Robert's unexpected appearance, the temptation was gone. It seemed as if in one fatal swoop of his mouth, Brett had broken all her walls. She would have agreed to be his mistress. Her fall would have been complete.

But she had this one last opportunity to change her destiny.

She pushed away all thoughts of Brett and what might have been, grabbing Robert by the arm. She looked at him again. Made certain that he was not some sort of fevered dream.

'Robert Clare, what are you doing here?' she said, kneeling down beside him. 'Why have you left school?'

Robert stood up and stuck his hands into his pockets. 'They punished me for things I didn't do. I had nothing to do with the stink bomb.'

'Doctor Allen sent a note. He believes you did. You should take your punishment.'

'He believes wrongly. It wasn't me. It was some other boy.' His hands balled into fists. 'They all said it was me.'

'Truly?' Diana crossed her arms. 'And who made a stink bomb in the kitchen this summer? Three times, Robert!'

'That was different. I was experimenting. Once I knew how it worked, it did not matter any more.'

'And if it was not from you, how did the boys get the information? You know what your father will say. You will never have the horse you long for.'

Robert gave a shrug and ran his toe in the dirt, but a single tear gleamed in his eye. Diana's heart squeezed. She wanted to scoop him up and hug him to her, but he had to learn his lesson. He could not simply leave school whenever he wanted. He could not give up.

'Is there some problem, Diana?' Brett came to stand at her shoulder. 'Who is this ragamuffin? One of the colliery children?'

'My nephew.' Diana glanced over her shoulder, up at Brett's questioning face. 'He has run away from school.'

'And I ain't going back…ever.' Robert's voice rose an octave and she could see his muscles begin to bunch. 'I came this way to say goodbye to Rose and Titch. They are the only ones who care about me.'

'Titch?' Brett asked quietly.

'Our terrier.'

Brett nodded and motioned for her to continue. Diana knelt down beside Robert.

'But, Robert, you love school. All this summer you spoke about how you longed to be back.' Diana reached out to hug him to her again.

'I hate school. Stupid school. Don't need it to ride horses.'

'Never underestimate education,' Brett commented in a matter-of-fact tone. 'Without it, you are ignorant.'

'I don't need an education to work.'

'Your father wants more for you then digging ditches or shovelling coal,' Brett said. 'Fathers are like that.'

'I am going to race horses.'

'You need to study. There is much you have to learn,' Brett said. 'There is more to life than racing horses.'

'I won't! I won't!' Robert screwed up his face and stamped his foot.

'Robert!' Diana said, thoroughly shocked. 'Please forgive my nephew. He is normally much better behaved than this. Apologise immediately to Lord Coltonby, Robert.'

Robert hung his head and mumbled an apology. Diana breathed more easily.

'What is the true difficulty, Robert?'

'Greek and Latin are only about dead people.'

The corner of Brett's mouth quirked upwards and Diana fought against the temptation to laugh. Robert was right, but that wasn't the point.

'The Romans were great engineers,' Brett remarked. 'They built bridges and aqueducts that remain standing today. They raced horses and built chariots.'

'I wouldn't know about that.' Robert hung his head.

'Your father sent you to school to learn,' Brett said quietly. 'You should go back.'

'Who...who are you?' Robert backed up against the wall.

'Lord Coltonby—he owns the Park now and he is a friend,' Diana said and prayed that Robert would listen to reason. He was too large for her to pick up and carry back. She had no idea how she was going to get him and Merlin back to the house. Then there was Simon to be faced.

'Lord Coltonby?' Robert's face jerked up. 'Your horses won the Derby and several other plates.'

'You know about the turf?'

'A few of the other boys do and so I joined in.'

'Yes, it was my horse that won. By two lengths.'

'Wait until I tell Rupert and Henry that I met Lord Coltonby and—'

'I thought you had finished with school,' Diana said quietly. 'How can you tell them? And why should they believe you?'

'That's true.' Robert stuck his hands in his pockets and made a circle in the dirt with the toe of his boot. 'I am done with it.'

'Robert, how did you get here?' Brett's voice was low, as if he was coaxing a wild animal.

'Got a lift from a drover. Thought he was nice and kind, like, but he weren't. He beat his horses.'

Diana glanced at Brett. Robert's story did not ring true. 'Robert, who suggested this?'

He drew another line in the dirt. 'Henry,' he whispered. 'Henry was going to come with me, only he didn't appear and the drover grabbed me. Said I owed him money.'

'And then what happened?' Brett asked.

'He threatened to beat me because I didn't have any money. I waited, and waited. Then I saw the Lion and Dove pub and knew I was close to home, so I escaped.'

Diana stifled a cry, and reached for Robert again. Brett motioned for her to be quiet.

'That was very resourceful of you.'

Robert tilted his head to one side. 'Was it?'

'You had a lucky escape and you know it,' Brett said. 'You are a bright boy, aren't you? You know what can happen to children who disappear.'

Robert shook his head—gone was the bravado. 'I do.'

'People will be worried about you.'

'I wanted…I wanted to come home,' Robert whispered. 'I missed it. I wanted to see Papa. He would put things right. A boy's father should put things right.'

'He should do, but sometimes fathers forget.' Brett's face was remote and his eyes faraway. He was speaking of another father. Diana's heart turned over for the little boy that he must have been once. Had he too run away from his school? What dangers had he faced and how had they made him into the man he was today?

'I think Papa is going to be very angry with me.' Robert scrubbed his eyes. 'I should go back to school now, before he discovers what I have done. He will be disappointed in me.'

'No, you face your father,' Brett said. 'You have come this far. You have a responsibility. You were the one to run away. You and you alone must face the consequences.'

'And if he sends me back?'

'I will take you in my carriage with my horses.'

Diana stared at Brett. The offer was so unexpected. Why should he do something for her nephew? Instinctively she knew that he was not making the offer to curry favour with her, but to help Robert make the right choice. He had a way with boys. She had seen that before with Jimmy Satterwaite.

Robert turned to Brett and held out his hand. 'I will consider your offer, sir. But first I must see my father. You are right. I do have responsibilities.'

'He is a good boy, Brett,' she whispered. 'He has had a bad fright. He does not mean to be rude.'

'I can see that. I was a boy like him once and my scrapes were far worse. Luckily his father is there to forgive him. Mine wasn't. His experience has probably taught him a more severe lesson than any punishment could have.' Brett took Robert's hand. 'The pact is made. My horses are at your disposal, should you require it, young Master Clare. You need only send word.'

'And how will we get you home, young man?' Diana regarded Robert, who hung his head.

'I hadn't considered it.' Then his back stiffened and his fists balled at his sides. When he looked like that, Diana could see the resemblance to Simon—the same pig-headed determination. 'I can run alongside.'

'You can ride in front of me,' Diana offered.

Robert gave a half-shrug.

'I suspect he would prefer to ride on Falcon,' Brett said.

'Can I?' Robert's face shone. 'I will be able to tell Henry and Rupert that I rode one of Lord Coltonby's horses. How many plates and cups have you won?'

'Me or my horses?'

'It amounts to the same thing.'

'There is a difference which you will understand when you get older. But for the record I have won two plates and seven cups, while my horses' number in the hundreds. It is the ones I won through my own efforts that I am most proud of.'

Diana's throat closed. She hoped one day Robert would understand what Brett was saying.

The boy's eyes grew round. 'But can I ride with you?'

'If your aunt agrees. She is the lady in charge.'

Diana nodded as her throat closed tight. Brett had known the exact words to say. She had thought to protect herself, but she wondered if it was too late. When the time came for them to part, she knew her heart would be in danger of shattering.

Diana pulled hard on Merlin's reins, forcing the horse to a slow walk. She had given in to Robert's request and she and Brett had raced slightly. But now, she obeyed the rules of the stable and walked the horses back.

Her heart sank as she rounded the corner towards the mounting block. Simon's carriage stood ready in the stable yard. She had half-hoped that he would have left for the colliery before they arrived back. It would have given her a chance to clean Robert up and find out more about his version of events. To prepare a story that would pass for the truth, but give the events in the best possible light.

Behind her, Robert's whoop of delight resounded as Brett made his stallion rear. And at that very instant she saw her brother walk out. He drew his eyebrows together as he jammed his top hat on.

'What is going on here?'

'Isn't it obvious, Simon? I have returned from my morning ride.' Diana kept her voice steady but her stomach clenched. With a few ill-chosen words, Simon could undo everything.

'Why is my son here?' Simon pointed with an accusatory finger. 'Why have you brought him here? Why isn't he at school where he belongs?'

Diana took her time dismounting from Merlin. With Simon in this sort of mood, she had to remain calm.

'I was out for my morning ride and encountered Brett and Robert. It seemed sensible to return here with them. Would you have preferred me to send your son elsewhere?'

'What is Coltonby doing with my son?' Simon thundered, grabbing her arm. 'Why is he riding with him? Why isn't he in Newcastle? At school where he belongs and where I pay good money for him to be.'

'Be civil,' Diana said in a furious undertone and

jerked her elbow away. 'Robert ran away from school. I discovered him out by the look-out point. I thought for a moment he might continue to run.'

'Robert ran away from school?' The colour drained from Simon's face. 'Why would he have cause to do that? Dr Allen's has an excellent reputation.'

'And he has had a bad time of it.'

'But why? What is the boy playing at? And where is Dr Allen? I pay him to look after Robert's safety, not to have the boy gallivanting all over the countryside.'

'You will have to ask your son.' Diana nodded to where Robert sat with Brett. 'Go on, call him. Talk to him.'

'Robert Clare!'

Robert slid down from Brett's horse and ran to Simon. 'Papa,' he said with a trembling voice. He stopped and started again. This time, his voice was stronger. 'Father, I have returned home. I was wrong, but I have come back.' He glanced up at Brett. 'Did I say it right?'

Simon did not say anything. He looked solemnly at Robert's bedraggled face. Diana willed him to hug his son, to acknowledge that he was pleased to see him. Anything. Simon placed a hand on Robert's shoulder for a brief instant. 'I will deal with you later, Robert Clare. No doubt your head-master will be in touch.'

'It wasn't my fault, Papa.'

'Once I know the full facts, then I can make a judgement. I warned you that I would not stand for any more tricks.'

'This isn't a trick, Papa. I will go back now.'

'You should never have left in the first place.'

'I know.' Robert hung his head.

'Were they unkind? Were they cruel?'

'I ran away because I did not want to be punished for something another boy did. I know a man should take his punishment, but only when it is just.'

Simon took out his fob watch, regarded it and then slid it back into his pocket. 'We will discuss this when I return from work, Robert. I am late.'

Diana went forward and caught the carriage door. 'Simon!' she said in an undertone. 'He is your son. Speak to him. He worships you.'

'He ran away rather than face his punishment.' Simon's knuckles shone white against the door. 'I have nothing but contempt for him.'

'He made a mistake. He was very nearly kid-napped.' Diana held out her hands, pleaded with her brother to understand. 'It is but by the grace of God that he is here.'

'Diana, I have a business to run. Allow me to handle him in my own way. You should have forced him to walk. He chose to come here. He should not be rewarded with a ride on Coltonby's horse.' He rapped on the roof of the carriage.

Diana stuffed a hand into her mouth and held back a sob. Who she felt sorrier for—Simon or Robert—she could not have said. All she knew was that this was a tragedy in the making. But she also knew that she could not make Simon do anything. He had to lead his life as he chose to. She glanced at Brett and saw a muscle jump in his cheek. 'Are you not going to thank Lord Coltonby?'

Simon stuck his head out of the window. The two men stared at each other. Neither moving a muscle.

'My gratitude, Coltonby, for returning the boy.'

'As your son has been returned safely to his parent, there is no need for me to remain here.' Brett addressed his words to Simon, but made no move to dismount.

'Thank you,' Diana mouthed. Brett gave a nod and his horse cantered away.

The stable yard was silent until long after his horse's hooves had faded. Simon's carriage, however, remained stationary. Diana went up to the door, opened it and looked at her brother's distressed face. She thought she saw a tiny tear in the corner of his eye, but Simon never cried, not even when he had told her about Jayne.

'Simon,' Diana whispered and willed him to respond to his son. 'You need to do something. He has had a scare. He has agreed to return. I don't think he will try it again. He was nearly kidnapped by drovers. He followed bad advice.'

'I can imagine what risks he took, Diana. It doesn't make it right.'

'You made mistakes when you were that age. I can remember the apple-tree incident. How many saplings did you break?'

'And what did Father do? Beat me! Within an inch of my life!' Simon drew in his breath.

'At least our father cared about your fate.'

'I would never whip Robert like that.'

She offered a small prayer up as the silence stretched again. Simon surely had to understand. Robert was only a boy. She felt a movement at her side and Robert pushed between her and Simon.

'Papa?' he said. 'I didn't mean to be bad. I wanted you to know the truth. I wanted you to think the best of me. I did not make a stink bomb. Henry did. But it was my fault that he knew how to do it. You are right. I should never have left. I should have stayed and accepted the punishment.'

Simon glanced down at Robert. His throat worked. 'Was it very smelly?'

'Terribly.' Robert's nose wrinkled. 'Henry had done the compound wrong. It exploded too early.'

Diana held her breath.

'I will write to Dr Allen. He might be persuaded to take you back, but I expect you to behave like a Clare should—with dignity and honour. It is not up to you to decide if a punishment is just or not. You leave that to your elders.'

'Yes, sir. I will.'

'We will speak about this later.' Simon nodded towards the coachman and the horses began to move.

Diana watched the carriage roll away, painfully aware that there was nothing she could do except hope that Simon would somehow see sense and not brand Robert as being exactly like his mother. There was much in him that was Clare. Simon had changed over the past few years, and she wasn't sure she even recognised him.

'I can't believe Robert did that,' Simon said later that evening after they had finished supper and Robert had gone to bed. 'Left school for such a small thing. He should have taken his punishment like a man.'

'But he *was* punished. He has learnt his

lesson.' She paused. 'He is only a boy. Give him time, Simon.'

'But why leave?' Simon held his ruby-red glass of port up to the light. 'All he had to do was to send me a letter. I would have read it.'

Would you have? Diana wondered. Suddenly it seemed after years of not questioning her brother and his motives, she had to break her silence. It was too easy to play it safe. It was as if Brett had awoken some devil within her, and she was tired of taking the sensible course. 'He probably wanted to make sure you understood the whole story.'

'I fear he takes after his mother and you know where her wildness led. Those last years of her life, all that pain and suffering… Diana, how could I want that for Robert?'

'Will Dr Allen allow him to return?' Diana asked. She held back the words explaining that Robert was only nine and could hardly be expected to play a man's part.

'I will write to the good doctor and explain the situation.'

'Why do you think he will agree?'

'I have donated enough money to that school. Dr Allen will hear me out. For the right sum, he will do as I ask. That much was made clear the last time Robert misbehaved.' Simon ran his hand through his hair as he paced up and down in the dining room. 'Robert and I will have a full and frank discussion. He will do as I say. We will have no more of that nonsense.'

Simon had forbidden her to be in the room when he confronted Robert. The boy had emerged white faced, but resolute. Diana longed to hug him to her, but he had clearly grown too old for such behaviour.

'We almost lost him, Simon.'

'I gave my promise to his mother that I would look after him and I have done so.'

Diana pressed her lips together. She knew what Simon believed and why. He had confessed everything about his marriage and his fears for Robert. At the same time she had been grateful that he had never questioned her about London. He'd just been glad that she had returned.

'Does he have to go back? There must be other schools we could send him to.'

'Dr Allen's is the best in the north-east. It is my decision. Robert will have the best, but his mother's tendencies have to be curtailed.'

'And who will take him back when he goes?'

'You can.' Simon waved his hand. 'I am busy with my engine. It is at a crucial stage. It moved two feet this afternoon. Robert will understand. He loved his time there last summer.'

'Simon, it would be better if you took him. You could speak with Dr Allen. Explain in person. It would mean so much to Robert.'

Simon looked at her and slowly shook his head. 'Please, Diana. You know I would give in. I want to be a different father than ours.'

Diana pressed her hands onto her thighs, regained control of her emotions. 'Very well, I will. I want to see him settled properly. Lord Coltonby has offered a ride in his carriage if it will make things easier.'

'Coltonby seeks to use my son for his own purposes.'

'Why…why do you say that?'

'It should be obvious to you what the man is about, why he is sniffing around here.' Simon's eyes raked her up and down. 'He will never marry you, Diana.'

'Did I say that he would? Why do you persist in thinking the worst of him? Cambridge was finished years ago.'

'He is doing this to get me to drop the price of the land. He will then go and sell the rights to Sir Norman Bolt. Don't think that I am not aware of how much Sir Norman needs that land.' Simon clasped his hand to his forehead. 'My God, to think I nearly gifted it to Biddlestone in exchange for investing in my engine. It was sheer providence.'

'I thought Lord Coltonby wanted the land for the view.'

'Ah ha, he says that, but he and Maurice Bolt have been as thick as thieves. Why else would they have raced? I overheard Bolt boasting about his father's new engine and you know it would give them access. I know Maurice Bolt wouldn't risk his father's prize mare for a boot-blacking receipt. There is more to it.'

'Simon, you are spouting nonsense. Lord Coltonby is not interested in engines. Or wagonways. He is interested in horses. You are wrong about him.'

'Then ask him. And while you are at it, ask why he is sniffing around a *tradesman's* sister. What were you thinking about by meeting him, Diana? You are playing into his hands.'

'You are hardly a tradesman, Simon.'

'In his eyes, I am and always will be. Do you really think your charms have beguiled him?'

'You are angry Simon. You seek to hurt someone.' Diana choked back the tears.

'Am I?' Simon whispered. 'Or am I seeing things clearly where you are wilfully blind? He is exactly like your misbegotten fiancé, out to get what he can.'

'I need to see my nephew. He is my first

concern, not your ongoing childish feud with Brett Farnham!' She walked with quick steps out of the dining room.

'That's right. Go on, Diana, run away from the truth.' Simon's voice floated after her. 'It is easier that way.'

Diana stopped on the stairs and sank down. She laid her head against her knees as Simon's vile words washed over her. He was wrong. Brett was not using her. He had never sought to use her. They were friends.

Brett surveyed the Ladywell Main colliery from his curricle. The machinery and men were laid out in front of him as the sound of the great pumping engines rang in his ears. The solid ponies pulled the carts along the wagon-way towards the landing on the Tyne from where the coal would be shipped to Newcastle and beyond. Prosperous. Clare cared more about his business and his machines than he cared about his son or his sister. He wanted investment in his engine. Very well, Brett would give him the money, pay over the odds for the land as well but, in exchange, he wanted Simon's co-operation with Diana. Together, they could make her understand that his offer was honourable, and why marriage was the only option.

Brett alighted from the curricle and tossed the ribbons to Jimmy Satterwaite. The lad showed real potential as a possible tiger, particularly as Brett's former tiger refused to settle in Northumberland and had returned to the bright lights of London. 'Look after them. They are skittish enough around machines. I'd send them back to Tattersalls but they are high steppers. This will not take long.'

A great roar drowned out the lad's comment. A huge black machine advanced out of the shed, puffing smoke and grinding along the cast-iron rails. Sparks flew up in a massive cloud, showering the machine with red gold. Jimmy cowered slightly and both horses pawed the ground.

'Look to the horses, Satterwaite,' Brett said sharply. 'If they go, there will be no stopping them. You want to be a tiger, don't you?'

'I will, sir, but that thing…' The lad pointed a trembling finger as his horses reared a second time. 'It frightens me. Me da were injured by one of them machines. Spent weeks off work.'

'Hardly a fiend from Hades, boy. Concentrate on the horses. Lead them away from here—slowly and steadily.'

The lad gave a half-nod and clung on to the bridles for dear life. He seemed to be in charge—

but barely. Brett turned his attention back to the screaming monster. He started forwards.

A burly man stepped in front of Brett, blocking his way. Brett glared at him.

'You ain't allowed here. No one is allowed here. Not while this here is happening.'

Brett raised an eyebrow. 'I am Lord Coltonby. I have business with your master.'

'I don't care who you say you are. Mr Clare has said no one is to be here. Not today. Today, we are closed.'

'Clare will see me now. Or face the consequences.' Brett regarded the man with a stern eye. Ice-cold fury washed through his veins.

The burly man pursed his mouth and shook his head. 'Mr Clare ain't going to like it.'

'I don't care if Mr Clare likes it or not.' Brett glanced over his shoulder and saw Jimmy struggling to hold the horses as the monster advanced towards him. 'What in the name of all that is holy is that?'

'Travelling engine, sir. That's what they call them. Loco Motives.' The man continued to block his way.

'I do not care what they call them. There is a problem.'

Brett watched in horror as the iron rails began to buckle and twist, splintering under the weight of the engine. He watched as the machine tilted and the fiery coal began to spill out over the wooden blocks that held the rails. The air became thick with oaths and screams as the men realised what was happening.

The foreman stood, stunned, watching in disbelief. Brett saw the flames begin to lick the engine.

'Do something! Get some water,' he yelled, but the man continued to stand there, rooted to the ground.

'He said it was safe.'

Brett ran forwards, shouting orders to the men who gathered around the disaster like fairgoers gawking at the latest marvel. 'Why are you standing there? That man needs your help.'

'We daren't go any closer. The master will have it under control right enough. He always does.'

'This has happened before?'

'Not as bad as this…'

Brett paid no heed to the man and raced forwards. The heat from the engine seared his face. Simon Clare stood propped up at the controls, eyes closed, seemingly oblivious to the carnage happening around him. He had courage, Brett would grant him that.

'This contraption is going to explode! Get out while you can.'

Clare glanced at him. 'Get away from here. You don't know what you are playing at, your lordship.

Go back and play with your horses. Leave this to the experts.'

'Neither do you!'

'I am perfectly safe. You will be in danger if you stand there.' Clare leant forwards and twisted a knob. The great machine heaved forward again with a grinding sound. Sparks flew up in greater arcs, covering Brett with a thousand pinpoints of light.

'Not as much danger as you are in.'

Without hesitating, Brett plunged in and pulled the man out. The infernal machine gave one last shudder and then the orange-red flames licked the spot where Clare had stood. He placed Clare on to the ground and turned his attention to the machine and the smouldering rails. The machine continued to puff smoke and steam in to the air.

'How do you stop it?'

Clare lay there, singed, a queer smile on his face. His features were blackened with soot, but his green eyes blazed. He struggled to stand up, stood there swaying back and forth as Brett examined the wreckage. 'What sort of mad man are you, Coltonby? I told you to get away from here. You and your bungling have destroyed everything.'

'No permission needed. No thanks required.' Brett leant closer, made sure that Clare could see his lips. 'You would have died in that machine.'

Clare's response was to land a punch on Brett's jaw. Brett staggered back, surprised.

'I don't forgive a man lightly when he reacts that way,' Brett said, fingering his jaw.

'You had no cause to rescue me.'

'You don't want to be rescued. Very well, then.' He picked the man up by his jacket, started to haul him towards the smouldering machine, then stopped. 'You are not worth it, Clare.'

'Let go of me,' Clare struggled.

The machine's groaning and creaking increased. The men who had been gathered round started to scatter.

Brett kept his grip tight around Clare's arm. In this mood, there was no telling what he might do. And he had no wish for Diana to accuse him of harming her brother.

'Let go of me, Coltonby. If I don't stop it, that boiler will blow.'

'Promise me you will be sensible.'

But Clare twisted and freed himself from Brett's grasp.

Brett gritted his teeth and watched Clare take three steps. With a gigantic roar, the boiler of the engine exploded. Brett watched in horror as Clare was hit. He staggered and fell to the ground. He got up on to his knees and tried to rise, only to fall again.

'I think I might have overestimated something.' He collapsed on the ground and lay still.

Brett leant down him over. Clare's face was pale white against the soot. He gave a funny gurgle and lay still. Brett put his ear to Clare's chest and heard the faint rattle of a breath.

'Get a doctor, quick!'

Chapter Fourteen

'Do I have to do my times table?' Robert looked up from the dining-room table. 'I am not at school, and the sun is shining.'

'You will be learning at home until Dr Allen says that you can return.' Diana regarded her nephew. She wanted to be elsewhere, as well. Not in here, stuck trying to remember how the eight times table went. The weather had turned slightly chillier and the sloes, blackberries and other hedge fruit were ready for picking. There were a thousand other things she longed to do, but her duty was to ensure Robert kept up with his school-work. If she concentrated on Robert, she could forget Simon's insidious accusations about Brett. His words kept going round and round in her brain. Why had Brett become interested in her? Why had he started paying her attention? She needed to know the answer, but it also frightened her. What if Simon was correct?

'But…but…'

'Do you want your school friends to see that you have fallen behind? Do you want them to laugh at you? I have always had trouble with my eights, in particular eight times seven.' She swallowed hard. He had to understand how easy it was to fail. 'I know how cruel people can be.'

'But I can already do up to the twelve times table, Aunt Diana,' Robert blurted out, holding out his paper. 'See! It is simple, particularly eight times seven. You write fifty-six equals seven times eight.'

Diana sighed, and reached for the paper. He had neatly written out all the times tables. The pain behind her eyes threatened to become a fully fledged headache. Despite having no expense spared on her education, her grasp of mathematics remained hazy. Abandoning maths might be the best plan. 'Shall we try geography, then? I will draw a map of Northumberland and you can put in the principal rivers and towns. And I want the handwriting legible, not ink stained.'

Robert groaned. Then his face brightened. 'I can hear horses. Someone is coming to visit.'

'Robert. You cannot hear the stables from the house. Sit back down.'

'No really, I can.' Robert rushed to the window. 'They are coming up the gravel path, but it looks like Papa's carriage.'

Diana's hand trembled slightly. There was no reason for Simon to return home so quickly. He had told her this morning at breakfast that he would not make the mid-day meal as he wanted to have a trial run of the engine. Her mind raced with all sorts of possibilities and she tried to hang on to the most rational—Robert was seeking an excuse to stop his schoolwork.

'What nonsense, Robert. Your father would never come up the gravel path. He always goes to the stables.' Diana pointed to the chair. 'Pick up your pen and concentrate.'

'But he is. I know my father's carriage.'

Diana went to stand next to her nephew. Simon's carriage was indeed turning up the drive. She pressed her lips together as the back of her neck prickled. 'Robert, I was wrong and you are right. Remain here while I see what is going on. And while I am away, you may recite your eight times table.'

Ignoring his groans, she walked quickly outside, in time to see Brett alighting from the carriage. His face was furrowed and his coat covered in soot. He made no move towards her. She tried for a smile, but he gave a brief shake of his head. She forced her legs to carry her out to the carriage.

'Is this some sort of joke?' Diana asked quietly. 'Why are you in Simon's carriage? Where is yours? You are scaring me, Brett.'

'No joke.' A great weariness hung over him. 'I have been to the colliery. There was an accident.'

Diana's mind raced. Fire damp? An exploding engine in the pump house? The colliery had a good safety record, but that counted for nothing. Pockets of dangerous gas could develop without warning. She had tried to tell Simon that he should find a solution to that problem, but he had only laughed and said that he would, after he'd managed to get the travelling engine to work. She swallowed hard and refused to let her mind wander down that path. 'And Simon? Where is he? What have you done with him? Is he…?'

Her throat closed and she could not ask the final question.

'Your brother lives. You must keep that in your mind. He is alive.' Brett nodded towards the carriage. 'I have brought him back to you.'

'Diana.' A voice croaked from the carriage.

Diana peered in and saw Simon sitting there with his face swathed in bandages. He held his arm awkwardly. His clothes were far more rumpled that Brett's and a distinct smell of smoke and grease hung about the carriage. 'What happened?'

'Coltonby will explain.' Simon closed his undamaged eye and leant back against the carriage seat.

'The travelling engine. Or rather the non-travelling engine. Your brother's attempts at Loco Motion have failed. Spectacularly.' Brett proceeded to explain the morning's events.

Diana listened with growing horror.

'I am grateful you arrived in time.'

'I would have sorted it!' came the yell from the carriage. 'Do not believe Coltonby, Diana! It was a triumph! A triumph! If he hadn't pulled me from the engine, I would have stopped it.'

'Or you would be dead. Nobody could have stopped the boiler from blowing.'

'Coltonby, you have no idea about engines.'

'I know enough.'

'I knew it! I knew it! You want to get that land cheap. You have done a deal with the Bolts. It is why you have been nosing around my sister.'

'I have no idea what you are talking about. I have made no arrangement with the Bolts.' Brett's voice was calm and measured.

'Brett?' Diana whispered. He wrapped his fingers about her hand and gave it a brief reassuring squeeze. Then let go.

'Your brother took a blow to the head, Diana. He is not in his right mind. Ignore what he says. Ignore everything he says about the land.'

She nodded, wanting to believe him, but she had also seen his eyes, seen the way they slid away from her.

'Your brother has been ranting and raving all the way home. I have paid it no mind. The doctor wanted someone with him. He is afraid that he might be suffering from shock. People in shock say things that are not to be believed.' Brett reached out and touched her hand. 'He will bear the scars of this day for the rest of his life.'

Diana's brow wrinkled. She knew vaguely of the term 'shock'. She had heard it used before, but had never actually seen the effects. She peered again into the gloom of the carriage. Her brother moved restlessly, irritably.

'Will he recover?'

'He has the luck of the devil. He is alive, Diana. He may lose the eye, but his limbs will heal eventually and the burns on his face will fade. But he will have to spend time resting.'

'Easier said than done with Simon.' Diana attempted a laugh, but it came out as a strangled cry. It was all too easy to imagine what had nearly happened. She had to be thankful for small mercies. Only an eye, when he could have lost his arm or worse. 'Simon hates to be ill. He sees it as a sign of weakness, that it is his duty to get up as soon as possible.'

'Why does that not surprise me?' Brett's lips turned upwards.

'And you are a good patient?'

'Guilty as charged.' Brett touched his hat. 'The doctor has given him some laudanum and it should help make him sleep. He will call later today to check on his patient.'

'I assume you used Dr MacFarlane, the colliery's physician. He is good, if a little old fashioned in his methods.'

'He was quite thorough.'

'And with you as well?'

'With me?' Brett gave a shrug. 'A few bruises and scrapes, but nothing life threatening.'

'I see.' Diana pressed her hands together, to prevent them from reaching out to him and discovering for herself his injuries. She had to remain discreet.

Diana motioned to several of the servants, who helped Simon from the carriage. At first, it appeared that Simon had fallen asleep, but he eventually rose and stumbled from the carriage.

Simon's face turned black and he pointed his

finger. 'That man interfered with my engine. Mine! And the land stays mine despite your sniffing around my sister. I know what you are on about, Coltonby.'

'Simon!'

'We were not all born with a golden spoon in our mouths. Some of us had to work for our fortunes.'

'We will discuss this later, Clare.' Brett turned to Diana, his face stern. 'Get him into the house before he does himself damage.'

Diana concentrated on getting Simon into the house and then settled into his bed. She tried to be efficient and not to cringe at the red welts on his arms and face, burns from the steam. Robert came rushing in, but halted, uncertain, by the door. Diana walked quickly over and shut it, telling Robert that his father was tired.

She had just turned to go when Simon croaked from the bed. 'That Coltonby, don't believe a word he says. Interfering fop!'

'You are overwrought, Simon, and very lucky that Lord Coltonby saw sense not to take offence. Such men settle slurs by duels.'

'I am the equal of him.' He struggled to sit up. 'Bring him on! He has insulted you, Diana. I can feel it. He only paid attention to you because he wants me to give him the land. It is why he came to the colliery. I am not afraid to avenge your honour, Diana. I can shoot straight.'

'I know you can,' Diana said soothingly and forced her mind from the knowledge that somehow Simon had worked out that Brett had seduced her. How? Had it been only a lucky guess? 'Now lie back down.'

She smoothed the bedclothes, tucking him as if he were no older than Robert. He turned to face the wall.

'You were right, Diana. Hedley did not let me have one that could be easily fixed.'

'I told you the engine wouldn't work. When are you going to abandon this dream?' She waited to hear his scathing remark. He swung his head around and stared at her, his good eye burning with an intense heat.

'It went, Diana. It moved. It is the rails that are wrong. I can feel it in my bones. It is not the engine that is the problem, but the rails it travels on.'

'You sleep now. We can speak later.' She brought the sheets up to his chin.

'You are a good person. Keep Coltonby away from here. He only wants to use you, Diana.'

Diana paused. 'I don't have any say over where Lord Coltonby goes. And you should be on your knees, thanking him for saving your life.'

'I would have had the engine under control, if he had not distracted me.' Simon raised his hand. 'The man's a fop for all his bravery. He is cut from the same cloth as all aristocrats.'

'You are wrong, Simon.'

'I know I am right.'

Diana closed the door with a decisive click. Simon wanted a fight, but she did not. Brett was different. He had to be. She retraced her steps and found Brett entertaining Robert in the dining room. The chairs were drawn up like a coach and four and Robert was perched on the end of the table. 'Robert Clare! Get down this instant.'

Robert slipped down from the table. Both he and Brett had the grace to hang their heads. Brett had discarded his coat. 'I thought he could use the distraction.'

'But on the table?'

'I needed to have the right perch, Aunt Diana. And Coltonby says that I am a natural with how I hold the ribbons.'

Diana gave Brett a hard look and he shrugged, unrepentant. 'It is all in the proper teaching. How is the patient?'

'Robert, go and see Rose,' Diana said. Robert looked as if he was about to protest, but took one glance at Brett and became quiet.

'We will continue with your driving lesson later.'

'Yes, Aunt Diana.' He left the room.

'I thought it would cheer him up.' Brett began to replace the chairs and restore the dining room to some semblance of order.

'But the dining room table?'

'It is solid.' He lowered his eyes. 'There are many uses a table can be put to.'

'You know them all.'

'One or three.'

Her insides tingled. Ruthlessly she suppressed the feelings. Without even waiting or asking, Brett had set about making himself indispensable. But why? Was Simon right? Did it have to do with the land?

'The fact remains that it should not have been used as a perch.'

'Your nephew is worried about his father. He needed a distraction.'

'And you sought to provide it? How obliging of you.' Diana crossed her arms.

'I do but try. You should see how very obliging I can be.' He made a smooth bow.

'Is that what you are to me—obliging?'

'You are upset, Diana.' He reached for her, but she stayed on the other side of the room. His eyes assessed her for a long moment and he ran his hand through his hair. 'My father was killed in a carriage accident when I was Robert's age. I know what it feels like to have a father who is more interested in machines and objects than in his son. He thought he could make a carriage that could travel on its own. Sheer madness.'

'Is this why you are against engines?'

'I am not against progress, Diana, simply against the all-consuming need to achieve it no matter the cost.'

'What happened after your father's death?'

'My mother remarried quickly, too quickly. My stepfather sent my brother and me off to Eton where I was beaten and learnt to make cheese on toast. My mother died in childbirth and my stepfather simply sent a terse note to tell us that we were now orphans. I know what it is like to be miserable at school and what needs to be done to survive. You wanted to know why I understand Robert—because I was once that boy! There, I have said it! Are you happy?'

'Brett, I am sorry.' Diana's throat closed. She could see the boy that Brett must have been. 'I had no idea.'

'I have never asked for anyone's pity. For a long time, all I had was my name, Diana. I had to make my own way in the world.'

'But I am sorry. And I am sorry that my

brother said such awful things about you. It was unforgivable.'

'You are upset. Your brother has been injured, but he will recover.' Brett resisted the temptation to take her into his arms. He drew a deep breath. 'Robert will grow up to be a fine young man.'

'Why were you at the colliery? Was it to speak with Simon about Robert?'

'I wanted to put my differences with your brother to one side. Why do you think I went there? I went there to speak to him about you and me, to beg him for his help. I wanted to settle matters between us.'

Diana looked up at him; her eyes had turned a glacial blue and flinched as if he had beaten her. 'You mean the land.'

'That's right, the land. I wanted the problem sorted out…before…'

'And that is why you started romancing me, isn't it? Your feud with my brother?'

Brett was silent for a long moment. He found it impossible to lie to her. And yet in this mood, he feared that she would refuse to understand. 'Do you want me to answer that?'

'Yes. I need the truth. I deserve the truth. Now.'

'Very well, then—the truth. I had planned on using our appearance together at the ball to force your brother to sell me the land. But it all changed once I actually encountered you. You must believe that, Diana. I sought you out because I liked you. The ball was a triumph for you. We came together because I desired you and you desired me. Think about that.'

'I don't want to think about that.' She put her hand to her head. 'I wish I had never met you.'

'And what would you have done if your brother had died in that accident?'

'Survive!' Diana's head came up, eyes blazing.

'Let me help you. Confide in me. I know you must be worried about your brother.' He reached out and caught her chin, forcing her blue-green gaze to meet his own grey one. She had to understand what he was saying. His motives might have been wrong at the beginning, but now he was acting from the best possible motives. 'I want to help. Diana, we are friends. Lovers!'

'You have done enough.' Diana wrenched her head away. She had believed in him and it had all been a lie. 'I think it is best if we part.'

Brett regarded Diana, and was tempted to draw her into his arms again, but retained control. Her head was high and her mouth pinched. It would only make matters worse. She had to understand how ashamed he was. How bitterly he regretted his earlier intentions, but how glad he was to know her now.

'There is much that is unsettled between us, Diana.' He held out his arms and willed her to walked into them and lay her head against his shoulder. She retreated to the window. 'Come away with me. Let us speak privately. We are good together.'

'There is no *us*. Today has shown me what my responsibilities are—my brother and his son.'

'Don't you have a responsibility towards yourself?' Brett continued on remorselessly. 'You were happy with me. I enjoyed spending time with you. You must believe that.'

'I have no idea what I believe any more.'

'We were good together, Diana, and we can be good again.'

'You have no right to say that to me.'

'I have every right! I claim the right…after what we shared.'

She held out her hand. 'Goodbye, Brett, I believe this is where it ends. There are times when one can't follow one's desires. I spent five years re-building my life. I do not intend to throw it away on some mistaken moment of passion.'

'It does not end, until I say it does.' Brett clenched his hands at his sides. He wanted to shake her, to make her see that she was trying to erect barriers between them. He had no intention of hurting her. He had never lifted a finger against a woman and he did not intend to start now.

'No, it ends now. I am no wanton woman. I am a lady. And I will not be used in this manner. Did you ever think about what you were doing to me?'

'I only thought about what you were doing to me, Diana. I…grew to like you.'

'You used me and our friendship. I will not be treated in this fashion!'

'And that is your final decision. Is there any way I can make it right?' Brett tried to force his lips to turn up and his voice to purr, but all he heard was the anguish and the despair.

'There is.' She gestured towards the door, unmoving, and unyielding. 'Jenkins will see you out. Go, Lord Coltonby, your presence is not required here. Ever.'

'As you wish.' Brett strode out of the room and did not dare look back.

'If you set the tray down much harder, you will wake the dead.' Simon's voice caused Diana to jump as she tiptoed in the next morning to leave a pot of tea.

'You were supposed to be asleep.'

'I have been awake for hours.' He flashed her a

smile. 'Your pacing about your bedroom did not help. You will wear a groove in the carpet.'

'Lord Coltonby made me angry. He…' Diana stopped. Her feelings were too new and vulnerable. She could not explain. All she knew was that he had started his seduction with the express intent of humiliating her. 'It does not matter now.'

'Lord Coltonby saved my life. I have been lying here thinking that. The boiler was already going when he pulled me from the engine. I misjudged the man. He is no fop whose only concern is his clothes and his horses. He risked his life to save me, a man who bore him ill will.' His green gaze pierced hers. 'He is an honourable man. If he says a thing, then he means it. I intend to sell him the land, Diana. I trust his motives.'

'But you said…' Diana stared at her brother in astonishment. He seemed more relaxed than he had in a long time, as he used to be before he had married Jayne.

'I was not thinking straight. Laudanum will do that to a man.' He held up his hand and gave a half-grimace, half-smile. 'Not an excuse, Diana, simply an explanation. I will live yesterday for the rest of my life, but all my men survived. It will be a long time before I touch another engine.'

'All those things you said.' Diana put her hand to her mouth. 'They were a lie?'

'Words of a man driven beyond his endurance. I have no proof that Coltonby and Bolt were in league together. None at all. I have no idea why Coltonby came to the colliery yesterday, but I am grateful that he did.'

'He went to speak to you about the land. You were right, Simon, and I was wrong. He was seeking to use me. He was going to humiliate me at the ball.'

'But he didn't.'

'No,' Diana replied slowly. 'But all the same, it is why he started paying me attention. I have been a fool, brother.'

'Diana.' Her brother held out his hand. She blindly groped for it. 'What has gone on between you two?'

'It does not matter, brother. It is over now. Finished.' Diana slipped her hand from his. She closed her eyes. Suddenly she felt old and tired. With the saying of the words, something within her had withered and died.

'If he ever harms a hair on your head, he is dead. I do not care that I owe my life to him. I would gladly sacrifice it for your honour.'

'It won't come to that.' A shiver went down her spine. 'I promise you that. Our friendship has finished.'

Chapter Fifteen

'Lord Coltonby promised to take me back in his carriage.' Robert's voice held a distinct whine as Diana attempted to persuade him into the carriage a week later. Doctor Allen had agreed that Robert could return and Simon had decreed that it was vital the boy continue his education. The constant banging of doors and heavy footsteps had made Simon's head pound.

'Your father has decided that you are returning to school today. I don't think we can bother Lord Coltonby again.' Diana kept her voice steady. She refused to think about the fight she and Brett had had.

She wished a thousand times that she could unsay those words, but they were there. She hadn't wanted him to go. She had wanted him to take her in his arms and whisper that he cared about her. And that it did not matter how it had begun, only that he cared for her now. She wanted to have a second chance, but Brett had never sent word and she had her pride.

Sleep had been far from her mind this last week. Simon had even commented on her listlessness. His burns were healing, but his temper was becoming shorter by the day. Nothing anyone did was right.

She had jumped at the chance to return Robert to school and gain some measure of freedom. With Robert gone, perhaps Simon would not complain as much about the disturbances and her life could begin to return to normal. The morning sun shone crisp and clear, a change from the incessant drizzle of the last five days. Diana took it as a sign to get on with the business of living.

Today was all about picking up the pieces of her life. It was better this way—ending before they had really begun. Brett would thank her in time. She knew that she now had a little compartment in her head marked *Brett Farnham* and *what might have been.* Six days ago, she had discovered that there would be no consequences to their joyous afternoon picnic. She knew she should be going down on her knees and thanking God that nothing worse had come of it, but she discovered that all she wanted to do was to forget and forgetting seemed beyond her.

'Please, get into the carriage and stop chattering about Lord Coltonby and his horses.'

'But why? He is an agreeable man. He liked me. I could tell.' Robert's bottom lip stuck out and he suddenly bore an uncanny resemblance to Simon when he had refused to take his medicine earlier that morning.

'You were able to ride on his horse. It will have to suffice.' She knew her voice was far too sharp, but she silently begged him to drop the subject.

'No one will believe me,' Robert muttered. 'And it is all your fault. You could have sent him a note. He said to send him word and he'd come.'

A note? She had the remnants of her pride. He had to apologise first. She looked up at the ceiling of the carriage and composed herself. 'Is that important? You know the truth.'

'Yes.' Robert climbed into the carriage and sat opposite her with a mutinous face and crossed arms. 'He promised, and you have neglected to tell him that we are leaving today. He would have let me sit next to him. He told me so. You made him break his promise.'

'Robert, you must refrain for asking for things.' Diana patted the seat next to her. 'Come, sit beside me and we will be on our way. I am sure the other boys will be anxious to speak to you about your adventures. And even if they are not, school is about more than adventures.'

Just then a yellow carriage pulled into the stable yard, blocking their exit. Brett jumped down from the coachman's position. Diana's heart leapt. Here. After all, as he had said. She wanted to rush out and apologise. She wanted him to scoop her into his arms and whisper words of remorse, of love. She made a face. She might as well ask for the moon. She remained in the carriage, her fingers gripping her reticule.

'I see I have arrived in time.' Brett opened the door to their carriage and peered in. His smile grew as he saw the occupants. 'It is well that word was sent.'

'No word was sent.'

He merely raised an eyebrow. 'This carriage looks to be a bit cramped. Mine will be better suited for our purposes.'

Robert immediately rushed from his seat and pushed past Brett. 'Your carriage, truly?'

'After you, my lady,' he said with an exaggerated bow. 'Your nephew has agreed with me.'

'We are not going with you.' She crossed her arms, but was absurdly pleased she had worn her deep crimson pelisse, the one with two shoulder capes and fashionable trim. 'Robert, we need to leave. I must return you to school today. I have promised your father.'

Robert paid no attention to her, but continued to regard Brett's carriage with awe. He started towards where the groom held the horses.

'It appears your nephew has other ideas.'

'My nephew should learn what is good for him.'

A faint smile played on Brett's lips. 'He reminds me of his aunt—strong willed.'

'You mean pig-headed.'

'You were the one to say the word.' His face sobered. 'I have missed you Diana, more than I dreamt possible.'

'The other day…' Diana paused and wondered how she could explain without betraying her feelings.

'You were upset over your brother. We will speak no more of it.' His eyes hardened. 'I am not proud of what I did, but if I hadn't, we would not have become friends. Thank you for having Robert send the note.'

'I…I never did.'

'Friends?' he asked. 'Can we start again? Properly this time? You and I?'

'Neighbours,' she answered and held out her hand.

His eyes lowered to her lips. 'I believe I will wait for your friendship.'

'You may have to wait a long time.'

'Or very little.' He leant forward and brushed her cheek. 'I have missed you, Diana.'

'Is this your carriage? I mean the one you use for the Four in Hand?' Robert asked in awe, breaking into the conversation. Diana slumped back against the seat back; her lips ached as if he had touched them. 'They are always yellow, or so Henry says. Henry Sowerby is going to be a whip when he grows up.'

'Henry Sowerby is the one who was responsible for the stink bomb, apparently,' Diana replied at Brett's questioning look. 'I can't tell if Henry is a person to be admired or despised.'

'Probably both in equal measure.' Brett gave a warm laugh and Diana felt her insides turn over.

'You don't have to take Robert. It is a long journey. Simon has agreed that I should use his carriage. It has all been arranged, even down to the coaching inn I should use if I become over-tired on the return journey.' Diana kept her voice firm. She had no idea why Brett was here or who had told him to come. Possibly Rose. But she refused to play his game.

'I gave my promise, Diana. I intend to keep it. It is his choice.' Brett's face became inscrutable. 'You may accompany us if you feel it necessary. I would welcome it.'

Diana stared at Brett. Why was he doing this? What was he asking?

'Aunt Diana?' Robert tugged at her skirt.

'Robert,' Diana said with firmness, 'Lord Coltonby has kindly offered to take us to Newcastle, but your father has lent us the carriage. I know what your father would want us to do.'

'I would like to go in Lord Coltonby's carriage, if you please, Aunt. Papa will be pleased as then he can use the carriage to go out to the colliery. He won't care how I go. He wants me gone.'

'Robert Clare! How dare you say such a thing about your dear papa.'

'But I heard him saying the very thing this morning, before breakfast.'

'His head pains him. He has lost sight in one eye.'

'But it is what he wants.'

'Good lad,' Brett murmured. 'And you will be joining us as well, won't you, Diana?'

Diana drew a deep breath. What exactly was Brett playing at? Go with him? Share a carriage with him there and back? Slowly she shook her head. 'I have promised my brother that I will see Robert safely returned to school. It will have to be in this carriage.'

'There is room in my carriage for you.'

'Please, Aunt.' Robert hung on her arm. 'You

did promise I could ride behind them. And it is a coach and four.'

'When, if not now?' Brett's eyes twinkled. 'You know you want to. I will drive and you may ride in the carriage.'

'But—' Diana tried to think of all the reasons why this was a bad idea, except she had missed his company. Going in the carriage while he drove would be no different from riding in the carriage when John drove.

'I will return you by nightfall, I promise. The horses are high steppers. They will easily make it to Newcastle and back. There will be no need for a coaching inn.'

'Oh, Aunt, please, please. You must come with me. It is the only way.'

'Please.' Brett's voice was no more than a breath.

Diana wondered for an instant if she had heard correctly. Was he begging her?

'It is impossible to fight you both. Robert, please inform your father that Lord Coltonby is here and we shall see what he says. I know he will agree with me.'

Robert ran off before she could stop him and they were left alone in the stable yard. Diana pretended interest in the clasp of her reticule as Brett silently watched her.

'What are you looking at?' she asked, feeling the colour on her cheeks begin to rise.

'I was merely wondering if the sensible Miss Clare was coming or if we were going to be treated to Diana.'

'I am always the same person. Miss Clare will suffice.'

'I much prefer Diana.' He lengthened the last word, rolled it in his mouth, giving it sensuous possibilities that she had never dreamt of.

Diana turned her head. Despite what he had done to her, it would be very easy to fall in love with this man. A fatal mistake. The last thing he wanted or desired was love. 'You spout pretty fables.'

'You have not taken to wearing a cap again. I wonder why that is.'

'Robert will be back soon.' Diana kept her voice steady. She refused to let him provoke her.

'He is a pleasant child—a credit to the woman who raised him.'

'I look on him as my own.'

'But he is your brother's.'

'Yes, he is. Sometimes, I wonder if my brother sees it. His wife, Jayne, was wild. It was not a happy marriage.'

'Does your brother's ill-considered marriage mean you are condemned to repeat the same mistakes?'

'I make my own mistakes.' Diana regarded the tassles on her reticule. 'There are some to whom marriage is an aspiration, but not to me. I have seen how easily a woman can be trapped.'

'Surely that depends on the spouse, rather than on the institution itself.'

'I could never marry solely for duty.'

'It is a good way to be.' His lips became a thin white line. 'Sometimes one does not have a choice.'

'One always has choices. It is the consequences that give trouble.'

'This is true. Are you suffering from any consequences?'

'None that I know of.'

'It is good to hear.'

An ice-cold fist closed around Diana's heart. Robert would be back in a few moments with Simon and everything would be over. Only she was not sure she wanted it to be.

'If we are indeed going in your carriage, things will have to be moved.' Diana turned her attention to making sure the basket of food and other essentials for Robert were transferred over into Brett's carriage. 'The sooner everything is properly stowed, the sooner we can leave.'

'I am yours to command.'

'Coltonby.' Simon's voice rang out across the

yard. 'My son says that you intend on returning him to school.'

'I made a promise.' Brett glared at Simon. Diana offered up a small prayer that they would not come to blows.

'So I understand.' Simon looked away and his shoulders hunched. 'You sent me a banker's draft.'

'It is for the land as we agreed.'

Diana looked between her brother and Brett. They had been in communication? Her brother had given Brett the land? A niggling suspicion rose within her. The mysterious note sender was standing in front of her, holding the banker's draft aloft like it was some trophy.

'It is twice what I originally asked for.' Simon held up the piece of paper, and tore it into shreds. 'You saved my life, Coltonby and my life is worth far more than a parcel of land.'

'Any man would have done what I did.'

'You hold yourself in too little esteem, Coltonby.'

Diana cleared her throat. 'I will go with Robert and make sure he is settled.'

'You will need a chaperon, Diana,' her brother said, his face becoming stern.

'I can take Rose.'

'Rose is needed here. She makes excellent

tisanes. If you are to be gone, who will look after me if my head should pain again?'

'I will return Miss Clare before nightfall. My horses can easily make the journey there and back.'

The men regarded each other and then Simon nodded. 'You bring her back—safely.'

'That is my intention,' Brett replied. 'I gave you my word at the ball, as a fellow Cantabrigian. I see no reason to break it.'

'I will hold you to it then. Diana, you see that Robert is properly settled at school.' Simon turned on his heel and went back inside the house.

Diana stared after him in astonishment while Brett looked at her with a smug expression on his face.

'Are you ready to go, Miss Diana?'

'It would appear everything has already been decided.' Diana started to mount the steps up to the carriage.

'Details can be important.' Brett saluted her with his whip.

'Can I ride on the top with Lord Coltonby?' Robert asked.

'You are too young,' Diana said firmly.

Robert raised both of his hands, but Brett shook his head. 'It would be a brave man who would go against your aunt. You will have plenty of time when you grow up.'

'But you might not be here.'

'I am planning on putting roots down in Northumberland.' He gave a significant look at Diana. 'It seems like a good place to raise children.'

'The fresh air is very good for them.'

'So I understand.'

'I wish you and your bride-to-be every happiness.' She kept her back straight and refused to think about what Brett's children might be like. She hated the thought of having to meet them and whoever his wife might be. But it would be far worse if she had accepted his half-hearted proposal. Then she would have had to suffer his growing indifference and to become little more than a wearisome burden inflicted upon him by his devotion to some misguided duty.

'Aren't you putting the cart before the horse? I have to marry first.'

'It is usually best.' She forced a laugh from her throat. 'No doubt next season's crop of débutantes will yield an appropriate countess.'

His eyes narrowed. 'We had best depart if you want to return before nightfall.'

'I definitely intend on returning before nightfall. You gave your word.'

'Unforeseen circumstances…'

'Unforeseen circumstances had best not happen.

I trust you to do everything in your power to prevent them.'

'Then you will allow Robert to ride up with me.'

'Do I have much choice?'

'No.' Brett lifted an eyebrow, but Diana kept her face composed. She refused to give in. She had put passion behind her. What had happened out by the grotto would not happen again. Today would be a test and she would succeed. 'You are always a pleasure to cross swords with, Diana. No one could accuse you of being boring.'

'I do my best.' Diana climbed into the carriage and sat down on the well-sprung seats as she ignored the sound of Brett's hearty laugh.

The trip to Newcastle sped by. Every so often she would hear Robert's excited voice and Brett's deeper, more gravelled one answering him. Never condescending or hurried, but firm and authoritative. She had to admit that Brett did know how to control the ribbons. He also appeared to have discovered the secret of controlling Robert.

When they arrived at the red brick school, she expected tears or at the very least protestations, but no sooner had the carriage stopped, than Robert climbed down and opened the door for her.

'I have promised to do my best, Aunt Diana,' he said. 'I won't let you down.'

'And remember, my promise,' Brett said, coming to stand by him. 'Be attentive to your lessons, and no more bad reports, then I will instruct you on the finer points of carriage driving.'

Diana looked from Brett to Robert. All through the journey, she had dreaded something like this. What could she say to him? She knew that it was a pie-crust promise. Brett would develop a new enthusiasm and Robert would face yet another disappointment. She kept her chin raised. There would be time enough to explain to Robert later.

'I do mean it, Diana,' Brett said softly. 'How else can I prove to you that I keep my word?'

The timely appearance of Dr Allen and the school's matron prevented Diana from answering.

'Will your horses be all right for the journey back?' Diana asked Brett after Robert had been settled back in school. 'How long do they need to rest?'

'They should be fine. I did not push them too hard to get here. Your nephew was enjoying the feeling of being a whip. You should have seen him holding the ribbons. The boy is a natural. He asked ever so many good questions. He made me think.'

'I saw his face. You have another worshipper, Brett.' Diana pressed her hands together. Simon might not be pleased when he discovered it, but it had certainly made the journey much less fraught. 'I wanted to thank you for what you did. You did not have to.'

'You mean arriving here with a great flourish and the horses going at full gallop?' Brett laughed. 'I can still remember what schoolboys love. I only wish I had thought to bring a mail coach's trumpet.'

'Why did you do it?'

'Because everyone needs someone to make a fuss of them.'

'He has me.'

His gaze travelled slowly down her form. 'You are not a man.'

Diana was grateful for her bonnet. 'I would have had a bad time of it without you and your antics. I thank you for that.'

'I am pleased you see some small use for me.'

'Yes, a small use,' she agreed with a laugh. 'I suppose we ought to go. It wouldn't do for Robert to think we were spying on him.' She covered her hand with her mouth. 'I wanted to apologise for what I said the other day. I had no right to question you like that.'

'Did I say anything?'

'You must understand—I refuse to be used in that fashion.' Her stomach trembled but she had said it.

'Intentions are different from actions, Diana. And my intentions changed, once I began to know you. You must believe that I have every intention of protecting you and your reputation.'

'I will believe that when it happens.'

'Allow me to prove it to you. Will you then admit it? Or are you too proud?'

'Why must we always argue?' Diana whispered. 'I much prefer it when we get along.'

Brett didn't answer. He simply stared down at her with his steady grey eyes, eyes that had nearly turned to silver.

'You are the most provoking of men.'

'I think I enjoy being provoking.'

'Well, I am not entirely sure that I enjoy it.' Diana opened the carriage door. She would end this conversation now, before that little piece of her insisted on continuing their relationship, before she begged for his kiss, before she began believing his promises.

'Which way shall we go back?' Brett asked.

Her hand trembled on the door frame. 'Do I have a choice?'

'We can go back a longer, more scenic route if you wish.' Brett's hand closed over hers. 'I promise to refrain from provoking you, well…not unless you *want* to be provoked.'

A tingle washed up her arm. The scenic route. A room in an anonymous inn. Brett and her. Together. It would be so easy. For a long time, she found it difficult to breathe. 'You promised to return to Ladywell by nightfall.'

'It could still happen.'

Diana gently withdrew her hand, and put the temptation far from her. She refused to do that. She had not sunk so far down into wanton wickedness that she used the return of her nephew to school as an excuse for a liaison with her lover.

The whole idea when she considered it held an unsavoury ring.

She had not sunk that low. She retained her principles. The madness that had enveloped her over the past few days would end. She held on to the thought and let it crowd out all her desires.

'I would like to return home as quickly as possible.' Her words tripped over each other in her rush to get them out. 'You may spare the horses, but Simon will want to hear about how Robert got on at school. He does care about his son.'

Aware that she was beginning to babble, Diana clamped her lips shut. She willed him to say something. To show that he understood. These feelings inside her were at war with each other. She desired him, but she needed more than desire. She needed more than a half-hearted proposal. She had seen the relief on his face when she had refused him.

Brett regarded her with clear grey gaze. He continued to stand close, too close. She watched the way the sunlight caught his buttons and turned them darker. 'A closed stuffy carriage or up beside the driver in the fresh air—where do you want to ride?'

Diana swallowed hard, turned her attention from the way his buttons looked against the crisp linen of his shirt. She knew if she rode within the carriage, she would not have a chance to speak with Brett. And she had missed him and his teasing tones more than she had thought possible. It would be the end of everything. Irrevocably.

She would end it after today. He would depart for somewhere unknown and, if they ever met again, they would be able to make polite meaningless conversation.

But would it do any lasting harm if she allowed herself to dream for one more afternoon? Within a few hours, they would be back in Ladywell and her life would continue on its preordained path.

'Up in the open air,' she whispered, her voice barely audible to her ears. She blinked, scarcely able to believe she had said the words aloud.

'Diana?' He leant forward and his breath kissed her lips. 'You were impossible to hear.'

'I will ride up beside you,' she said quickly before she changed her mind. A queer fizzing excitement went through her veins. 'I want to see how you handle the ribbons of a Four in Hand. I may be able to learn something in case I should ever encounter an obstacle course again.'

He gave a half-smile. 'Ever the sensible Miss Clare.'

'Is it sensible to ride up next to the driver?' She peeked up from under her eyelashes. 'It is the first time I have heard that.'

'Oh, very sensible. Quite the best option. You get a whole new view of life when you sit beside the driver.'

'I thought you promised not to provoke me.'

'I said that I would do my best. That is a different promise entirely.'

'Is it? Are you going to twist your words?'

'Can I help it if a certain woman persists in forgetting the exact nature of the words?' His face became a picture of injured innocence.

'And if that woman considered him to be a supreme twister of words?'

'Then she'd be wrong…as she has been wrong about so many things.'

'About so many things?' she whispered and tried to ignore the racing of her heart.

'We need to go if you wish to return to Ladywell before nightfall.'

He helped her up to the perch and then clambered up beside her. Diana had to squeeze over to one side. Brett's leg pressed against hers and all her resolutions appeared to fade away like the mist in front of the sun. He leant forward and his knuckles grazed her breast as he reached for the reins. She drew in her breath sharply.

He said nothing, but gave her an eloquent look before concentrating on arranging the ribbons. Diana bit her lip and decided a dignified silence was her best option.

The coach began to roll away from the school and back into the Newcastle traffic.

The view from up top was entirely different from the view through the carriage window. Tops of carriages, second-floor windows where clerks worked busily at their desks, bonnets covered in flowers and silk intermingled with top hats and flat caps.

She half-turned in her perch. Robert's school was rapidly swallowed up in the traffic of the city. Carts and carriages crowded the streets, suddenly moving forwards and closing spaces where a breath before the road had been clear. Twice Diana was certain they would hit a delivery van or a cart. She sucked in her breath and shrank as the carriage passed through an impossibly narrow gap. Brett put an arm about her shoulders, but she rapidly sat up straight and folded her hands in her lap.

'Impressive driving.' She tried for a calm and measured tone, ignoring his slightly triumphant look. 'There are very few who could make it through that.'

'It is easy once you know the trick. As I explained to Robert, carriage driving is like life. You need to keep your attention focused. And your concentration far enough ahead. It is all about anticipating obstacles. And there are always potholes to trip up the unwary or inattentive.'

'I worry that I might get in your way. Perhaps you ought to stop and I will go below.'

'As long as you don't make a sudden lunge for the ribbons, we will be fine.'

He gave a little flick and the horses increased their speed as they left the smoke-shrouded city behind. It seemed as if they were in their own world, up here on the coachman's perch. Diana shivered slightly as the chill of the wind hit her, and wished she had thought to bring her thick shawl as well as her crimson pelisse. That had to be the cause. It was never a shiver of anticipation, a reaction to her leg nestled against his, her shoulder touching his.

'Are you cold?'

'I will be fine. I thought I would be riding in the carriage and did not bring a shawl.'

'You can go down there, if you want. I will stop the horses.'

'No, I like the view from up here.'

He put his arm around her and drew her into the circle of his arms. 'Is this better?'

She relaxed against his body and rested her cheek on his chest, listening to his heart thump. Warm, comforting and altogether far too enticing. She closed her eyes and sought to hang on to every detail. When this was all over, she would keep the image fresh.

'What are you doing?' he asked when she opened her eyes. 'You have the most intent expression on your face.'

'Making a memory.' She struggled to sit upright. 'I will be fine now. The air is quite pleasant in the sunshine.'

'I am honoured that you want to remember this moment.'

Their gaze caught and held for a long moment. Diana felt the inexorable pull towards him, towards the slippery slope called—falling in love. She also knew the ending and the heartache that came with it. She started to say something, but finally opted for a light tone. 'How many times do I get to see an expert in action?'

'How many times indeed?' He flicked the reins and the horses started moving faster, their hooves beating against the stones.

Diana watched as his hands expertly controlled everything. She knew in the hands of a less-experienced driver, the horses would be running away, out of control, but with Brett, they obeyed the least flicker of the ribbons.

As they approached a village, he pulled the thundering horses back. Immediately they slowed.

A cart loomed ahead, blocking half of the road. A labourer was busy loading barrels. Nothing untowards. Diana sucked in her breath as she saw a bright blue pinafore dart out into the road.

'Brett!' Her hand reached out instinctively to steady herself, but tangled with the ribbons.

Brett cursed long and loud. He pulled back hard. Diana felt her body slam into the railing as the carriage turned sharply, colliding with the cart. Everything slowed down and seemed to take an age.

Images flashed—the little girl in blue, the ball, the lead horse rearing, Brett's arms straining against the ribbons as he struggled to avoid the girl. A piercing scream resounded in the air, followed by the slow crunch of wood. With the noise, the speed started to move double quick and Diana felt the carriage lurch to one side and then the other. Everything hurtled forwards and then stopped. The world became dark.

Diana risked a breath and found her lungs could fill without an ache. She raised a shaking hand and pushed her bonnet back from her forehead.

'Are you injured?' Brett asked, his dark grey eyes peering into hers.

'I am fine, a little shaken.' Diana put her hand to her face. 'I never meant to…'

'It was an accident. You must not think about it.'

'How is the little girl? And the horses?'

'I will see to the horses now, but the child appears unharmed. Her mother pulled her to safety.' Brett lightly jumped down from his perch.

'I still don't know how you missed her.'

'I drive to the inch. There is a practical reason for it.'

A farmer hung on to the bridle of the lead horse. Diana could see a pregnant woman had scooped the child up and was cradling her in her arms. Everything would be fine. It was only objects that were damaged. Not people. The accident could have been much worse.

Diana sank back against the seat, trembling. She heard the farmer's raised voice, the wail of the child and Brett's measured tones. Everything flowed over her as a late butterfly fluttered a few inches from her nose. Silently, she pleaded that everything would be fine and they would quickly continue on their way.

'Everything is solved, Diana, but you need to get down.' Brett reached up a hand to help her down. He wanted to gather her into his arms. The accident could have been so much worse. All he could see was how she had very nearly fallen, but had clung on. The images played over and over in his mind and he knew that he faced many nights waking up in a cold sweat, haunted by what might have happened. Today was not supposed to have been about losing her, but regaining her trust, demonstrating in the only way he knew how that he cared and wanted to start again. He wished to think that friendship was enough.

'Yes, I think I will ride inside the carriage.'

'It won't be possible. Not yet,' Brett said gravely. He gave a wave to the farm labourer. The farmer's cart bore some signs of damage, but it was the wheels of the carriage that needed to be repaired.

'Is the carriage all right? You managed to stop before any lasting damage was done.' Diana's smile faded. 'Will we be able to continue on our journey? We will return to Ladywell today.'

'There will be a delay. The wheels need to be seen to. I will not drive an unsafe carriage, Diana, not even for you.'

'How long of a delay?' Her eyes showed alarm. 'I wanted to get back to Ladywell tonight.'

'There is an inn down the road—the Angel. Respectable, but not fashionable. I will get you a private room.' Brett willed her to understand. He had no desire to compromise her. He wished now that he had thought to bring her maid, someone to make the stay respectable. But he had been certain that time alone would be the correct way to woo her.

'Your version of respectable may differ from mine.'

'Or the farmer's.' Brett reached over and read-justed her bonnet so it was sitting more firmly on her head. 'The mail coach stops there. It is the best the village has to offer. The only place. You will have to brave it, as will I. The village is quiet and so we should be able to get rooms.'

'Can I take the mail coach?' The words tumbled out, tripping over each other in her rush to get them out. 'Rose and Simon will be expecting me home today. They will wonder what has happened.'

'It has departed.'

'Departed?' Her hands went to her bonnet, straightening it and re-straightening it. 'How could it have already departed? It was my best hope of returning to Ladywell. You promised.'

'Are you saying that I somehow planned the accident?'

'No, no. There was nothing you could have done about it.'

He pressed his lips together, feeling a great pit open in his stomach. He wanted her, but he needed her to want him in her life as well as in her bed. This time when he proposed, she would be left in no doubt that his proposal went beyond lip service to duty.

'Your plans will be delayed.' He held up his hands, cutting off her protest. 'Your brother is aware how long it takes to get back from Newcastle and the hazards on the road. How many times has your brother arrived home later than first anticipated?'

'I suppose you are correct.' Diana swallowed hard. The image of Brett and her together, limbs intertwined danced in front of her eyes. She screwed them up and banished it. He had said rooms—plural. She had to concentrate on being sensible. What had been between them had flared briefly and then vanished. All that remained were the embers of a friendship.

'I know I am correct. It is beyond my control.'

'It seems so pat—the rake and the broken carriage. My brother may fear for my reputation.'

'You were the one who grabbed my arm. Perhaps I should fear for mine.' He gave a half-smile. 'I made a promise to your brother. I will protect you.'

'What exactly has happened to the carriage?' Diana wrapped her arms about her waist. 'Will it take long to fix? A delay of an hour or two will not make too much of a difference. We can still arrive back when it is not too late.'

'One of the wheels has come loose and the horses have suffered a bad fright. It would be folly to continue on today.'

But was it folly to remain here? Somehow their fate had been decided against her plea. She seemed to be drawn inexorably into his arms. And she knew that this time, her heart would go with her.

'I see.' Diana tightened her hold on her reticule. 'It is important to make sure the carriage is adequately fixed. I would hate to be delayed longer.'

'It would be far worse if we set out with it in ill repair.' Brett's fingers tightened on her elbow, leading her away from the carriage and towards the Angel and its creaking sign. 'There are some risks I refuse to take.'

Chapter Sixteen

'There you go, hinny, a nice cup of tea to restore you.'

Diana gave the landlady a trembling smile. She cautiously took a sip and allowed the hot strong sugary brew to wash through her system. Although the tea was far sweeter than she would normally take it, it had a restorative effect. 'It is very fine.'

'A good cup of tea does a body good, despite what the doctors say.' The landlady smoothed her skirts. 'There is nothing like a singing kettle to put me in a good mood.'

Diana gazed about the room. It was simple but comfortable. Far more than she had hoped for. A small fire glowed in the grate and there was even a mirror over the dressing table. She set the cup down on the small table next to the armchair.

'Yes, I like a cup of tea.'

'You looked like the sort.' The landlady bustled around the room. 'Your man has ordered a private meal for you. He thought you might find it easier. We tend to get a few drovers come through on their way home from the Hexham cattle market. They are harmless, mostly.'

'Thank you.' Diana held back the words explaining that Brett was far from being her man. Neither did she like to think about the few cattle drovers who were not harmless.

'It is good that you have someone like that looking after you.'

Diana took a careful sip of her tea. 'Yes, he has his uses. Were there enough rooms for him?'

The woman gave her a sharp look and Diana cursed her tongue. 'He will be in the stables. It is the proper place for coachmen.' She gave a loud sniff as if she had heard about Diana riding up beside him, rather than within the carriage.

Diana fought the temptation to laugh. It was probably better that Brett had done that. If it became known that Lord Coltonby and she had become stranded, she doubted that anyone would believe the innocence of it. But the landlady's outrage at the merest suggestion that a coachman should have a private room threatened to send her into fits of barely suppressed laughter. No doubt, it would be a story that would be chewed over and over again by Brett's friends. How he had outwitted a landlady and made her believe he was a coachman.

'Yes, it is the proper place for a coachman. Hopefully the carriage will be speedily repaired. I wish to continue on with my journey tomorrow.'

'You should be able to. It didn't sound too bad and Joe the blacksmith is a right good one.' The landlady dropped her voice. 'At first I worried that you and he might be escaping to the Headless Cross at Gretna Green. There are quite a few couples who come this way, you know. And I don't want any midnight knocking on doors. I run a respectable establishment.'

'We were returning my nephew to his school in Newcastle, and I am on my way home.'

'You can't be too careful. Still, I could see why you might be tempted with that one. He has a very fine manner for a coachman.'

'I think I am far too old to be contemplating such behaviour.' Diana shifted uneasily. Brett could never come up here to her room. The gossip would spread through the village and from the village to other areas—all speaking about the lady in the yellow carriage who had entertained her coachman. He had promised to safeguard her reputation.

'You're only too old, when you're dead.'

Diana opened and closed her mouth several times. 'I think it would be best if I waited in the parlour. I want to know the extent of the carriage's damage and how long it will take to repair. Please inform him of my request when he returns.'

The woman appraised her. A crafty gleam came into her eye and Diana shifted uncomfortably, feeling the heat grow on her cheeks. She had not made a decision yet. All she knew was that she did not want to wait in her room like some short-heeled wench who only needed the gentlest of pushes to fall on her back. 'Aye, there is one. You can wait there if you like.'

'I would prefer it. It is more seemly, somehow.'

'More seemly. Aye, it is that.'

She followed the woman down to the back parlour. The landlady bustled about the room, straightening the pillows on the sofa. Another pot of tea and plate of shortbread were produced and placed in front of the fire. The landlady held out a claw-like hand as her eyes became crafty. 'I will need extra for the room. For your privacy. You won't want disturbing, will you?'

Diana kept her back straight as she gritted her teeth. Always money. She dug into the bottom of her reticule and held out a few coins. The woman frowned, but pocketed them. 'Once I have spoken to my coachman, I will return up to my room.'

Then she politely but firmly turned the conversation towards the inn and when the mail coach would leave in the morning. If the carriage had not been fixed, she knew she would have to leave anyway.

'And would you like me to send up the scullery maid to help you with your clothes when you are ready?'

'Thankfully, I am wearing a simple gown so I shall manage myself.' Diana kept her chin high.

The landlady gave a nod and tapped her nose. 'I will let your man know where you are when he comes in.'

'I appreciate it.' Diana sat down, and began sipping her tea as she watched the coals burn brightly in the parlour's fire.

The coals had become embers, but Brett had still not appeared or sent word. She picked up the poker and stirred the fire. It erupted into a glorious blaze of colour, but soon burnt down. An indication of her relationship with Brett? A brilliant blaze of intense heat and then nothing?

She glanced out of the window and saw the night had drawn in. To her right, the distant clangs of the bar sounded as more and more men gathered. And even though she knew it was silly to wish it, she felt disappointed that Brett had failed to come to see her. He had to have been finished with the blacksmith by now. The sky only held the few last remaining rays of sunlight. No one worked that late. She dug her nails into the palm of her hand. He was avoiding her. Once again she had misread everything. This journey had been about his promise to Robert, rather than him seeking to repair their damaged friendship.

She lifted the bell, ready to ring for the landlady and to have protection going up the stairs. When she next encountered Brett, she would be distant. Today had taught her the necessity of that. This long agonising wait, this pointless wait—and for what?

Her whole life seemed to stretch out in front of her, grey and colourless, as she grew ever older and eventually even Robert and Simon would stop needing her.

Today's accident had taught her how quickly things could change. How precious life was. It was strange that Simon never saw that. All he seemed obsessed with was creating this engine and making it move. His brush with death had only made him more stubborn, but hers had changed her.

She gave one last glimpse at the dying fire. She wasn't willing to sit there waiting any longer.

Heavy footsteps sounded in the hall. Her hand stilled, waited for the footstep to move onwards.

A discreet knock echoed in the room. Diana tilted her head. The footsteps weren't right. Should she answer the door? The knock came again, this time heavier and more impatient. She opened it a crack and a heavy-set man stood there, swaying and grinning. She went to slam the door, but he stuck his fingers out and caught it.

'You don't have protection.' His words were slurred and the stench of beer assaulted Diana's nose. 'A woman such as yourself should have protection.'

His words sent shivers down her spine. He should have said lady, not woman. What did he take her for?

'I would suggest you return to the bar or wherever you came from.' Diana stood blocking the doorway. She measured the distance from the door to the fire grate and the poker. Did she dare run for it? 'I am waiting for someone. He will not be best pleased to see you.'

'I think you want company.' The man wiped his hand across his mouth. 'Women like you always want company. Mrs Dawkins thought you might, seeing as you was still here.'

Women like her? Diana blinked. He had made

a serious mistake, but she had made a worse one. She had thought herself safe in this room.

'You will leave this instant.' Diana used her sternest voice and pointed in the direction of the bar.

'I like them feisty.'

He started towards her. Diana backed away. One step at a time. She would prevail and when she emerged, she would never ever have anything to do with Brett Farnham again. Respectable inn? Hah!

'I am asking politely—go now, please.'

'How are you going to make me, a little scrap like you?'

She reached behind her and her hand closed over the poker. She drew a breath and summoned her courage. She would have one chance, one blow. She lifted the poker slightly, adjusted her handgrip, steadied her legs. 'Go.'

'The lady has asked you to leave. Politely,' Brett's lazy voice drawled. 'I recommend you take up her suggestion.'

Diana felt the poker slip from her hands. Brett was here, lounging against the doorframe. His body appeared relaxed, but his eyes burnt with a steely determination.

'And if I don't?'

'I will not be responsible for the state of your short-term health.'

'You southerners are all alike. You think you can come up here and make a big noise. All wind and no bottle.'

'I wouldn't concentrate on thinking. It is not a drunkard's strong point.'

'Are you insulting me?' The heavy ox turned, balling his anvil-like fists.

'You were insulting the lady.' Brett straightened his cuffs, as a sardonic smile twisted his lips. 'I returned the coin with interest.'

The man pursed his lips and flexed his huge hands. 'Someone ought to teach you manners. You ought not to talk to your betters like that.'

'It is amazing how we think alike.' Brett's fist connected with the underside of the man's jaw, sending him reeling backwards. 'I did warn him.'

'Did I say a word?' Diana kept her eyes on the fight, but tried to grab the poker again.

The man staggered back, shook his great bull-like head and rushed forwards, fists flailing. Brett easily sidestepped him. The man stopped and then turned, meeting Brett's next punch in his stomach. He doubled over. 'Here, there was no cause to do that,' he spluttered.

'We appear to have a difference of opinion about that.' Brett blew on his knuckles.

'I was going. There is only way out of the room, unless I go by the window,' the man protested.

'Do not tempt me.'

'I was only trying to protect this here piece of fancy.'

'Go, please go.' Diana gestured towards the door. 'Do not make it worse on yourself.'

'But this is the room Mrs Dawkins always puts her girls in. Always the parlour when one of them's free.'

'Not tonight.'

The man seemed to sober. His eyes travelled between Diana and Brett. 'I appear to have made a mistake.'

'Do not compound it by remaining.'

The man started towards the door, mumbling.

'Apologise to the lady. And kindly inform Mrs Dawkins that this lady is not to be disturbed for the rest of the evening.'

'I am very sorry, but she was asking for it.' The man looked truculent. 'Can I go now?'

Brett grabbed the lapels of the man's coat, stared him in the eye.

'You will humbly crave her pardon. You will never do such a thing again.' Then he released the man's lapels.

'I humbly whatever he says.' The man practically ran out of the room. His footsteps could be heard clumping down the hall.

Brett shut the door with a decisive click, locking it behind him.

'Is it over?' Diana whispered and brought the poker around in front of her. Her fingers refused to let it go. 'I was frightened.'

'It is over,' Brett said. 'The man was drunk. He didn't know what he was saying.'

'But do you think that landlady rents out this room as…as…?'

'I didn't enquire.' He ran his hand through his hair. 'You were supposed to be up in your private room, away from this.'

'The landlady seemed disapproving, and I wanted to find out about the carriage.' She was aware that her cheeks were flaming. 'I could hardly ask her to send my coachman up. What would she think? It would not have been seemly.'

'So you came down here to this room.'

'How was I to know? I expected you back long before now.'

Brett came over. His hand closed around hers. Gently he removed the poker. 'You should return to your room.'

'Yes, I should.' Her feet refused to move. 'Will you escort me there?'

He raised an eyebrow. 'If you think it necessary—I doubt your gentleman caller will return in a hurry. Shall I ring for the landlady?'

'I don't think there is any need to bother Mrs. Dawkins.' She ran her tongue over her parched lips and hoped he'd understand. 'The inn appears full tonight.'

'As you wish.'

He held the door open and she went out of the little room. Her heart pounded so loudly that she thought he must hear it. She led the way up the narrow back passage and heard him follow her. She breathed more easily when she had reached her room, opened the door and gone in. A few remaining coals glowed faintly in the gloom.

He bent over the embers, stirred them up and placed more coal on top. The fire blazed into life, sending shadows playing on the walls. 'It will take the chill off the room.'

Diana stood watching him. She noticed how his muscles moved under his coat. 'Thank you.'

'Think nothing of it.' He stood in front of the fire. 'I came back from the blacksmith's to discover this—the entire inn full of drunken drovers. It was not what I had envisioned.'

'You weren't to know.'

'I should have considered.' His mouth became a thin white line. 'How did he get into the parlour?'

'He knocked. I thought it might be you. The landlady said that she would tell you where I was and that I wanted to speak with you.' Diana gave a half-shrug. 'He put his foot in the door, and… this is all my fault.'

'It is not your fault, Diana, you weren't to know.' He made a face. 'I blame myself.'

'Shall we now argue over who is at fault?'

'Has he harmed you?'

She shook her head and crossed her arms about her, tried to banish the image from her mind. The old Diana would have been curled up in a ball. Her days of being timid and scared of life had truly ended. She knew she would have hit the man with a poker, if he had landed one punch on Brett. 'You arrived in time.'

'Thank heaven for small mercies.' He gave a crooked smile. 'I had given up on divine intervention, but I am willing to concede, Diana Clare, that you have a guardian angel looking after you.'

'How is the carriage?'

'Mended. We can leave at first light, and you will be back home before noon.' He pressed his fingertips together and his brow became furrowed as if he was struggling for control. 'I can station myself outside your door if you wish. Regardless of what people might say, it will be safer that way.'

Outside the door. He was about to walk out of her life.

Diana stared up at the ceiling. It had to come from her. The decision she had made before no longer counted. She wanted to be with this man. She wanted to show her desire for him. She had no wish to bind him to her, merely to create memories that would sustain her when she was old and grey, to think that once her life had been a bubble of happiness. 'Please stay with me tonight.'

'I don't think it would be wise.'

'Why think?' she whispered. She ran her hands down her sides and licked her lips.

'You have had a traumatic day.'

'I know what I am doing. Stay here with me.' She took a step forwards, caressed his jaw with her hand and felt the graze of his stubble against her fingers. 'Please?'

His fingers traced the outline of her jaw, featherlight, delicate as if he was memorising it. 'Are you sure?'

Was he going to make it difficult for her? She was no good at seduction. She wanted to show him that she needed to have him in her life, for as long as it lasted. She nodded towards the bed, attempted a joke. 'It has linen sheets.'

'I had not even considered the bed, but you're right, it does.'

'You did promise and you always keep your promises.'

'That I do.' His eyes held a strange light.

'What happens next?' she whispered and stared at the floor, rather than at him. 'I am a beginner at wickedness.'

'Let me watch you undress.' He breathed in her ear.

'Undress?' Her hands went to her gown. She rapidly undid the buttons before she had time to think, before she had time to worry that she was doing it wrong. Tonight was about seduction, and wantonness. It was not about her normal world. It was as if she was trembling on the brink of a threshold. 'Like this?'

He stepped away from her. His eyes became inscrutable. 'Continue.'

'I don't follow.'

'Let me watch you.'

She started to take off her gown, stopped, feeling her cheeks grow hot under his dark gaze. 'It is impossible.'

'Try.' His voice flowed from the shadows.

She did it suddenly, lifting her arms and pulling

off the gown, painfully aware that he must have watched other women, women who could make undressing a seduction. And her efforts were clumsy. Her fingers tugged at the stays, and managed only to pull the bow tighter. She gave a little exclamation and tried again.

'You see, I am hopeless at this.'

'Far from hopeless.' His husky rasp wrapped itself around her innards. 'And what would you do next?'

'Plait my hair.'

'Sit down on that stool in front of the mirror, begin plaiting.'

'Are we playing a game?'

'Of sorts.' His eyes crinkled at the corners. 'Indulge me in this fantasy. For tonight.'

She sat down and obeyed, concentrating on her hair rather than on him or the mirror. A simple little action, one which steadied her nerves. If it was fantasy, then it bore no relation to her life. Indulge him? Indulge herself, and the dreams that had woken her over the past few nights and filled her with a nameless ache. 'Am I doing this right?'

'Yes.' The word was no more than a hiss of air.

She glanced in the mirror and saw him standing behind her. The heat from his body warmed her back. 'I want to touch you, Diana. Touch you and watch you watching me.'

She gave a hesitant nod.

His hands came around her, grasped her aching breasts and his lips nuzzled her neck. She watched in the mirror as his hands pressed against her and her nipples stood out, tightly furled and dark rose under the thin cloth. He rolled his fingers over them, increasing the ache. She met his eyes in the mirror, saw her own heavy with passion. Her back arched and she felt his hard body pressing against her, leaving her in no doubt of his arousal.

One of his hands reached inside her shift, found the apex of her thighs. It hovered there as his mouth moved to an earlobe, nibbling, sucking. One finger traced the length of her crease. A jolt of fire went through her.

'Do you like what I am doing to you?' His hot breath teased her skin.

She could only nod. His fingers went deeper, caressing her as his other arm became an iron band holding her in place. She gave her body up to the exquisite torture. The ache within her grew. She twisted against the arm as she felt herself teeter on the brink. Her whole life had come down to this delicious ache. Her hands went up and caught his head, held him there. A mewling cry erupted from her throat.

'Shall I stop?' His hand paused, his fingers skimming her curls, playing in them.

'Continue.' She wet her lips. 'Please continue. Does that make me utterly wicked?'

'Only if you want to be.'

'With you.'

He gave a very masculine laugh. His tongue traced the edge of her ear. 'We are well suited. Think what it will be like to have my mouth there. Warm. Wet.'

His fingers slid inside her, making her buckle. Her hands pushed against the strength of his arm as a deep shudder went through her.

'I need…' she whispered. His finger stroked more and the world tilted.

His hands shifted. He scooped her up and she was held against his chest. She clung to him, regaining a sense of balance.

'I don't even want to think about how close I came to losing you today,' he murmured against her hair.

'You didn't lose me.' Her hand cupped his cheeks and he turned his lips to brush it. 'And I didn't lose you. We have tonight.'

'I know. I am greedy, though.' He bent his head and his lips teased hers. 'I want it all.'

He carried her to the bed and laid her down gently, arranging her limbs. 'I do keep my word.'

She refused to think as his lips sank lower, as they followed the path he had promised. His tongue flicked into her belly button, lingering—circling and teasing. Her body arched up off the bed. He glanced up at her, nodded in approval and moved his lips lower still.

His hands cupped her legs, opening them wider. His hot breath touched her crease, then his tongue parted it, delved deeper. Her head thrashed about on the pillow and little mewling cries came from her throat.

'Please,' she whispered and wasn't sure if she wanted him to speed up or to take his time. All she knew was that if he didn't continue, she'd die.

He took his time, swirling and teasing her until she thought she must surely shatter. Her hands clenched the linen sheets. Then he stopped and swiftly undid his breeches, divested his shirt so that his gleaming body shone bronze in the firelight. He nestled himself between her thighs and powerfully drove inside her.

Diana began to rock, to follow the age-old rhythm. She knew her body was telling him things, and his was answering, driving her to higher peaks.

'Brett,' she whispered.

He paused and looked down at her. 'Yes?'

'This is everything,' she whispered. His only response was to hold her tighter as a great shuddering engulfed them both.

* * *

Brett raised his body up on one elbow and looked down at her sleeping form. Gently he smoothed a tendril of hair from her cheek.

It seemed incredible that within a few short weeks, this woman had come to mean so much to him. He wondered how much her declaration was passion and how much was for real. He wanted to feel that she cared for him.

When they returned to Ladywell, he would ask her properly. He would make her understand that it was not duty that drove him to ask. It was his own fault that he had allowed his passion for her to cloud the issue. He had never meant to take her like this here.

She murmured in her sleep and her body sought his again.

'Soon, soon,' he whispered and kissed her temple. He had not asked for tonight, but he would use it. If necessary, he would join forces with her brother; together they would make her see that tonight changed everything. Marriage to him was her only option.

Chapter Seventeen

The cold early morning sunlight shone into the little room. Diana woke to find the bed next to her empty. She looked about her, confused. Then she saw Brett standing in front of the remains of the fire, fully dressed, his black Hessians gleaming and his riding cape immaculate. He was watching her. Her face coloured and she resisted the urge to dive back under the covers.

'If I had not fallen before, I certainly have now,' she said, with a hesitant smile, hoping he would understand. It was one thing to make love in a field, and quite another to make love in an inn. She wasn't quite sure why it was different, but it felt different. She wished that she had woken in his arms. Somehow it would have been all right. But she hadn't and it changed everything. She raised her arms above her head, stretched and tried to show she was unconcerned. 'Truly a pretty wench, rather than a lady.'

No answering smile flitted across his face. If anything, his expression became stern. 'We need to get you home as soon as possible, Diana. I gave your brother a promise.'

'But don't you agree about me being a pretty wench?' She peeped at him from under her lashes.

'I was wrong to call you that when we first met.' A deep frown showed between his brows. 'It was unforgivable and I did apologise. You are no pretty wench. You have always been a lady.'

'But…' Diana concentrated on the remains of the fire. Where had her tender lover gone? She had expected soft words, and instead he appeared cold and distant. She had thought that somehow last night had settled everything between them, but it seemed like everything had been destroyed. He had taken his pleasure and now wanted to leave her. Her passion had led her astray. Again.

'You should get dressed. We have far to go today.'

'The bed remains warm and the cock has not yet crowed.' The pit in her stomach was growing with every breath she took. She knew that she could not play a mistress. Every move she made seemed gauche and awkward.

'I am dressed for a reason, Diana. We need to get

you back to the Lodge, back to your life. Inns like these are not made for the likes of you. I made an error of judgement last evening.'

Diana bit her lip. She had said too much. It had been she who had asked him to stay with her. Even her words sought to tie him. She had been the one to seduce him. Thankfully, he had not noted the need behind her seduction. She took a breath and regained her composure. 'Not made for the likes of me. The landlady was happy enough to take my coin last evening. And it was my coin as well. This is *my* room.'

He raised an eyebrow. 'I would have paid for you.'

'She thought you a coachman.'

'Yes, she did, and hopefully that will keep her mouth quiet. Otherwise, her tale will be repeated in every hostelry between Carlisle and Newcastle and up to the borders. And that is nothing to be desired.'

Diana pressed her knuckles against her mouth. 'I gave a false name.'

'That doesn't matter. People will guess.'

'Then you had best go and see to the horses, if you are the coachman. I will dress as quickly as possible.' She paused and swallowed hard. She had not even considered people talking and gossiping. She had thought herself safe. 'I will ride in the carriage. There may be some talk, but not full-blown scandal.' She paused and made sure her voice did not tremble. 'It would be best if you leave me now. I can cope.'

'As you wish…'

'I do wish.'

'Shall I send a woman up to help you dress?'

She shook her head, blinking rapidly. Correct. Polite, but distant. She could not fault him, but she would have preferred the warmth of last night. 'I am reasonably self-sufficient. My gown is easy to put on and my hair simply dressed. Rose despairs. But it is one of the advantages of being an ape-leader—not keeping up with the latest fashions.'

'You were never destined to be an ape-leader.' A faint smile touched his lips. 'You are far too alive for that fate.'

'So you say.' She gave her head a little toss and stuck her chin out defiantly. Inside, her stomach knotted and she felt her heart shatter into a thousand pieces. All she wanted was one word and she'd be in his arms, but she had to know that he wanted her to be there. She needed the security of knowledge. 'I will meet you down at the carriage.'

A muscle jumped in his cheek and his lips parted, but he clamped them together.

'I do not intend to have a sordid affair, Diana.'

'I know how to be discreet, Brett.' She made

shooing motions with her hands. 'You were the one who said we had to leave. Now, let me get dressed.'

His boots echoed against the wooden floor. He paused at the door. 'There may be consequences from last night.'

'I will face the consequences when they happen.' She attempted a bright smile, but her stomach turned over. Was it wicked of her to hope for a child? She should be shocked by the thought, but the only thing she could think about was holding a baby in her arms and being able to bestow all her love. She raised her chin. 'Such things are by no means certain. Babies do not happen every time a man and a woman couple. I shall have to hope for the best.'

'You are taking a remarkably forthright attitude.' His eyes had deepened to slate grey and his mouth had become a thin white line.

Diana swallowed hard. 'It is better than weeping and wailing. I knew what I was doing last night, and what the consequences could be. I acted of my own free will with no expectation of being priest-linked.'

'Is that what you want?'

'I want to go back to my old safe life,' Diana lied. She could not bring herself to say the words to Brett, not until she knew how he felt. His derision or indifference would kill her. It seemed she was destined to keep repeating her mistakes. The last thing she wanted was for Brett to be cruel. 'If it makes it any easier, I did not intend for last night to happen. Events overtook me.'

'But it did happen, Diana, and will keep on happening. Think about that. Events will keep overtaking both of us. You must make a decision—do you desire respectability or not? What is it that you want? You need to tell me, for I am at a loss.'

'Not if we stop meeting.' Diana looked at her hands. It was far too soon for that, her heart protested, and her life seemed to stretch out before her. Bleaker. More correct than ever. 'If we stop meeting, become distant friends, then the temptation will be put beyond the both of us.'

'Is that what you want, what you truly want?'

'It is the only way.' Diana kept her head held high. She would not beg him to repeat his offer of marriage. She would not trap him like an animal. She had her pride. 'It is the sensible way. We have never pretended anything more than friendship exists between us.'

He closed the door with a decisive click. And she knew she had lost him, that she had never really had him in the first place. It had been some dream, a dream that she had now woken from.

Diana resisted the urge to throw something at the

door. It was her fault for wanting it all. She refused to marry for anything but love. He had to care about her. She had to give him his freedom.

Brett kept his eyes on a point beyond the horses' ears. A steady rain beat down on him, chilling him to the bone and matching his mood. The journey was passing far too swiftly. Normally, driving gave him ideas, but this time his mind was a blank. Each scheme he considered seemed more preposterous than the last. And he had come no closer to solving his problem—Diana seemed implacable. She might desire his body, but she had no desire for his hand.

At the Ladywell crossroads, he had been very tempted to continue on the road to Gretna Green and force her into a marriage over the anvil. He had even started the carriage down the road when he had pulled the horses up and turned them on to the correct path.

For the first time in a long time, he knew he was not in control of the situation. He had allowed someone else to have power over him. Everything he had worked so hard to achieve counted for nothing if Diana was not by his side.

Despite his dawdling, the Lodge's chimneys appeared far too quickly. A carriage passed them on the drive, spraying water and gravel. Brett raised his hat to Lady Bolt. The woman's eyes slid away from him and the Honourable Miranda stuck her nose in the air as their coachman whipped the horses into a faster trot.

The incident had happened so quickly that Brett hoped Diana had been unaware. He concentrated on bringing the horses to a standstill and tried not to think how she would have reacted to the cut.

Brett's innards tightened. He would hold true to his resolve. He would explain to Clare that even though he was the last person he had ever envisioned as a brother-in-law, Brett was going to marry his sister. They would have to set aside their differences for her sake. It was going to be done properly. Together, they could convince Diana where her duty lay. He did not relish the prospect, but it would have to be done.

The door to the Lodge stood open and Clare with his bandaged face gleaming in sun stood, moodily surveying the scene. Brett concentrated on bringing the horses to a complete standstill, before he jumped down from his perch.

'Coltonby!' Simon thundered before Brett had been able to open the carriage door. 'What have you done with my sister? You have ruined her! You promised to have her back before nightfall. On my life I trusted you, Coltonby.'

'There was a carriage accident with a farm cart. We were delayed,' Brett bit out each word. 'Sometimes, these things happen, despite one's plans.'

Diana emerged from the carriage, pale faced but resolute. Brett gave her an encouraging nod but she turned her face from him. He thought he glimpsed the glimmer of tears. He swore softly. She had seen the cut. She knew what was coming. He had wanted to spare her that. He would spend the rest of his life making amends.

'You, one of the most noted whips in the country? Involved in an accident with a farm cart? The truth, Coltonby.'

'Which truth is that?'

'You seduced my sister. You seduced her and intend to let her live a life of sin. You never change, Coltonby.'

Diana's cheek turned bright pink against the white of her skin. 'You have no cause to say that, brother. You have no proof.'

'Your very countenance shows it, Diana. This man will be made to marry you or I will blacken his name from here to the ends of the earth.'

'I have called men out for less,' Brett ground out.

'Name your date and time.' Clare's eyes blazed at him.

Brett stared at him in disbelief. Clare took a step towards him, and raised his fists. 'I will defend myself, Clare. You may count on that, but I have no wish to duel with you.'

'Stop it! Stop it, you two!' Diana came between them, her hands out, pushing them apart. 'I will not have it. I refuse. Simon, you are behaving like a child. Drag your mind out of the gutter.'

'He must be made to marry you, Diana. He dishonoured you.' Simon Clare looked him up and down with a curl to his lip. 'I know his kind. You cannot say that I didn't warn you.'

'No one must be made to do anything.' Diana put her hands on her hips. 'An accident happened. Lord Coltonby swerved to miss a little girl and the carriage was damaged. He has shown me nothing but kindness and consideration. Your prejudice blinds you, brother. Brett Farnham is a gentleman and always has been.'

Brett stared at Diana. Did she intend to brazen out the disgrace? With a word, or maybe even a gesture, he could ensure it. He remained absolutely still. He refused to get her acceptance that way. He could not tell Clare what had passed between them. Just as Diana had refused his earlier offer, he would not have her marry him simply because her brother demanded. He refused to achieve his ends this way. He loved her too much. She had to love him in return. She had to want to marry him.

'The lady has spoken,' he said slowly, almost not recognising his own voice. 'She has done nothing to be ashamed about.'

'Nothing except spend the night with a notorious rake in God knows what sort of hell hole! The disgraceful baggage!'

'You overstep the mark, Clare. Has your sister ever done anything to make you ashamed? Everything she has done has been predicated on you and your business. She is a lady and should be treated as such. She should never have had to live this half-life you condemned her to—reduced to a nurse, caring for your son.'

'I dare because she is my sister.' Simon advanced towards Brett. His hands clenched into fists. 'This has been a long time coming. I tried to ignore the rumours and slurs. But I can't any longer.'

'You wish to drag my name through the mud? Your own sister's?' Diana shook her head. 'Forgive me, Simon, but I don't think you want to do that.'

'I want you to be safe,' her brother whispered. 'I have striven to keep you and your reputation safe.'

'You have done what you did because it was

easier than looking for another wife.' Diana held out her hands to her brother, willed him to understand. 'But Brett is wrong. I did enjoy my life. I have no regrets about raising Robert and I love him as if he were my own.'

'Then you will understand why, for the sake of Robert, I have to ask you to leave unless you promise me never to have anything more to do with Coltonby again.'

'Are you asking me to choose?'

'Do not make her do this, Clare.' Brett's voice rang out.

'You keep out of it.'

'Diana?' She heard Simon's voice. 'I need to know. You have brought us to the edge of ruin. Will you give up this man? Or will you destroy Robert's chance in life as well as your own?'

'What do you know about Robert's chances, Simon? You have never bothered to be a father, not properly.' She watched Simon blanch, but knew the truth in her words. She met his green gaze and he was the first to look away. 'He is your son, Simon. Be his father. He has already lost one parent.'

Diana looked towards the house. For so long she had thought it a place of refuge, but, if she allowed it to be, it would become her prison. She looked to where Brett stood, the breeze slightly ruffling his travelling coat. Freedom and life. It was far more important than security. She knew that now. 'Brett, take me with you.'

'What are you asking?'

She held out her hands. Tears streamed down her face. 'Take me with you as your mistress.'

Behind her, she heard Simon's curse and ignored it. She had reached the point in her life at which she had to stop running. Her breath caught in her throat as she waited for his answer.

'No.'

She stared at him in stunned disbelief. 'No?' She swallowed hard. The word had come from Brett. 'What do you mean?'

Brett's lips turned up in a thin smile. 'No.'

Diana felt her world turn upside down. Had he truly meant to end it? Here and now? She had lost everything. She stood there stunned. Unable to take it in.

'Even your lover has more sense than you, Diana.' Simon's scornful words floated on the breeze.

'Please, Brett,' she whispered as her heart broke into a thousand shards. 'Tell me why. Surely I am owed that.'

'Is it me you want, or the idea of me?' he asked in a harsh rasp. His grey eyes had become silver arrows piercing into her soul. 'What exactly is it you want? Love comes at a cost.'

The idea of him? She stared at Brett, confused. She wanted him. Then her mind cleared. She knew what he was asking. She had spent years thinking about him as the prince of rakes, a man around whom scandal and gossip swirled, but that wasn't Brett Farnham at all. Brett was something more— a loyal friend, someone she could depend on, a man who kept his promises. Her idea of him was very different than society's and she knew that she had discerned the true man.

'You,' she said without hesitation. 'I want you. I want my life full of passion and emotion.'

Brett nodded and she knew she had said the right words. He would take her with him. They could go on together, for as long as things lasted. And then when it ended, she'd face the future. She held out her hands. 'I promise to be a good and faithful mistress for as long as it lasts.'

'You cannot have me that way.' His face darkened like thunder and she took an involuntary step backwards. 'I refuse.'

'Why not?' She tilted her head to one side. Her whole being trembled. He could not be planning on repudiating her here, in front of Simon. 'It is what you want. Why are you not agreeing?'

'Because I love you, Diana. I have loved you from the moment you drove away from the mud pool, leaving me standing there with a book in my hand. And then the feeling was reinforced when I met you again, wearing that ridiculous cap and struggling so hard to deny yourself all pleasure. I tried to say that it was simply to spite your brother, but I was fooling myself. I wanted to spend time with you.'

'But if you love me…'

Brett strode three steps to her, caught her hands and went down on one knee. 'I want to marry you and have you by my side for the rest of my life. Please say that you will be my wife.'

'You want to marry me? Out of duty?'

'Duty has nothing to do with it. I don't want you to marry me because your brother insists, or because you think society demands it. I want you to marry me because it is what you desire above everything else. I love you Diana.'

'You love me?' She tugged at his hand and he stood. Her fingers curled around his.

'I have been trying to show you, and now I am telling you. I love you, Diana Clare, with all my heart and all my soul. And I want to marry you for the right reason, the only reason—I need you in my life for all time. Please.'

'Brett, I will. I love you with all my heart and

soul and to be parted now would be more than I could bear.' She threw her arms around him and gave herself up to his kiss.

'You will have to bear it for a little while, sweetheart.' His eyes crinkled and he gave a heart stopping smile. 'No midnight gallop to Gretna Green for us. We marry in the parish church with the banns properly read and your brother giving you away. I will have no one speak out about this marriage, Diana.'

'If it must be done that way, then so be it. But let it be a simple wedding.'

'Whatever your heart desires, my very dearest lady.' He lowered his mouth and Diana forgot about everything for a long while.

* * * * *

HISTORICAL

LARGE PRINT

MISS WINBOLT AND THE FORTUNE HUNTER

Sylvia Andrew

Respected spinster Miss Emily Winbolt, so cool and cynical with would-be suitors, puts her reputation at risk after tumbling into a stranger's arms. Her rescuer is none other than Sir William Ashenden, a man of some distinction. He needs to marry – and Emily yearns to believe that he wants her not for her fortune but for herself…

CAPTAIN FAWLEY'S INNOCENT BRIDE

Annie Burrows

Battle-scarred Captain Robert Fawley was under no illusion that women found him attractive. None would ever agree to marry him – except perhaps Miss Deborah Gillies, a woman so down on her luck that a convenient marriage might improve her circumstances. Deborah accepted his pragmatic proposal – because she was already halfway to falling in love with him…

THE RAKE'S REBELLIOUS LADY

Anne Herries

Tomboy Caroline Holbrook is used to running riot, and can't imagine settling into a dull, respectable marriage. But her zest for life and alluring innocence draw the attention of Sir Frederick Rathbone – who is far from dull! In fact, he's the most exciting man Caroline has ever met. But should she resist the attentions of this rakish bachelor…?

™ MILLS & BOON®

Pure reading pleasure™

HIST0409 LP

THE CAPTAIN'S FORBIDDEN MISS

Margaret McPhee

Captain Pierre Dammartin is a man of honour, but his captive, Josephine Mallington, is the daughter of his sworn enemy… She is the one woman he should hate, yet her innocence brings hope to his battle-weary heart. As the Peninsular War rages on, can the strength of their love conquer all that divides them?

THE EARL AND THE HOYDEN

Mary Nichols

Miss Charlotte Cartwright has never forgotten Roland Temple's contemptuous rejection of her hand in marriage. And she's not about to forgive, either – even if Roland, the new Earl of Amerleigh, is now older, wiser and ten times more handsome! But Roland is determined to right the wrongs of the past – and this time the hoyden will be his bride…

FROM GOVERNESS TO SOCIETY BRIDE

Helen Dickson

Lord Lucas Stainton is in need of a governess. The man is ruthless, rude beyond belief, and Eve Brody wishes him to the devil – but the position is hers if she'll accept… As sparks fly between Eve and the magnificent man of the house she learns that the dark-hearted Lord is carrying the weight of ruin on his broad shoulders. So she offers him a proposal…

MILLS & BOON
Pure reading pleasure

HIST0509 LP

HISTORICAL

LARGE PRINT

MARRYING THE MISTRESS

Juliet Landon

Helene Follet hasn't had close contact with Lord Burl
Winterson since she left to care for his brother. Now Burl
has become guardian to her son she is forced to live under
his protection. He has become cynical, while Helene hides
behind a calm, cool front. Neither can admit how affected
they are by the memory of a long-ago night…

TO DECEIVE A DUKE

Amanda McCabe

Clio Chase left for Sicily trying to forget the mysterious
Duke of Averton and the strange effect he has on her.
However, when he suddenly appears and warns her of
danger, her peace of mind is shattered. Under the
mysterious threat they are thrown together in intimate
circumstances…for how long can she resist?

KNIGHT OF GRACE

Sophia James

Grace knew that the safety of her home depended on her
betrothal to Laird Lachlan Kerr. She did not expect his
kindness, strength or care. Against his expectations, the
cynical Laird is increasingly intrigued by Grace's quiet
bravery. Used to betrayal at every turn, her faith in
him is somehow oddly seductive…

⊚™ MILLS & BOON®
Pure reading pleasure™

HIST0609 LP

HISTORICAL

LARGE PRINT

THE RAKE'S DEFIANT MISTRESS

Mary Brendan

Snowbound with notorious rake Sir Clayton Powell,
defiant Ruth Hayden manages to resist falling into
his arms. But Clayton hides the pain of past betrayal
behind his charm, and even Ruth, no stranger to scandal,
is shocked by the vicious gossip about him. Recklessly,
she seeks to silence his critics – by announcing
their engagement…

THE VISCOUNT CLAIMS HIS BRIDE

Bronwyn Scott

Viscount Valerian Inglemoore has been a secret agent on
the war-torn Continent for years. Now he has returned
for Philippa Stratten – the woman he was forced to leave
behind. But Philippa, deeply hurt by his rejection, is
unwilling to risk her heart again. Valerian realises he'll
have to fight a fiercer battle to win her as his bride…

THE MAJOR AND THE COUNTRY MISS

Dorothy Elbury

Returning hero Major William Maitland finds himself
tasked with the strangest mission – hunting down the
lost heir to his uncle's fortune. While searching in
Warwickshire for the twenty-year-old secret he meets
the beautiful but secretive Georgianne Venables, who
may prove to be his personal Waterloo…

MILLS & BOON®
Pure reading pleasure™

HIST0709 LP